MUNDANIA CLOSE

WILLIAM HATCHETT

A Wild Wolf Publication

Published by Wild Wolf Publishing in 2025

Copyright © 2025 William Hatchett

First print

ISBN: 979-8307765647
Also available as an E-book

www.wildwolfpublishing.com

She makes sport with the sons of man, and conceives from them through their dreams, from the male desire, and she attaches herself to them. She takes the desire, and nothing more, and from that desire she conceives and brings forth all kinds of demons into the world. And those sons she bears from men visit the women of humankind, who then conceive from them and give birth to spirits.

Raphael Patai, The Hebrew Goddess, Wayne State University Press, 1990

According to Lurianic Kabbalah, Lilith, Samael, and Asmodeus are both independent entities and interrelated and interdependent. They correspond to three levels of reality: Lilith to the world of action, Samael to the world of formation, Asmodeus to the world of creation.

Deliriums Realm, Essays on Good and Evil, website

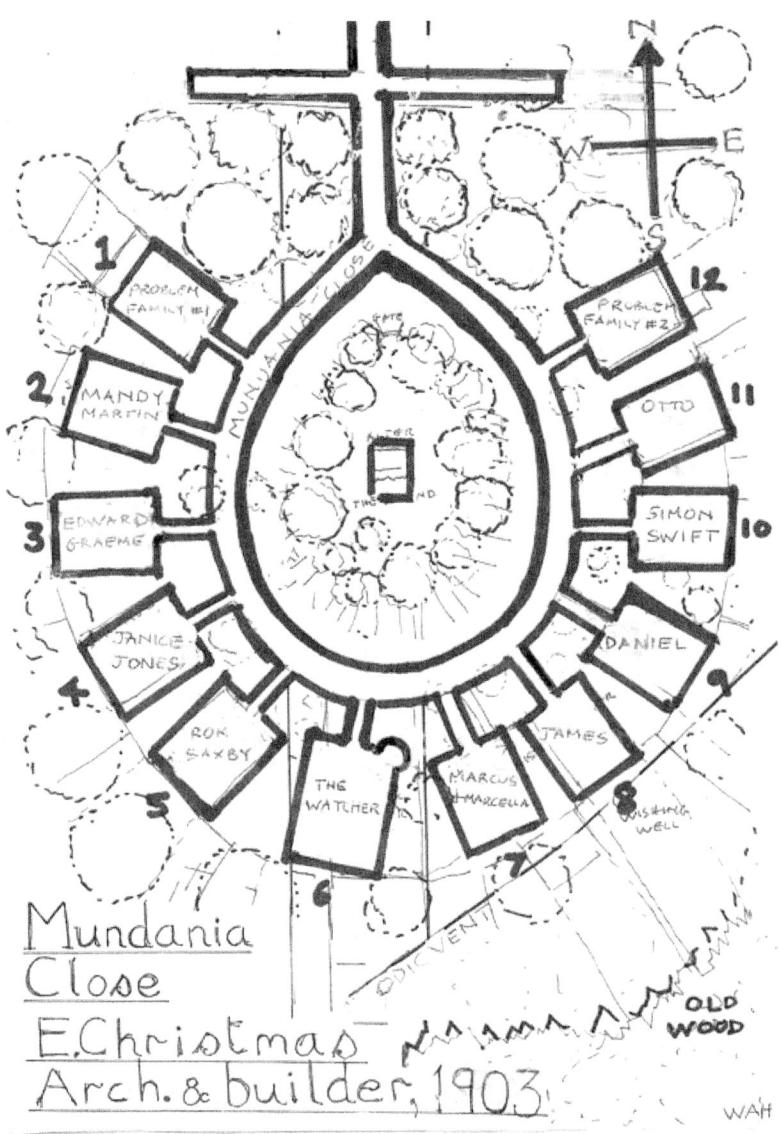

Mundania
Close

E.Christmas
Arch. & builder, 1903

4

Prologue

I am the Watcher. With my consort, Violet, I have looked over Mundania Close since I officially died. That was more than a century ago. Do you see the forest of marks that I have made on the wall, like the pencil flicks in a game of Hangman's Noose? They record the days, weeks, months, years and decades that I have spent here. I have watched, from this room, as saplings grew into broad-girthed giants, shading the close and filling it with their seeds.

The twelve houses that form this community have weathered well. They were supposed to, designed, as they were, to suit our English weather. Their foundations are stout enough to withstand incursions from the roots of wisteria and ivy. Even their original oak barge boards and fascias have survived, albeit with multiple coats of paint. The man whose firm built them took pride in his work. He used only the best materials and he had an innate feel for proportion and the decorative felicities of Arts and Crafts architecture. These houses are his memorial. He is buried in the foundations of number nine.

How long will Mundania Close last? For a thousand years? Eventually, it will revert to atoms and be reclaimed by the wild wood. My life is contingent upon the physical survival of this dwelling, number six. I am condemned to watch a world in which I have no agency. I am made of light and dust. You see, I am eternal – but only if I never leave this house. That is the covenant that Violet and I have made with the Ancient One.

•••

I observed, from my tower, as my neighbours' dwellings changed hands. Families moved in with their bright hopes, perambulators and motor cars. They sired children, grandchildren and great grandchildren. I observed them, from the highest window in this turret, through dark glass, making sure I could never be seen.

The late 1960s were congenial to me. I could not always see clearly what was going on. But I could imagine hedonists in bright clothing copulating on the mound in the centre of the close and smoking hashish. Their minds had been opened. Their summer parties often lasted for days.

Subsequent decades brought more powerful amplification and new intoxicants. But, to my ears, music became repetitive and mechanical. I yearned for the former wild, long-haired dithyrambs of drums and guitars. Perhaps those days will return. History moves in the cycles or Apollo and Dionysius. As I have seen, the rules that govern social behaviour, culture and clothing are strict, relaxed then strict again.

•••

The truth is, Violet and I are tired of merely watching and ticking off the years. We wish to participate in human life, as we once did. Change is coming. I can feel it in my bones. The new occupants of number seven are to be my Lords of Chaos – disruptors. They contacted me through the simple medium of a Ouija Board. The soon-to-arrive newcomers, the Gardners, who are currently living in Putney in west London, are adepts of sex magic, using the texts of Aleister Crowley as their manual.

The Gardners' parties are far too wild for their current address. The anonymity of this obscure suburb will suit them. They are neophytes of the occult but I shall soon teach them the true ways of the Left Hand Path. To invoke the Dark Lord will require powerful magic. They will help me to complete my unfinished business.

A new life is beckoning. The sun on our backs. Violet and I await, with anticipation, the coming of the new residents of Mundania Close. Lucifer will be our star. The bars of this prison will melt. Soon, we shall enjoy unfettered freedom!

Theophilus William Williams
Honor Oak, London, 9th January, 2022

1

The Arrival

Monday 10th January 2022, 10.01am
Daniel, The Writer

'Daniel Robbins, journalist, author and blogger', it says on my website. I used to travel to work every day, for a magazine that you probably won't have heard of, in an office close to the River Thames. Now, my front room is my office – one with a sound system (okay, a record player), comfortable furniture, photos and paintings. This room is on the first floor of my house, number nine Mundania Close.

It's a lovely place, Honor Oak, in a desirable part of town. I admit it's not Hampstead, or Crouch End, or Stoke Newington, all 'north of the river', as we say down here, but I like south-east London for its homely ordinariness – a badge that it wears with pride.

This quadrant of London has council estates with terrifying reputations, in which teenagers battle each other over postcodes and the colour of their bandannas. It has enclaves of the extremely wealthy, some tucked away, almost invisibly, down unmade roads. But mostly it's the in-between people who live here – you know, teachers, telecoms engineers, social workers, orchestral musicians, in almost identical Victorian and Edwardian houses, built over a few crowded decades around railway stations.

It's so quiet where I live that when I first moved in, I couldn't believe it. It's proper, middle-of-the-countryside quiet, apart from one thing. Foxes scream in the night, like babies being tortured. When Covid came, the skies emptied. An even more crushing silence pressed down on our heads. We started to hear bird song at unfamiliar times of day. It was nature saying 'look, I'm still here! Listen'.

•••

I used to be a music journalist. My working time was spent in sweaty dives with sticky floors, in Camden or Islington, or the West End.

Taking advantage of what was then a close friendship with someone I had gone to school with, I wrote a biography of a rising pop star.

He became unfeasibly wealthy and famous. People said it was a good book. But my friend's pals spread poison about me and he disowned me. He won't talk to me now. Amazingly, the book bought me this house. It was optioned by a streaming channel for a documentary that was never made – peanuts for them, a small fortune for me. I moved to Mundania Close with my partner. I was very happy. She wasn't. We split up. I had a breakdown.

Yeah, I know, there is no 'normal'. We are all on the spectrum of something or other. All I know is, I ended up in the psychiatric equivalent of A&E. I was prescribed a drug as effective as applying jump leads to a dead battery. Over the next two years, I medicated and therapised my way back to the point where I felt that there was, actually, a reason to get out of bed.

As a freelance journalist, author and blogger, I'll dabble my toes in pretty much anything. My first degree was in biology, and I find myself more and more interested in nature, which I guess is a bit odd for someone who made their living writing about music played in places where 'the sun don't shine'.

Here, as I work, on the first floor of number nine, I look out through my window at the horseshoe-shaped community of Mundania Close. I can see pretty much every house and every tree. That rectangle of light is a palette upon which I impose my moods – or is it the other way round?

•••

The days shape-shift in tiny increments. Most people don't notice small changes as their elements reconfigure. Sounds are important. Over the years, I have absorbed the diurnal, weekly and even annual rhythms of the close. They are my internal clock – the metallic, alien warning of the bin lorry as it reverses on Monday mornings and, in the afternoons, the clatter of crates from supermarket delivery vans.

Suburbs like this one resemble deserts – terrains in which life is present but largely invisible, at least to the untrained eye. Occasionally, creatures emerge into the light and scurry to somewhere else. Those who have chosen to spend time there have suspended hope of what their lives could be.

The person who lives at number five is a builder with a large belly who drives an ugly four by four. His name is Ron Saxby. He has a teenage son, Nigel. No one knows what has happened to his wife. She was Swedish – a harassed creature whose sparkle was rubbed off by her association with Ron.

Perhaps she's left him. Perhaps he killed her and buried her in the garden. She hasn't been seen for a long time. Infuriatingly for his dad, Nigel has the blond hair, eyes and gappy teeth of his mum.

Saxby is the only person in the close to have slathered the space at the front of his house with concrete. He has, instead of grass and flowers, four sad-looking plastic tubs containing generic-looking plants. Two concrete lions, symmetrically arranged, guard his front door.

Number six, the largest house in the close with an imposing corner turret, has been unoccupied for years. No-one knows why. It looks neglected. Number seven, empty at present, is regularly re-sold. Everybody's wondering who is going to move in next. Renovations have been taking place since before Christmas.

Huge volumes of chewed-up clay were removed, indicating that large-scale building work was taking place – perhaps a basement extension? The scale of the work has aroused great curiosity in the close as to the identity of the new owner.

In January, semi-mature trees and plants – exotic specimens one would expect to find in a warmer country – were carried through the house by men in overalls. This increased anticipation to fever pitch. Perhaps an oligarch or a rock star had bought the house?

But why here? I mean, this is Mundania Close, not Holland Park.

•••

It's the big day. Mundania Close's new residents are arriving! I can see a man from my window. He's a tall, slightly stooped fellow with ginger hair, a wispy beard and pale skin.

He's wearing a cravat. Despite the touch of spring frost in the air, he's opted sandals as footwear, with woollen socks.

It's that 'I don't give a fuck what you think about my appearance' attitude that makes the English great, in my opinion. A woman is standing behind him, reaching into the back of a car. She is petite, barely reaching his shoulder, with dark bobbed hair, a yellow

9

cardigan and bright red lipstick. Pretty. Definitely a lot younger than him.

She's wearing startlingly tight jeans.

They notice that I am watching them. Christ! I don't want to be branded a curtain twitcher. Why not introduce myself? I decide to walk round the pavement to affect a chance meeting.

This is uncharacteristic of me – normally I rarely venture from my house. I'm risking a humiliating brush off. It's happened before, several times in the close, and that has made me wary. Wariness is the default state of the suburban mind.

However, this time, I decide to depart from my normal habits. I'm not sure why. Perhaps an instinct tells me that this arrival is an unusually significant event in the life of this reluctant community.

I have decided to become its ambassador.

•••

'Hi.' Her voice is bright and friendly.

'Hi,' I echo.

'We're your new neighbours.'

'So I see.'

'My name is Marcella and this is Marcus.'

'I'm Daniel.'

Marcus smiles. He looks at me with the beady eye of a cormorant.

'Daniel or Dan?'

'Either, I don't mind. Most people call me Dan.'

'What do you do?'

'I'm a writer.'

He is showing interest. The people who live here are never interested in anything. Sometimes there isn't even a follow-up question. Lack of curiosity is a prerequisite of suburbia.

'What do you write?'

My answer is certain to extinguish any further curiosity.

'Marcus, for God's sake, leave the poor man alone.' I notice that Marcella has a slight American accent. 'He doesn't want to be interrogated!'

'It's OK,' I say. 'Honestly.'

10

'Even so, one should not impose upon people.' She speaks a subtly anglified form of US English, with slightly elongated vowels, like Sylvia Plath did. It's attractive.

'You certainly like books,' I said. Boxes of them are lined up on the pavement.

'We certainly do,' the woman says. 'Marcus is an academic.'

There's something Middle Eastern about her face, I note – the elegantly arched eyebrows, the finely sculpted nose. Her face cream hides the fine wrinkles of the third decade of life, but she is no puffy-lipped Instagram pin-up. I am drawn to her deep chocolate brown eyes, her delicate, almost feline features.

'What does he study?'

'Magic.'

It is Marcus who speaks.

'You mean, like magic tricks?'

'No, not that kind of magic.' He laughs.

'Would you like to come in for tea?' Marcella asks. 'We have coffee too. I know you'll be curious about what we've done with the house. You're far too English to show it.'

I follow her into number seven. Marcus places his hand on my shoulder. For some reason, this doesn't seem out of place.

The hallway has black and white chequered tiles and a huge gilt-framed mirror. The house has been beautifully and tastefully kitted out. Does Marcus mind that I am admiring his wife's shapely figure?

Saturday 22nd January, 11.54am
James, The Set Designer

'It had to be this house', Marcella explains. 'It simply had to be.'

We are drinking coffee, sitting in the kitchen of number seven. We've only met four times, once over the fence, but have already become friends. Daniel, the writer at number nine, my other neighbour, gave me a flattering description of the exotic incomer. I have filled in more detail for myself.

Marcella has told me about her background. She comes from a Middle Eastern family but was born in New England. Her family moved to the west coast when she was a child where, later, she met Marcus. He's an Englishman from a wealthy family. He was

11

Professor of Anthropology and Ancient Religions at Berkeley University, where she was studying Art History. Despite their age difference, they decided to get married and move to England. When Marcus' aunt died, they inherited a large sum of money.

Her kitchen is luxurious. Attached to it is a large, airy conservatory. It has cane furniture and is filled with plants, including fragrant pelargoniums and ferns. Marcella's sleek Persian cats, Krystelle and Jacinta, divide their time between kitchen and conservatory.

We are sitting on either side of that must-have kitchen feature known as an 'island' although, in this case, it's actually an isthmus, attached at one end to a wall. Marcella is an artist. She's shown me some of her brightly coloured but slightly disturbing abstract paintings. There's an easel in the conservatory. She intends, she's told me, to use it as a studio.

'But why this house, here?' I ask. It isn't the first time I've posed the question. 'You could easily have afforded somewhere a lot grander.'

'Oh James. Alexa...' she breaks off to talk to her digital assistant... 'make us another pot of coffee, would you.' Clearly, she is trying to change the subject.

She teases back a strand of hair as she turns her head. Her fingernails are painted scarlet.

'Alexa, for God's sake!' she says, impatiently. I've noticed that she often treats the device like an incapable servant. We hear a gurgle as an aroma of Arabica beans floats into the air.

I persist. Why would one move to south-east London when one could afford an equally large house in a smarter part of town?

'There were special factors,' she says, vaguely.

'Hi.' It is Marcus' voice. He's been standing in the doorway, watching us.

He is wearing a Paisley dressing gown with a black silk collar and suede moccasins.

'To answer your question, we were bored with south-west London,' he interjects. 'I needed somewhere quiet for my studies. Marcella loves painting and gardening. This is perfect for us.'

He steps into the kitchen, savouring the smell of coffee.

'You can certainly get more for your money round here,' I remark.

'Oh, you do James,' Marcella comments. 'Mundania Close is a gem. And it has such a fascinating history.'

Marcus pulls a slim silver case from his breast pocket.

'Darling,' says Marcella. 'You've come down to smoke in the conservatory, haven't you? I suggest you do so and leave us in peace. I need to talk to James about the party.'

We have met, specifically, to discuss the arrangements for this proposed social event. The party is intended to reassure those neighbours who are curious or fearful about the new arrivals. It will be held in the Gardners' back garden.

There will be delicious food and appropriate music. Marcella intends that everyone who lives on the close will be made welcome. I'm not sure if this is a good idea, but I haven't told her that. Perhaps Marcus' charm and her confident self-assurance will be able to carry it off.

Marcus smiles.

'Please don't let me stop you, my dears. I do apologize for interrupting your conversation. I shall go back to my den.'

He turns and disappears into the hallway.

'Now, where were we?' Marcella says. 'Shall we carry on planning our party? Didn't you tell me that one of our neighbours is a composer, James? Perhaps he could provide the music.'

'Oh, you mean Otto at number eleven. Yes, he is a composer but I don't think his music would be really suitable.'

'Why not?'

'The stuff he writes is experimental. Some of it isn't even music, in my opinion. It's just weird noises. It's certainly not party music. Anyway, Otto isn't very friendly, I don't think he likes people. I doubt he'd come.'

'Well I hope he does. He sounds fascinating. Where's he from?'

'I'm guessing Germany. I've never asked.'

I have a thought.

'I have a friend, Dom, who's a DJ. He's into rave music, but I know he does weddings sometimes. He's really cool. I'm sure he'd bring his decks.'

'You mean deck shoes?'

'No, you know, record turntables.'

'That sounds perfect. So, who else should we invite?'

I mentally review those who live in the close. There's the family with the unruly children at number one – holy terrors with ginger hair. The social media influencer, Mandy, at number two does makeup tutorials on YouTube. She wears very tight white trousers. She's the kind who loves a party. She's full on. Too full on.

The guy at number three is an appalling snob. He's a musician in an orchestra. I explain that I'm pretty sure he'll come, because he'll be curious about who's moved in – whether they are above or beneath him in the social hierarchy. He will want to check them out.

Then there's the lady at number four, who used to be a famous pop singer. She is very overweight and not very well. She rarely goes out. She probably won't come.

Nobody knows who lives at number six. Weirdly, lights occasionally go on and off, but no one has ever been seen going in or out of the house.

She seems fascinated. 'A recluse?'

'I guess so.'

'That's intriguing. Perhaps now's a good time to find out who they are.'

'Perhaps.'

'So, who else?'

'There's my neighbour at number nine, Dan. He's very nosy so he's bound to accept.'

'I've met him. He introduced himself to us the day we moved in. He came in and talked to us. He seems charming.'

'He seems nice but be careful what you tell him.'

'Why?'

'He's a journalist.'

'I'll remember that.'

I continue the tour of potential guests. There's the bicycle man at number ten, Simon Swift. He's always leaving and arriving, in his ridged helmet with its all-seeing camera. I have only ever seen him wearing flesh-hugging Lycra shorts. There's a bulge at the front in a kind of woven pocket, like a glove puppet. It's hard to take your eyes off it.

She laughs. 'I know what you mean,' she says. 'It's funny when men wear Lycra, isn't it?! Those bulges look like medieval codpieces.'

'They do, don't they,' I agree.

Otto, the composer at number eleven is also a cyclist. But he never speaks to Simon. He doesn't like him.

'I wouldn't invite number twelve,' I say.

'Why not?'

I explain that the single mother who lives there is depressed and withdrawn. Her two teenage sons are a nightmare. Both of them have been in trouble with the police.

'What for?' She looks alarmed.

'The usual. Drugs, stealing. I'm not really sure.'

'They wouldn't steal from the close, would they?'

'I don't think so. It would be a bit close to home.'

'That's a relief.'

'Alexa – more coffee please. Would you like another, James?'

I look at my watch.

'Yeah, why not.'

We hear a gurgle. 'Thank you, Alexa. Would you like a muffin?'

'Well yes, but only one.'

'I guess you have to watch your figure, like I do.'

'I certainly do.'

She slides off her stool, bends, and reaches down to open the oven. The movement unleashes a delicious buttery smell and reveals an expanse of toned flesh – a golden meridian between her jeans and her blouse. There's a tiny tattoo on her back. It could be a symbol or an insect – a beetle or a scorpion.

She places a tray on the island, standing extremely close. Her scent is musky and sensuous. Breathing in her rare perfume and the nostalgic smell of baking, I feel myself becoming aroused. Women have never attracted me in that way. Does she know?

I bite into the cake, reaching an exquisite core of melting berries.

'Good?'

'Mmmm. So, when are we holding this party?'

'Oh, that's easy, in March, for Ostara.'

'Ostara?'

She seems surprised that I don't recognise the word.

'It's the celebration of the Spring Solstice, darling. That's going to be on Saturday 19th March. There's a full moon the night before but I always think that Saturdays are best for parties, don't you?'

I am too preoccupied by the heaven in my mouth to reply.

'Are you enjoying my muffin?'

I nod.

'Would you like another?'

I shake my head.

•••

Neither of us has mentioned the elephant in the room – number five, the dreadful Ron Saxby, owner of Saxons the builders. Everything about him is wrong – his huge truck, his plastic-framed windows and concreted-over drive. He even has an unpleasant, aggressive dog.

'Are you going to invite number five?' I ask, tentatively.

'Well, I think we have to, don't you? I have to say though, I do think he's awful. He seems to be in a bad temper all the time. Last week, I said hello to him and he ignored me!'

'Yes, that's happened to me a few times,' I confide. 'He's a hater. When he's in his truck he's even worse. I once saw him almost kill a Deliveroo rider.' I pause. 'I suppose the thing to do is invite him and hope he doesn't come.'

'That's so English James. Is he married?'

'He was but his wife has gone.'

'Gone where?'

'No-one knows. Most people think she couldn't take being bullied anymore, so she just left him.'

'Perhaps he buried her under that dreadful concrete in front of his house.'

'It's quite possible.'

•••

We've sorted out the music and discussed the guest list for the party. There's still the decoration, lighting and catering to finalise. This takes up the rest of the morning. I have two more coffees and, feeling guilty, another muffin.

She asks me about my job and colleagues at the Royal Opera House. I confide some of their peculiarities and those of the precious, overpaid prima donnas who appear on the stage, whose every whim we must obey.

16

I enjoy being in her company. We like to gossip and we laugh at the same things. There's something that disturbs me – I'm starting to find her attractive, in a physical way. *Watch yourself James!*

Next week, the party invites will be delivered. There's no going back.

Sunday 23rd January, 11.25am
Daniel, The Writer

Suburbs are odd, unnatural places. It seems to me, from the evidence of this one, that their inhabitants rarely venture outside apart from at particular times, like Sunday mornings for gardening or washing cars, or on allotted recycling days which are strictly observed in a vicarious form of religious observance. Although my desk is by a window and I am there from early in the morning until late in the evening, I hardly ever see my neighbours.

It is one of the great mysteries. No-one ever seems to go out, like I do, to sniff the air or to walk to the local shop on the main road for an impromptu purchase of biscuits or chocolate, or a bottle of wine, or just to stand in the garden and marvel at the complexity and beauty of the universe.

So when does bin pushing, food purchasing and marvelling take place? It's an enigma that would challenge David Attenborough in one of his nature documentaries. Sometimes, I think everyone who lives on this close has been trapped by giant spiders in web cocoons. They are husks, their dead eyes seeing nothing, their flesh desiccating.

Normally, I try to avoid close contact with the people who live here. I prefer to observe them through my window. During the Covid pandemic, that policy broke down. To mark our solidarity with the NHS and our victimhood, some of us banged on saucepans with wooden spoons on Thursday nights, in a gentile version of a prison riot. Next, a WhatsApp group was formed. Its presence on my phone has annoyed me ever since. At its best, it's useful for sharing useful practical information. At its worst, it's a conduit for finger wagging and prissy nosiness. I wish I could leave the group unobtrusively, without anybody noticing, like sneaking out of a really bad play.

Through the WhatsApp group, I have learned that one of my neighbours, at number two, Mandy – aka 'the Mooks' – who always dresses in white, has an extreme aversion to the foxes who share the close with humans. She wants every fox to be eradicated. She alleges that there's a 'foxes' nest' at the rear of number four. She maintains that it was a disease spread by the foxes that killed her precious white poodle, Sandy.

In front of number three, the orchestra snob's house, a plum tree is growing through the grass verge. That tree is a marvel. Every autumn, it produces a profusion of dusky, deliciously sweet fruits. Most of them are squashed by cars and pedestrians, as if a swarm of giant, blood sucking insects has been crushed. The orchestra snob hates the tree because of the mess it makes. At that time of year, he is often to be seen resentfully jet-washing the pavement.

Once, I posted a photo of the tree with its ripe, juicy plums in the WhatsApp group. 'Free jam or wine!', I suggested. Number three responded that the tree should be cut down and this opinion was endorsed by number two. I was saddened by these responses, but I knew that resistance would be futile. I withdrew from the debate.

Although he doesn't do What'sApp, I know the builder at number five would love to root out and chop up every tree in the close – because of the sap and bird poo that fall on his monstrous car. The ugly vehicle has giant bull bars, chrome fog lamps and bloated wheels. The thing can be remotely controlled. Its owner often ostentatiously turns on the engine before he climbs aboard. His incongruous four by four commands the southern end of the close, purring, like a menacing Komodo dragon.

2

The First Event

Monday 14th March, 7.30am
Ron, The Builder

Come on Nigel for fuck's sake I haven't got all day! Why is he always fucking late? That air freshener is way too strong. It's sickly. Fuck. I think I'll... Oh, here he is, finally!

Nigel closes the door behind him. It's brand new, battleship grey. Mirror-effect glass. Doorbell camera. On each side of the door a lion stands proudly on a plinth. They are lions rampant. Classic.

The lad looks smart. Black blazer. Black and tie. Crisp. Shoes polished.

I wait as he crosses the treble-width drive. It is faced in pearl-effect Portland concrete.

Come on! Nigel buckles himself into the back seat of the motor. It's a Jeep Gladiator, 285 HP, rugged looks with modern comfort.

'You showed up then.' I catch his eyes in the rear-view mirror. Silence. Moody. Like his mum.

'Look, sunshine. I don't pay twenty grand a year in school fees to wait while you make yourself look beautiful. That's not how it works.'

Nigel shrugs. The silent treatment. His fucking mum all over.

'What the fuck is going on with your hair?'

The top is gelled, it looks like twisted rope. The sides are shaved, with weird patterns cut into them. Footballer's hair.

'Do they allow hair like that at school?'

'Yes.'

'Well I don't like it, I didn't like it yesterday and I don't fucking like it today. It makes you look like a fucking ponce.'

'There's no need to...'

'Shut it! I don't wanna hear it okay! You've made us both late, again. I'm telling you it's the last fucking time. Do you understand?'

Silence.

'Do you understand me?'

A small sound.

'Sorry, didn't get that.'

'Yes, I understand, father.'

Father. Not dad. I fire the engine up. It's V6 supercharged. Smooth as a whisper. You can barely fucking hear it.

Poncy gardens. Trees. Blossoms. Flowers. Twats. Why would a boy want a fucking horse, for fuck's sake? Turn left. People waiting at the bus stop. Losers.

'I'll get it for you, okay.'

'Get what?'

'The horse. If that's what you want.'

'Oh.'

'Do you know how much it's going to cost to stable and feed it?'

'No.'

'A lot. Well?'

'Well, what?'

'Can't you say thank you?'

'Thank you. Father.'

Gripping the wheel. South Circular Road. In town, she purrs like a thoroughbred. But she can tackle the most rugged terrain, and just wait till she opens up!

eyes. Silent treatment.

Fucking prick trying to cut me up! This is *my* fucking lane. Fuck off! Well?'

'Well, what?'

'Aren't you going to fucking say anything? Your mum used to do this.'

'Do what?'

'Lock me out.'

Silence.

'Don't talk about Mum!'

Oh Christ, his lower lip is trembling.

'Don't ever talk about Mum!'

Here we go. The waterworks.

School. Dulwich fucking College. Red terracotta. Green fields. Cricket.

'Don't they do boxing or martial arts at this school?'

I fucking love this car. Should I have got the red one? Not sure. Black is good. Yeah.

Twat. Get out of my fucking... Stop. Oops. Might be a teacher.

'Goodbye then... Nigel.'

Frozen stare.

'Bye.'

'Thanks dad.' I remind him. 'I'll say it for you shall I? Don't they teach you manners in this fucking school?'

'Thank you.'

Jesus. Can't he move any fucking quicker? Twat.

Tuesday 15th March, 6pm
Mandy Martin, The Social Media Influencer

Come on Mooks. I'm so tired but gotta do the socials. I wish I had someone to help me. Daniel at number nine? He has plenty of time on his hands and he's supposed to be a writer. I reckon he's a snob though. He doesn't like the Mooks. His loss. Right. Lights. Camera. Action. Let's do it.

Hi my lovelies, so in today's session, I'm gonna give you some pro-tips on skin prep, especially in that crucial under-eye area, so that we get some hydration in there and get a really beautiful natural glow. I'm going to show you the moisturisers I love to use, it's an oil-free range that I'm really excited about right now, before we move to our concealers and contourers and then, something I know you're dying for me to talk about – it's the fabulous new foundation range I told you about yesterday. Let me tell you something. It's going to work for you whatever your skin type. It's going to give your skin that glowing super-natural look that I know you all love. Healthy, natural skin! Like mine.

Don't worry, all the products that I mention are going to be listed below. These are the best products you can buy. Believe me. But you won't find them in any of the salons. Remember to follow me, Mandy Martin, on all my social media channels – Instagram, Tik Tok and Facebook. By the way, if you haven't used this channel before we have live chat time. That's on Saturday mornings. I know for a lot of you that's the special day when you're going out and you need a little help... It's going to be for me, as is it happens, this Saturday. Yes, the Mooks is going to a party!

Chat time is for my subscribers only and for them I can offer special discounts on some of the products that I recommend. Remember, like I said, you won't find them in the salons. Now...

Tuesday 15th March, 7pm

Daniel, The Writer

Ron Saxby is dead. It's hard to compute. But it's true. Normally, deaths in suburbia are discrete, unobserved affairs, the body quietly removed under a blanket on a wheeled stretcher and taken away. This one certainly wasn't.

So, here's what happened. It's 5am and I'm awake. This is a common occurrence. I often wake up early or, rather, I never really get to sleep. Before it is fully light but when my brain is active, I often have ideas.

I feel the need to write them down. What the hell, I think. I'm awake so why not go downstairs and commit the scribblings in my bedside notebook to my computer? Surprisingly often, these gifts from the unconscious evolve into something useful.

My days often begin like this. And so it happens that, today, I'm sitting at my desk as dawn is coming up. It's an odd part of the day, both in and out of time – one that foxes, with their sharp eyes and curious noses, exploit to the full.

An hour later, I'm still sitting at my desk, writing an article for a green business website. The light has come up, but it is still too early for anyone to be about.

Then something strange happens. At first, it registers as a throaty engine note. The sound becomes louder. Suddenly, Ron Saxby's four by four comes into view. It thunders past my house with its fog lamps blazing. Christ. What the hell! The car, a pretend pickup truck, barely makes the sharp turn at the northern end of the close. It clips the mound and skids onto the front gardens of number one and two, before getting its wheels back onto the tarmac.

Something mind-bendingly weird is happening. Ron Saxby has two concrete lions, purchased from a local garden centre, on either side of his front door. The animals are running behind the four by four as it careers around the close, like flesh and blood creatures, followed by his dog. The lions are pursuing their quarry with the relentless, pumping determination of predators on the Serengeti.

The car's second circuit of the close is, if anything, even faster, the lions still following. This leads to more damage as the metal beast negotiates the bend between numbers twelve and one. With a screech of tortured rubber, it sideswipes some trees. It regains momentum, lurching across grass and flower beds, leaving deep striations from its oversized tyres, knocking wheelie bins asunder. Holy fuck.

•••

On the third circuit, I notice a peculiar and alarming fact. There is no-one in the driving seat! I turn my head to see Ron Saxby standing on the paved drive in front of number five, waving his arms like a lunatic. This is the time of the morning when he normally drives his son to school. He must have sent him back into the house to avoid being crushed by the thundering beast that his vehicle has become.

Why does Ron step onto the pavement? Does he think that by sheer force of personality he can stop his four-wheeled monster? It's inviting disaster. I am convinced now that the machine has assumed volition – a menacing intent. That's the only way to explain what happens next.

The truck fractionally shifts its course as it veers round the southern perimeter of the close. It hits the burly builder square on. Ron is flung into the air, as if he is weightless. He lands on his back in the front garden of number eight, James' house.

The car shudders to a halt, just before it smashes into the house. Had it been a bull, its nostrils would have dilated, as it pawed the ground. It neatly reverses. In an arena, the crowd would have fallen silent, awaiting the coup de grâce. Ron's pit bull is rearing up, defending its master. One of the lions despatches the animal with a snapping crunch to the neck and flings it back over its head.

Evidently injured, Ron assumes a position on his hands and knees and attempts to escape. But nothing will save him. The truck has him in its cross hairs. It pushes him like a snow plough and drives him into the ground.

Now blocked, the beast reverses again. It makes contact with its victim for a third time with a slow, sadistic deliberation. Ron disappears beneath his nemesis, as it partially mounts him. The engine dies. Ron's head has been inserted into a flowerbed. The remainder of his not-inconsiderable bulk is above the surface. He has become an inverted iceberg.

The lions stroll back calmly to their previous positions. They jump onto the plinths and solidify, standing guard over their master's house.

The close comes to life. Several doors open. The clarinet player at number three moves to the scene in a curious walk that approximates to a run. He must be appalled by the damage caused by the truck. It looks as if Mundania Close has been hit by a hurricane.

Otto, the composer, is standing in his front garden talking into his phone. It never occurred to me to call an ambulance. For me, there was an inevitability about the spectacle. It was only going to end one way – either the car or the man would die. The car enjoyed three advantages over Ron – namely its power, size and intelligence.

•••

The irony of the sticker on the back of Ron's car, 'All Lives matter', occurs to many of those who visit the close over the next few hours. Two police cars arrive, followed by an ambulance.

Once it has been established that Ron is dead, the pace of events slows. The body is covered by a blanket, then a tarpaulin. The entrance to the close is sealed off with and white tape. Police officers knock on doors to take statements. We have become a crime scene!

Should I tell the police what I've witnessed? How can I? It was too weird.

In due course, I speak to a policewoman. I lie, saying that I only looked out of my window when I heard a collision. The car had up-to-date electronics, I observe. Perhaps a malfunction occurred. The policewoman nods. She tells me that family support officers are comforting Saxby's son, Nigel, in number five. I say this is a good thing. What a terrible tragedy. Yes, isn't it. I don't mention the lions.

Events outside proceed as we have all seen in innumerable crime dramas. Photographs are taken, police officers of increasing seniority arrive, forensic examinations are carried out by people in white zip-up suits.

A reporter and photographer turn up from our illustrious local paper, the News Shopper. I wonder what will happen to Nigel. Will the police find his mum? She could be back in Sweden.

Wednesday 16th March, 9.31am
Edward Graeme, The Orchestral Clarinettist

God. What a hideous mess. Who the hell is going to clean it up? Not content with burying himself in the ground, he has to dig up half the close and leave patches of oil from his ghastly car all over the road. At least they've towed the damn thing away. I wonder if his insurance company will pay for the damage. How would one get the details? From the police I suppose. I should have asked them.

Strange to receive a party invitation, on the day that someone died. Typical. There are no standards anymore. Good manners and respect have gone out the window. No doubt my dreadful neighbour will be there, with her pouting lips and her trowelled-on make-up. I shall have to pretend to be friendly to her. So will a-tonal Otto. I shall probably have to talk to them and the man who watches from his window and thinks that I can't see him, that alleged journalist.

At least the new people at number seven look respectable. I wonder whether they would be keen on reviving the Mundania Road Residents' Association? I shall ask them on Saturday. I could be chairman again. We can re-adopt the old standing orders. Perhaps one of them could be treasurer, or the secretary, to take minutes. Proper minutes. I shall ask them.

Wednesday 16th March, 12.03pm
Mundania Close WhatsApp Group

Marcella
What a terrible tragedy at #5. Marcus and I are devastated.
Mooks
He was a grumpy old cuss!
James
Yeah but we loved him didn't we ☺.
Mooks
Did we???? 😉☺ BTW is the party going ahead on the 19th? ☐
Marcella
What does everyone think? Perhaps it's inappropriate?
James
Well I've already got my outfit!
Mooks
Me too!!!!
James
Also, DJ and caterers booked. Short notice. So hard to cancel !

Mooks

It's what #5 would have wanted!

James

Yeh right! 😠

Marcella

So should we go ahead then??

James

IMO yes

Mooks

Of course yes. Let's make it a party that he would have loved!

James

Hard to imagine, but yes. Let's...

Marcella

Well, if you're both sure???

Mooks

The Mooks is never wrong! What about music?

James

We've booked a DJ.

Mooks

Great. I'm soooooooooo excited. ☐ ☐ ☐

James

Me too!! ☐

Friday 18th March, 11.03am
James, The Set Designer

'It's such a terrible thing,' says Marcella. It is mid-morning. We are sitting, as usual, at the breakfast bar. Alexa is making us coffee. Her TV is on, with the sound down.

'Did you see it happen? I mean, the accident.'

'No,' I reply. 'No-one did.'

'Not even Daniel? He sees everything.'

'Apparently he didn't. It was very early in the morning. Ron was taking his son to school.'

'Poor Nigel.'

'At least there'll be no-one to bully and shout at him now.'

'Yes, there is that.'

'And we don't have to worry about Ron coming to the party and picking fights with the other guests.'

Marcella laughs. She's dressed all in white today, like almond blossom. The sun is shining. One could almost say that spring has arrived. But, of course, in England, it's never that simple.

'Do you think that the weather will hold for tomorrow?' she asks.

'The forecast is good but that's no guarantee.'

'Oh James, you're such a pessimist.'

'Just a realist.'

'Right.' She places a cup of coffee in front of me. Now she is in business mode. She consults a memo she's made on her iPhone.

'So, let me tell you who has confirmed for tomorrow from the invitations you delivered. Just number three, the clarinet player. He pushed a note through our door. It was on headed notepaper. We were impressed.'

'That's Edward,' I say. 'He's old school.'

'We know, from What'sApp, that the lovely Mandy, she of the makeup tips at number two, is coming.'

'Do you think that the famous composer will come?'

'He isn't really famous and, no, he won't.'

'Are you sure?'

'Yes. But Daniel is a definite yes. I spoke to him yesterday. And he told me that Simon from number ten is coming with his wife.'

'He's the bicycle man, right?'

'That's the one.'

Simon Swift is the most boring man in the world. His main topic of conversation is how urban traffic flow can be managed to encourage bicycles. I think he works for the council but I have no idea what he actually does.

Once he's trapped a victim, there is no escape. He expands upon his theme until their eyes glaze over. Soon, they're begging that death will take them – a painless death – so that they can be released from the tedium of his company. His wife dresses unobtrusively. She rarely speaks. The poor creature is forced to listen.

'He's the guy with the large crotch', Marcella informs me, although I wish she hadn't.

'That's right...' *It's hard not to notice.*

'Of course, it could just be padding under that Lycra.'

'Maybe we'll find out tomorrow?'

27

'Oh James,' she says, her eyes widening, 'it won't be that kind of party.'

'I'm disappointed.'

'Of course you are.'

'Dom is coming,' I say.

'Who is Dom?'

He's the DJ, remember? He'll be rocking up at six with his decks and PA.'

'He has a personal assistant?'

'It means sound system.' She looks alarmed. 'Don't worry, it won't be too loud. The vibes will be mellow. Dom is cool like that. He can read the room. He knows when people want to chill out and when they want to boogie.'

'That's good,' she says. 'What about lights?'

'I'll ask him to bring some.'

I have a thought. 'You know, it's probably only six people, not including you, me and Marcus, seven if Janice comes.'

'Who is Janice again?'

'JJ, she's the Jamaican lady at number four – Janice Jones. She was a professional singer back in the 1960s. She rarely goes out now.'

'Do you think she could handle a party?'

'Yes, I think she'd love it. I'll check on her tomorrow, to see if she's OK.'

'James, you are such a sweetie!'

That silky dark brown hair. The tawny skin. The swish of silver bangles. The gleam of turquoise and amber. And her scent. It's not just fresh flowers, it's... It's dangerous. No, I'm not attracted to her. I can't be. Not in that way.

'James!'

'What?'

'Pay attention my darling.'

'Sorry.'

'So, let's see. Number one haven't RSVP'd either.'

'That doesn't surprise me,' I say, 'they're hippies. I bet they didn't even see the invitation. He's some kind of labourer. I gave him a job as a gardener once. He smelled of weed and he'd been drinking. Never again. She's also stoned most of the time. But it's hard to tell. She spends all the time running after their dreadful children.'

'Did you say the family at number twelve also have problems?'

'I did.'

'We should invite both one and twelve, yes?'

From the front door, number one exudes odours of skunk, boiled lentils and rancid cat food. As for number twelve, I carefully avoid eye contact with the two boys who live there – or are they men? It's hard to tell. They wear trainers and baggy sports clothes. They are man boys. Sometimes, black or silver cars with tinted windows appear in front of their house and emit a low, thudding noise.

Generally, to everybody's relief, these vehicles soon move back to deeper waters, like basking sharks visiting a shallow lagoon. I don't want to know what they get up to. The less I know the better. Instinct tells me that to attempt to establish any kind of familiarity with the wannabe gangsters at number twelve would invite disaster. I feel sorry for their mother. They've worn her down. She is beyond help. But it's her life.

'Look,' I say. 'I delivered the invitations, as you asked. Even to number six and no-one knows who lives there.' I am lying. I did not deliver an invitation to number twelve. I'm not an idiot.

'That's all we can do. If they come, they come.'

'Good, James.' She says, definitively.

'It's still, what, only seven people, if Janice comes.'

'Don't worry,' she says. 'Marcus and I have invited a few other people. We have friends you know.'

'I'm sure you do.'

'I think you'll like them. Two of them are, well, quite old but we've invited some young people that we know too. We met them when we were living in Putney.'

'Are you sure they'll be able to find their way to south-east London?'

'I don't think that'll be a problem.'

'Unless there's a train or tube strike.'

'You're doing it again.'

'Doing what?

'Being a pessimist. Anyway, don't be silly. They'll be coming by Uber, I imagine.'

'Well, that's great,' I say.

'Marcus and I are so excited. It will be the Feast of Ostara in our little close. James?' She sighs. 'You haven't touched your coffee. You need a fresh one.'

She shouts at Alexa: 'Alexa we would like some coffee please. Coffee!'

She talks to the device as if she's instructing a child.

Saturday 19th March, 4.07pm
Daniel, The Writer

Ron's car was winched onto a low loader and taken away on Wednesday night, under the eerie yellow glow of one the close's under-powered streetlights. There was something furtive about this exercise. Why did they do it at night? We can all go back to normal now. And we shall, of course. We're English.

The extraordinary event that has taken place – the death – will soon be assimilated into the life of the close. The repairs to its damaged fabric – the ruptured trees, the ugly scars of tyre tracks, have already begun. The close will heal itself, like a cat licking a wound. The event will be normalised with the balm of words. *Tragic accident, how ironic, what a shame, how terrible for his son.* We will all repeat these phrases, like a litany.

It's Saturday. Party day. This afternoon a large van parked in front of number seven. White plastic chairs and tables were removed with professional efficiency and carried through the house. Later, another van arrived. It was the caterers. I watched as Marcella carefully supervised the unloading of crates and Tupperware boxes. I saw her glance at the ugly grey lacuna in front of number five – Ron's empty parking space – and his tasteless concrete lions.

Did I really watch those lions come to life and chase Ron's truck round the close? Did I actually see his body fly into the air and land on a flower bed, like a crumpled rag doll? I'm sure I did. Marcella's glance rests on the too-clean drive and the incongruous lions. I seem to notice in her expression a very faint smile. Or am I imagining it?

3

The Feast of Ostara

Saturday 19th March, 11.16am
James, The Set Designer

That's strange. The door to number four isn't locked. Weird. Should I go in? Yes, why not... It's dark inside. It smells musty – and it's cold.

'Janice?'

No answer. You can tell she moved to the close in the 1980s, when she had money. The décor, with its busily patterned carpets and a colour palette of brown, coffee and orange has never changed. It's a relic of the time when people had large wooden sideboards and huge TV sets with screens like spectacle lenses.

I enter the kitchen. It's empty.

'Janice?' Silence.

I know, from previous visits, that she lives on the ground floor, shuffling from room to room on her Zimmer frame. She can look after herself. She still takes pride in her clothes and her jewellery. But she's become agoraphobic, retreating behind huge dark glasses that cover most of her face. Janice's life has contracted to four rooms. No-one visits her, not even her showbiz friends. Most of them are dead. Her nephews and nieces live a long way away. She has photos of them in the front room – girls in white dresses and toothy boys, with pictures of saints.

It is the room I'm familiar with. This is Janice's visiting salon, her parlour. The room is always over-heated. The carpet is too bright. There's a wooden radiogram with a sunray cut out of the front of the speaker. Tightly packed vinyl records live here – beige-voiced crooners, women in frothy chiffon dresses. One of them is JJ's LP. Their sleeves have faded, even though they're never touched by sunlight.

She has a drinks cabinet, in which syrupy and brightly-coloured liquids are kept for special occasions. On the walls are photos and playbills from her show biz days. When she started performing, there were still variety shows. She told me that her career ended because of her first husband. He didn't like her working.

Her career revived in the 1980s but she was now performing in small places, sometimes pubs. Janice was a singer who people half-remembered. She had a nasty fall soon after her second husband died – the nice one who loved her. She is a large lady now, stubbornly clinging to her frame, happy to entertain, but rarely going out.

I have never been in her bedroom. I tap on the door. No response.

'Janice?'

Nothing. I open the door. Stale, stuffy smell. Dark. Curtains drawn. Gleam of white pillows. There is a shape under the bed clothes. Janice? I move closer. Her hair is grey bristle. I touch her face. Her mouth has fallen in. Her skin feels like ice.

Saturday 19th March, 2.09pm
Mandy Martin, The Social Media Influencer

Hi my lovelies, well, it's Saturday – the big day, the day of the party. Now, I know that a lot of you have days like this – it could be a wedding, it could be a family party. You want that healthy look of fresh natural skin. Well, today, my lovelies, the Mooks is going to tell you exactly how to get that look, without breaking the bank! 🙂

All the products I mention today are listed below. These are the best products you can buy. You won't find them in the salons, believe me. Don't worry, I can get special deals on these products for you, my lovelies, because of my top industry contacts. Remember to follow me, Mandy Martin, the Mooks, on all of my social media channels – Instagram, Tik-Tok and Facebook.

Right, so you have hydrated that all-important under-eye area. The skin does get dry in that area, doesn't it? You've done your concealers and contourers, just like I've showed you. So, what comes next? Yes, that all-important layer – your foundation.

So, you know this fabulous new foundation range that I've been telling you about? Well, it arrived this morning and I'm going to be showing it to you – today!

By the way, it comes in seven matte, pearly and luminescent shades. I've already done a patch test to find out which one works best for me. So, here goes. Remember, my lovelies. Do your preparation but be bold, like I've shown you. The skin is your canvas. If you want a lovely fresh, natural look, you're going to need a little help. The Mooks does.

So take the brush and...it may feel a little tingly at first, like this one does, so...oh...oh. That's smarting a little...but...oh, oh...oh God... that's...oh...oh...I...oh...oh!

Sunday 20th March, 11.01am
Daniel, The Writer

I'm the first to arrive at the party. Marcella's dress is spectacular. It is black and clinging and far more flesh than dress is on view. Her eyes are shining unnaturally. Cocaine? Her scent has been increased in its scintillating allure by at least three notches. Marcus has dressed as if for a country house weekend, in pale brown corduroy trousers and polished brogues. He wears a tweed jacket over a well-pressed white shirt, with a pale cravat around his neck.

He greets me like a long-lost friend, asking me what I'm writing about at the moment. He seems to be genuinely curious. It's an article on foraging, I explain, the new fashion for looking for food in hedgerows that's spreading through the London suburbs.

As usual, Marcella curtails our conversation and draws me into the kitchen. Here, the main attraction is a tray of champagne glasses waiting to be filled. She has hired help for the evening – a local girl. She stands by, tensely, waiting to be instructed in her duties.

'Would you like to see the garden, Daniel?' Marcella asks.

'I would.'

It's well lit, although the night is not yet entirely dark. The garden offers a vision of order and calm – patches of emerald grass which glow like tropical islands, paved areas, palms and ferns in pots, and tasteful classical statuary. Many of these decorations are somewhat risqué – nymphs and goddesses with sensuously rounded buttocks.

At the end of garden, beneath a canopy of mature oak trees which grow on the other side of the fence, James' friend, Dom, has set up his decks. The music has not yet started. He wears a vibrantly coloured short-sleeved shirt and many festival wristbands coursing up his forearms. He's cupping an over-sized headphone to his ear, like a conch shell. Like Orpheus, he's focused on his important task – to bewitch the party guests with sound.

Marcella acknowledges him with a wave.

'Dom is a sweetie. What a great find. And we're so lucky with the weather, aren't we?'

I murmur my agreement. I turn to look back at the house. In the conservatory are two figures, like shadows.

•••

Marcella leads me back down the path to introduce me to these guests. He is a very old man in a formal suit with a waistcoat. His hair is silvery grey, his skin is sallow and covered with a network of fine creases, like a sheet that's been boiled too many times. His eyes are watery.

His companion wears a black floor-length dress nipped in at the waist. One would call it demure and old-fashioned apart from the fact that it thrusts up her virtually exposed breasts. I can see she's a woman of great vitality. Her eyes sparkle. Her dyed hair is the colour of a rusty bucket.

'Theo and Violet, I'm so glad you could come,' Marcella enthuses. The man barely registers her greeting but the woman gushes a 'hellooo'.

'Daniel, these are our friends. Theo is a book collector.'

The man stares through me as we shake hands. He has the eyes of a lizard. Perhaps he's blind?

His breath touches my face. It's foetid. I move back slightly but he doesn't seem to notice.

Violet registers no surprise.

'Where have you been hiding this handsome young man?' she demands of her hostess.

'He was the first person who welcomed Marcus and me to the close when we arrived,' replies Marcella. 'He has always been charming. And so English. Daniel's a writer.'

'Oh, a writer!'

Violet quizzes me for the next few minutes as if I'm a guest speaker at a book club. She has an old-fashioned London accent, with vowel sounds that one no longer hears. The man clutches the top of his cane facing the garden, his legs slightly apart. He is unnaturally still. He seems to be looking *at* the glass, not through it.

Marcella flits back into the kitchen. Marcus watches. One senses in him the calm, still centre of a man who is at ease with himself.

•••

Parties tend to follow the same well-defined stages. The first phase is the arrival, the greeting, the taking and placing of coats; the early guests are often shy, or don't really want to be there. Marcella is the greeter, a role that she is well equipped for. Her low-cut black dress, extreme friendliness and powerful scent make an overwhelming impression.

The first beneficiaries are bicycle man Simon Swift from number ten and his wife, Susan. For once, he isn't wearing Lycra. Susan's clothing is designed not to make an impression. Nevertheless, Marcella compliments her upon it. Her greeting overwhelms the couple. They quickly make their way down the hallway to the kitchen, seeking to escape. Marcus is here, like a suave maître d'hôtel, presiding over a rich array of food and drink.

I am in situ, savouring the complex notes of a glass of 2005 Burgundy – a good year, Marcus has told me.

More guests arrive. The next one is a surprise – Otto de Bont, who lives at number eleven, the composer of music guaranteed to alienate the untutored listener. He is wearing a collarless shirt and black cardigan and round frameless spectacles. How old is he? Forty, fifty? It's hard to tell. He's done well from his lonely vocation, hence his upmarket but minimally furnished house and extremely expensive bicycle.

The guests mill about looking awkwardly at each other. Otto and the Swifts would normally have nothing to talk about. They usually avoid each other like the plague. However, Ron Saxby's recent untimely death offers a safe topic of conversation. Marcus interjects comments and makes sure that glasses are filled.

Edward, the clarinettist, arrives next. He is the last of the first guests. He is wearing a suit with narrow lapels and a tightly knotted tie. His hair is slicked down with oil. This, or the defunct aftershave he's wearing, gives him an odd smell. The bottle of wine he is carrying, while expensive, is no match for anything in the cellar of number seven.

Edward and Marcus begin to talk. The clarinettist smiles. He has found, he thinks, a soul mate – an intelligent and cultured man, with a charming wife, who will restore the gravitas and culture that the close has lost – the dinner parties, the swapped classical CDs, the outdoor chamber music recitals.

Marcus is not attempting to escape. On the contrary. He's listening to Edward and nodding. Edward is laying out the prospectus for a renewed residents' association – a body that could rise, like a phoenix, from the ashes of its predecessor, designed to impose, with its carefully-minuted meetings, structure to the life of this secluded community.

•••

The music begins – a low, insistent repetitive thud, from the bottom of the garden. Edward registers surprise. Music and darkness offer some of initial guests of any party a diversion and means of escape. Some of the shyest and most reluctant will leave early.

Others from this group will be drawn into the spirit of the occasion, as the mild intoxication of their first drink kicks in. They'll wonder why they didn't want to come. They may even begin, horror of horrors, to enjoy themselves! Not Edward. The throbbing of Dom's speakers brings a nervous tic to his smooth-shaven face.

At half past seven, James drops in, smiling and shower fresh. He is wearing a lime green open-necked shirt and carrying a shop-bought cake, in a white box. He and Marcella air kiss and exchange compliments.

Mandy, aka 'the Mooks', should have arrived by now. She is nowhere to be seen. The joke is that she is still 'putting on her make-up'.

Poor Otto. He's escaped from Simon's droning, bicycle-themed monologue. He is standing alone in the garden, listening to a kind of music that he despises. Simon attempts to engage me on the street-by-street details of the borough's latest traffic plan, as Susan dreamily picks at party food.

Soon, I will deploy the excuse of needing to relieve my bladder and take a plate of canapes and a third glass of Burgundy into the garden. I'll chat to James and Dom. I know the DJ from previous parties. Normally, he's just returned from Ibiza. He's tanned like James and has a permanent smile – presumably from the effects of MDMA. I like him.

By eight o'clock, the sparsity of guests has become embarrassing. The Swifts have left. Edward and Otto are conversing, in a desultory fashion, in the garden. They're talking about 'modern music' and failing, utterly, to find common ground – picking at each other like two crustacea.

In the kitchen, I'm having an interesting conversation with Marcus. It has ranged over local evidence of Roman Britain, the geology of the London basin and ley lines. Marcella and James are locked in an intimate huddle, working their way through a seemingly inexhaustible supply of Champagne and speculating about the Mooks' absence. But this isn't really a party – it's more like an alcoholic-assisted coffee morning.

•••

At half past nine, I'm wondering whether to politely make my excuses and leave. But just as this rather restrained gathering is reaching a natural crescendo, something unexpected happens – a fresh group of guests arrives, like a company of troops making a beach landing. It's what often happens at parties. Recklessly late, they are already intoxicated, their pupils dilated from pills or powder. They don't do the stiff greetings and the fumbling with coats of the first arrivals. They plunge straight in, reviving the flagging guests in the kitchen, who have run out of things to say, and the jaded ravers in the back garden.

Each ring of the doorbell brings more arrivals – evidently Marcella and Marcus' friends from west London. Let me describe the women, as best I can. There are blonde Viking lovelies with perfect white teeth and eyes, dark-eyed Latin flesh pressers who rival Jennifer Lopez in curvaceousness.

All of them wear unfeasibly skimpy dresses that become smaller as the night progresses. Their perfume has the potency of industrially-manufactured pheromones. From around midnight, women wearing little more than their underwear arrive. Soon one of them is dancing naked in the garden to Dom's beats – floating like a cloud between the guests (or did I imagine it?).

Some of the guests follow the BDSM dress code. Others are Club-Med-style swingers, the men displaying their half-dressed wives for public consumption, like dangled car keys. The party reaches its crescendo just after eleven o'clock. Dom cranks up the volume and Mundania Close starts shaking to the trance, Afrobeat, rave mashup that he's cooking up.

I am pleasantly drunk and stoned. A mellow sense of sun-drenched wellbeing has been induced by Marcus' Burgundy. I have partaken liberally of the holy weed – lungfuls of sweet smoke from spliffs toked with James and Dom in a shadowy part of the garden. And the pills. Dom is a connoisseur in such matters. Perhaps they're pure MDMA, perhaps good old-fashioned ecstasy or designer LSD, or something even more bespoke. Who knows?

I'm not tripping. But I'm close. Dom's music is happening mostly inside my head. It is manifesting in my neural pathways like insane Catherine wheels and Roman candles showering arcs of fluorescent light in all directions. I have encountered Marcella at different points in the evening, straining to exchange words that can compete with the pounding assault of the music, like workers in an iron foundry. All of these conversations blur into one. As have those I've had with the Viking warrior maidens who seem to have stepped straight out of Netflix, their hair smelling like apples, and sun-ripened Italian sex sirens from half-remembered Fellini films.

Two weird vignettes that frame the party stand out. Did they really happen? I was so out of my head by the end that I have no idea. The first is in the conservatory. Theo, the ancient man with the foul breath, is holding court. His stories are captivating and hilarious. Everybody is hanging onto his every word, laughing. Marcus and Marcella lead the cheerleaders. Marcus' hand is placed high on Marcella's thigh. Theo's pink tongue licks his ancient, cracked lips. His consort Violet, attired in the funereal black and white lace of Queen Victoria, shrieks with laughter.

In the second vignette, I am in the garden, lying on my back. My eyes are closed. Dom's music presses into my brain in an assault of garish colours. I open my eyes. I see tangled limbs writhing, like those of a single organism. They're having sex. Are they really having sex? I don't know. Am I one of them? I have no idea. It really doesn't matter. I've joined the cosmos – the starlit sky that spins above Mundania Close, a fat full moon leering above it, as yellow as old laundry.

Sunday 20th March, 12.13am
Edward, The Orchestral Clarinettist

Good God, what an appalling night. I am… appalled. The noise! I imagine that is what an artillery bombardment would sound like.

What time did it stop? First at two o'clock in the morning, after the police finally arrived. Then, fifteen minutes later, it started again. But they were clever – they kept it to a level that was just below the pain threshold.

They didn't finally turn off that damned noise until after eleven! I'm glad I kept a log. We simply cannot have this kind of thing in Mundania Close. We cannot… What about people with children?! What about…?! I shall complain, in the strongest possible… complain… cannot have… this kind of… the close… artillery…

Sunday 20ᵗʰ March, 11.30pm
Daniel, The Writer

Poor Edward. I didn't like him. No-one did. But, even so, he didn't deserve such an undignified and public termination. This morning, I was sitting at my desk, trying to slow down the horses that were galloping through my head, when I looked out of the window.

Edward had appeared in his unnaturally neat front garden a couple of times. At midday, I saw him simply staring at Marcella and Marcus' house. He was shaking his head in disbelief. I could tell what he was thinking.

Saturday evening had started so well for him. I had watched him arrive at the party in his best suit, with his impressive bottle of wine, bought from a proper vintner. I'd listened as he had conversed with the polite and equally well-dressed Marcus.

They had been talking about digging up Ron Saxby's ugly driveway and re-planting the space. Roses, Edward had suggested. With their sharp thorns, they would provide both beauty and protection – a natural barrier. Marcus had agreed.

Edward had left the party at nine-thirty presumably close to his bedtime, content and well-vittled. The true party had not started by then. He had appeared again just after eleven – baffled and angered by the noise and the raucous shrieks of the guests who were now arriving every few minutes in white Ubers, like gulls alighting on a rubbish dump.

He had demanded to see Marcus. But Marcus could not be found. So he strode into the back garden. It was pulsing with light and sound. One female guest had removed her clothes. Unsavoury things were going on, some in the bushes, some in plain sight. It was like a Roman orgy. His mouth had opened but no words came out. He'd left.

•••

Today, after midday, he appeared outside his own house at number three. He was in full gardening mode – thick gloves, hiking boots, pruning shears, clippers, heavy duty waste bags and… a chainsaw. Edward mowed his grass for the first time this year and methodically began to cut back and tidy plants that were already tidy. It was easy to see what was going on. He was establishing order in the part of the close that he directly controlled, to restore his psychological equilibrium.

But what was the chainsaw for? It was too large for a small suburban garden. Was he going to break into the house of his neighbours, at number seven, the orgiasts, and cut them to pieces, so that that the quarry tiles of their beautiful kitchen would be awash with blood?

I soon found out the purpose of the device. Edward was going to cut down the plum tree that grew in front of his house because of the mess that its squashed fruits made every year on the pavement.

Fate had provided him with an excuse. You see, the tree had been badly damaged when Ron Saxby's van collided with it on Tuesday. It had nearly been cut in two by the careering vehicle. Now, he was going to do the decent thing and finish it off.

I could see that the chainsaw was far too big for this purpose. He'd have been better off with an old-fashioned handsaw. But he was making a point. I watched as he pulled the cord and the chainsaw barked into life. There was a fixed, determined look on his face. He was going to settle this damned tree for good.

•••

I was not prepared for what happened next. Observing Edward as he sloppily filled the chainsaw with petrol, spilling much of it, I saw him place the bright red fuel can too close to where he was working. His brain was a ball of rage. He wasn't thinking properly.

The catastrophe was sudden. A moment after the chainsaw's motor filled the close with its searing whine, a sea of orange flame washed over Edward and the tree, as a cloud of petrol vapour ignited. Man and tree were starkly defined in black on orange, like a silhouette drawing. Edward did not move. The chainsaw was lodged in a branch. He never relaxed his bulldog grip.

The flame flared in a thick column and flakes of grey ash drifted across the close. The conflagration reared up again as the petrol can exploded, like a dragon's breath. It was over quickly. The charred body of the clarinettist resembled an ancient mummy, attached to the scorched tree trunk.

•••

I'm standing outside, next to James and Otto. The fire has locked Edward's expression. He looks angry. His black lips are pulled back from his teeth. His eyes are caves.

Mundania Close becomes a crime scene again as it fills with vehicles – an unmarked quick response vehicle with flashing blue lights, an ambulance and two police cars. Blue and white plastic tape is unrolled – again. People in high-vis tabards guard the perimeter – perhaps the same ones who had been deployed on Tuesday after Ron was run over by his own truck.

A fire engine arrives and water is sprayed onto the blackened prairie of Edward's lawn. It sizzles as a cloud of white steam rises, like the dry ice fumes at a heavy metal concert.

People look at Edward's corpse and scratch their heads. The morbid spectacle, like a still from World War Two of a flame thrower victim, is photographed, both officially and unofficially.

A police officer comes into my house to take a statement. He tells me I was the only person to have witnessed what is already being described as 'the accident'.

While we're talking, we hear a commotion outside. More emergency vehicles are arriving. The reason becomes apparent when a body is wheeled out of number two by four people wearing hazmat suits and full face masks.

It must be the Mooks! Her body is driven away in an ambulance with blue lights flashing, followed by two motorbikes. Armed police officers guard her door.

Later, after midnight, our peace is invaded by a helicopter that hovers menacingly overhead like an angry hornet. A captioned aerial image is soon featured on rolling news, which reveals that four deaths in neighbouring houses have taken place in a quiet suburb of south-east London over the course of five days. Coincidence?

Our little community has been re-christened Catastrophe and Calamity Close, in several languages.

4

Eye in the Sky

Wednesday 23nd March
Strange deaths in Calamity Close
by Sandy Blythe
News Shopper

For once Lewisham has made the national news. But for all the wrong reasons. No wonder they are calling it Calamity Close. On Tuesday, a builder who lived at number five died, after running himself over in his own four by four. Accident?

On Saturday, Mandy Martin, or 'the Mooks', the well-known social media influencer, who lived at number two, died while she was applying her make up, live online. It seemed to dissolve her face. On the same day, the body of another resident was discovered – 75-year-old Janice Jones, once a well-known pop star, at number four. Coincidence?

As JJ, she recorded the UK's first ska hit in 1964, aged only 17. Called Sweet 'n Mighty it reached number two in the charts. JJ appeared on Top of the Pops, in a leather mini skirt. It was to be her only TV appearance. The former celebrity had lived quietly as a recluse in Mundania Close for almost 40 years. Nobody knew about her past life, apart from a few close friends.

Next day, the emergency services were back. Edward Graeme, aged 57, principal clarinettist with the London Symphony Orchestra had died while gardening on Sunday morning. Edward, who was known as 'Egg' by his friends, lived alone. He incinerated himself, in a bizarre accident involving a chainsaw.

It was the fourth death in five days. Staggering coincidence? Mundania Close has twelve houses. Now death has visited a third of them. Four neighbouring properties – numbers two, three, four and five – are empty. Understandably, the other residents are feeling rather worried. They are not inclined to talk to journalists.

These closely-spaced fatalities are arousing deep suspicion. Coroners' verdicts will tell us more. The saga of Mundania Close will continue. Perhaps, one day, they'll put it on Netflix!

Saturday 26th March, 9.11 pm
Daniel, The writer

A week ago, no-one had heard of us – we were an obscure corner of an unfashionable part of London – and now… Blame Sky News and its helicopter for days of cretinous stories rehashing the same Agatha Christie-themed crap. On Tuesday blah blah blah, on Saturday… Coincidence?

The story is still the lead item on TV and radio news bulletins. It has been reported that Mandy Martin's death while applying an apparently toxic face cream was watched by 1.7 million people online, before the video was taken down. The clip of her face melting had already escaped into the no-mans' land of social media. It's still out there annotated by endlessly proliferating memes and exclamation marks.

We've been in lockdown for most of the week. We were 'advised' by the police on Monday not to leave our houses, as forensic examinations were conducted at number two. Food was brought in. The close was under siege. The police were holding off waves of film crews and reporters from all over the world, as they investigated a 'potential terrorist incident'.

On Tuesday afternoon, a press conference was held. We learned, with relief, that no traces of nerve agent had been found at number two. The close was partially re-opened. We could leave… but that meant being harassed by world's press. There was a mobile catering van out there. Perma-tanned men and women with unnaturally white teeth were endlessly recording cheesy pieces to camera with the police cordon in the background – 'They are calling it "Calamity Close". In this quiet corner of London, nothing normally happens …' Horseshit.

•••

I have been thinking a lot about the deaths. Take Mandy. Maybe she suffered from an extreme anaphylactic shock, due to an allergy. Perfectly plausible. Edward, the egg man, should not have been operating a chainsaw stressed out as he was. JJ, the soul queen, could easily have suffered from a nocturnal coronary disaster. She was severely overweight, from years of asting white rice and fatty food.

And Ron Saxby? The man was a walking disaster – only one road rage incident from meeting his maker. Then again, I saw his monster truck come to life, like a beast, and push his head into a flower bed. Or did I? Was I dreaming? I must have been dreaming. The Calamity Close thing is all flim-flam – media-created hysteria.

I think that most of the viewing and reading public are sick of the story by now. I have noticed how it is migrating from the top of the evening news to the close. It is becoming a quirky tail-ender, designed to vaguely interest people before bedtime. A consensus seems to be emerging, that what happened last week was 'an incredible coincidence'. If the police had found out anything, they would surely have announced it by now – or arrested somebody?

The truth, 'incredible coincidence' or not, is that almost half of the households in Mundania Close have now suffered a bereavement. Numbers one and twelve, the Swifts, Otto, James and I are the survivors. Oh, and Marcus and Marcella. They have been lying low. No-one has seen or talked to them since the party. No-one is posting on the WhatsApp group. It's a sad place since the Mooks moved on. Perhaps I can leave the group now without anyone noticing?

The police are managing to keep most of the purveyors of news away. Anyway, they will lose interest pretty soon. But it's a different matter in the digital playground, or is it a cesspit? I have the largest online footprint of anyone in the close because of my blog. I'm not hard to find. Someone from a newspaper that I don't like has e-mailed me four times. Her name is Lottie something. She says that she will pay me money, 'for my trouble', hinting at a largish amount.

I nearly forgot, last night at about eleven, I saw something strange. A faint yellow rectangle of light appeared on the second floor of number six. I wouldn't swear by it but I'm almost certain that someone was moving around inside. Now that is odd.

Sunday 27ᵗʰ March, 8.26pm
Daniel, The Writer

The day is a time for doing, the night for dreaming. But often, when my mind is troubled, day and night bleed into each other. You see, I don't have the same routines as a normal person. Covid normalised this. It turned me into a vampire. To some extent, I can wake up and go to sleep when I want. It is when I am neither awake nor asleep that strange ideas come to the surface of my mind, fragments of the unconscious that have broken free like globules from a lava lamp.

Sometimes, words and phrases come. I force myself to become fully awake and to write them down in my bedside notebook. At times, I am trapped in a weird world between wakefulness and sleep. I know that I am dreaming but I am unable to break free. It is my lack of control that makes this kind of dream a nightmare.

Last night and this morning were like that. Thoughts that I have harvested have been captured in the semi-legible scribbles of my notebook. I do not keep a diary. There is no point. Mundania Close is a continuous actuality – a Möbius loop of trivial events and futile volitions. Neither do I keep a dream diary – my notebook is not an orderly narrative of actual dreams. It records the flashes of inspiration of lucid or self-conscious visions.

Last Saturday's party has been turning round a lot in my head. I have viewed it from all angles, remembered scraps of conversation and things that I saw. By the end of the party, I was almost hallucinating – which is not surprising considering the strength of Dom's weed and the ingredients of the pills that I had consumed. My thoughts keep returning to the strange couple in the conservatory – the old man with bad breath, the elderly lady in black, who shrieked with glee, like a child.

This couple did not fit in with the other guests. I did not see them outside, once drugs and loud music had turned the party into a bacchanalia, only at the beginning. They were black and white, shadowy – like holograms. The man did not appear to be in the actual present. He was there and not there. It was if he was not a physical entity bur a ghost. Ghosts don't have bad breath do they?

•••

Sundays are for lying in bed with the newspapers and another person, to bring tea to and to converse with. But not for me. I cross my living room. I place a mug of coffee, my smartphone and my notebook on my desk. I open the book at the page with the latest jottings. Immediately, I see two names – Theo and Violet.

I have written them down several times, to make sure that I remember them. The screen of my MacBook resolves into a plain blue background for the jumble of folders, Word files and jpegs that make up my working and imaginative life. My first action is to click on my Mail icon.

Two e-mails are waiting in my inbox. The first is from the unappealing Lottie from the Mail on Sunday, begging me, again, to give her an interview. I have checked her out. Her by-line photo has been manipulated to take twenty years off her age. Lack of empathy, and small-minded spitefulness are her trademarks.

The second is from someone I remember vaguely, a man called Adrian Bulow. He's a local historian. I met him on a Saturday morning at the open day of nature reserve in a small patch of local woodland. We spent a couple of hours together, chatting and cutting back brambles. I liked him. We exchanged details.

I read his e-mail.

Hi Dan,

I have been following, with fascination, the saga of Mundania Close on the news. It must be strange for you to be living in the middle of what looks like a media circus ☺. I remember us talking that day at the Garthorne Road nature reserve about local history. I've actually written about Mundania Close. I thought that you might be interested in this article. It's on my blog – Trees and mysteries: tales of south-east London (see link).

Please feel free to phone me (number below) at any time, if you would like to have a chat. Or perhaps we could meet for a coffee?

Best regards
Adrian

I click on the link.

Road with a 'Devilish' history

Mundania Close, it's an intriguing address and an interesting part of our local urban fabric – a delightful group of detached Edwardian house, built in the arts and crafts style. Somewhat tucked away, they are arranged in an unusual horseshoe-shaped layout around an open, communal area. The houses, which were completed in 1904, are grade two listed, thanks to the efforts of the Honor Oak Society. But do you know who created them?

It was a builder, once well known locally, called E.C. Christmas. His houses are still treasured for their ornate fireplaces, elaborate stairs and fine roof detailing, as well as their high ceilings, and beautiful tiled hallways. Christmas began his working life as a carpenter and was a highly skilled joiner.

This attractive little group was commissioned by a man called Theophilus William Williams, a local politician, who was to become infamous. He was in interesting character. Few things about Williams are what they appear to be.

Charismatic

Born in a workhouse, Williams rose from clerk to businessman, married a wealthy woman and entered local government. He became Mayor of Lewisham in 1900, at the age of 53. By that time, he had set up the first of his newspapers and several other businesses that had prospered. He was a very wealthy man.

In fact, he was a swindler who burned through his wife's inheritance and defrauded his investors. His life collapsed when he was declared bankrupt in 1904. Williams died at his own hand a few weeks later, on the day that he was summoned to appear at Greenwich Magistrates' Court, to be tried for embezzlement.

Williams commissioned E.C. Christmas to design and build a group of twelve houses, on behalf of a consortium of local businessmen. Naturally, he reserved the best house in the close, number six, for himself. It is the largest and most imposing property, with a first-floor drawing room that was large enough to be described, somewhat pretentiously, as a 'ball room'.

Society of the Ancients

We know that Williams and his associates formed a group, the Society of the Ancients. Few surviving records reveal its nature. Williams burned nearly all of his papers and business records just before his arrest, in an attempt to cover his tracks.

So, what do we know of the society? Well, we know that it included, as secretary, a man called Dixon Granger, who was the editor of one of one of Williams' newspapers, The Woodsman, based in Forest Hill. Other members were Cyril Butterworth a successful wine merchant, and a local property developer called Simon Ruddy, from Chislehurst.

Granger was a man of wide interests. His articles in The Woodsman frequently touched upon spiritualism, comparative religions, archaeology and folklore. We know, from Granger's writings, that he attended séances at which he believed that spiritual entities from 'beyond the veil' manifested themselves.

Curiously, all of the society's founding members died or disappeared in curious circumstances. In 1903, Butterworth, who had put up some of capital for the project, suffered a heart attack, Christmas simply vanished, Ruddy, another investor, was declared insane and interred in a lunatic asylum. Granger left London in 1904, the year that Williams took his own life.

A spooky address

Today number six is clothed in ivy. It is empty and boarded up. Two features offer clues to its former uses. Above the front door is a pediment. Moulded into it is the distinct impression of a square and compass – the universal symbol of Freemasonry.

It should come as no surprise that Williams was a Freemason – it explains how he rose to eminence so quickly – and that his imposing house served as a lodge for the craft. No doubt rituals took place inside, which may, by the ignorant, have been conflated with something more sinister.

A further clue, perhaps, lies in the name of number six. It is Sheol, an Old Testament word meaning 'place of darkness'. For Jews, Sheol is the realm of the dead. In Greek mythology, it is Tartarus, a dungeon of torment, the deepest part of the underworld. In the New Testament, it is Hades, or Hell.

Interestingly, I should note, in passing, that the layout of the close corresponds to an ankh – a cross connected to a slightly flattened loop. The ankh was a symbol imbued with deep meaning in ancient Egypt. I suspect that this charming but unobtrusive gem of suburban architecture, Mundania Close, has other secrets that are waiting to be discovered. I am happy to pass on the baton to someone else!

•••

I reach for my coffee, intrigued. Mundania Close has acquired a narrative. An absurd possibility takes shape in my mind. What if Theophilus William Williams – Theo to his friends – never died. What if he is up to murky goings-on with his new friends, Marcus and Marcella, who live at number seven?

By the most innocent reading, they are 'swingers' – people who like having sex with strangers. A more sinister interpretation would read them as practitioners of some kind of black magic. Could that explain the recent deaths?

I have a check to make. I leave my house and make my way to number six. Partially screened by a couple of gloomy looking yew trees, the house always seems to be in darkness, even on bright days. Its window frames are rotting. House buyers come to view it occasionally, but they never come back.

It is the decaying pride of the close – the largest house – directly facing the southern end of the mound. The windows are sealed from the inside. It's blurry and hard to see, covered by thick layers of paint. But there it is, just as Adrian described, a faint impression of the Freemasons' square and compass.

The name of house, moulded on a concrete panel on the front wall, has been almost obliterated by erosion. My eyes strain to decode the faint letters. That is certainly an S and there is a faint O, and an L. The H is illegible but the word that the letters form is clear – Sheol.

Am I dreaming? No, I am definitely awake. I look up at the first floor. So, that's where Society of the Ancients held their meetings. I can feel my skin tingling. The house has always seemed creepy. Now I know why.

•••

Sunday morning is not a bad time to take Adrian up on his offer. I call my friend while I am still standing outside number six. He picks up straight away.

'Hi Dan. Are you calling about the Mail on Sunday?'

'No, what do you mean?'

'They've done a big number on Mundania Close. I've got a copy in front of me.'

'No way.'

50

'Yeh, listen. WORLD EXCLUSIVE Life on Calamity Close by Lottie Baxter. That's at the top of the front page. There's four pages inside. Loads of pictures.'

'Pictures of what?'

'This very smart, affluent-looking couple. It's very like OK magazine – you know, gushing, sycophantic prose. There's an exterior shot of the close, with captions explaining who died.'

'Are there pictures of any other residents?'

'No, just this toothy looking woman and a bloke in a tweed jacket.'

'Marcella and Marcus.'

'That's them. There are some external shots. There's a picture that shows the front of number five, where the builder died and the front of number six.'

'That's where I am now…'

'Really?'

'Thanks for the article you sent me by the way.'

'That's OK. Was it useful?'

'Extremely. So, you've been to the close?'

'I have. It was a few years ago, in 2018. I don't imagine it's changed very much.'

'It hasn't. Apart from the fact that fewer people live here.'

'Indeed.

'Did you get a weird vibe, from number six?'

'I did, yes. Theophilus William Williams who had it built was a strange character.'

'You mean apart from being an embezzler and a Freemason?'

'I know that he collected Medieval grimoires. They are basically books of spells for invoking demons. And that he liked the ladies. I'm pretty sure that he practised what can only be described as sex magic.'

'Did it happen in the close?'

'One would imagine. You may have noticed that the close is laid out like an ankh, which represents the female reproductive system. In its centre is a mound, a mons pubis. Some people think that the Chapel of Venus that Williams had built is hidden there, beneath the vegetation.'

'Do you think so, Adrian?'

'Who knows? It's possible.'

'Is this information in the Mail on Sunday?'

He laughs. 'God, no. They don't know half of it. I am the only person who knows about any of this stuff. And I have only published a fraction of what I know.'

'How do you know it?'

'Mainly from Dixon Granger's memoir, published in 1924. It was published privately and only a few copies were printed. My wife found a very rare copy in in a bookshop in Blackheath.'

'I know it – the one the corner, by the heath. I love that shop. I often go there.'

'So do I.'

'Was Granger into weird stuff?'

'Yes and no. From what I can make out, he was just a harmless spiritualist, a table rapper. He believed in entities that live on the astral plane. It was all about fairies and ectoplasm for him. That was the problem.'

'What do you mean?'

'Well, it's clear from reading the memoir, that Granger and Williams fell out. It seems that Williams intended Mundania Close to be a kind of free love commune. Granger was going to buy a house in the development, yours actually, number nine. But he never did. Before he moved in, they had an argument.'

'Why?'

'Like I told you, Granger was a spiritualist. He was simply into talking to the dead, not sex magic. He spilled the beans on Williams to the authorities, including to senior Freemasons, which contributed to his own downfall, but not before a few more people around him had died mysteriously.'

I decide not to tell Adrian that I have met Theophilus and his partner, Violet, and, in fact, that I have talked to them. *Maybe later.*

'Well, that's an amazing story.'

'Yeh, it is.'

'Are you going to do anything with it.'

'Christ no. I wrote about in on my blog. I did start to write a book. It was called The Lewisham Love Cult. I was convinced that it was going to be a best-seller. I was half way through the research, and then…'

'What?'

'Someone broke into my house. They stole my MacBook, memory sticks, the drafts of the manuscript, all of my research files.'

'Christ.'

'Listen, you're obviously interested in this stuff. I'd love to help you.'

'Really?'

'Yeh. I can lend you Dixon's Granger's memoir. The robbers didn't steal that. I think you'll find it interesting.'

My heart begins to beat faster.

'Could we meet?'

'I don't see why not. There's no time like the present. My wife and I are having lunch at the Nag's Head in Lower Sydenham. We're just about to leave. Would you like to join us, Dan? I know that Charlotte would love to meet you. We'll bring Granger's book.'

'That's very kind of you. Thank you. I could meet you there at one. I can pop over on my bike.'

'That's great.'

'Cool. See you there.'

I'm excited. I don't wear Lycra to ride my bike, just my normal clothes. 'Pop' is not exactly the right word. The bike weighs a ton and most of the gears don't work. I tell people that's why it has never been stolen, claiming that this is a good thing.

•••

On the way to Sydenham, I stop off at Mundania Close's local shop. It stays open all hours and sells basic items at inflated prices. I purchase a copy of the Mail on Sunday.

The Mail franchise sticks to what it's good at – tickling the fancies of the voyeuristic and aspirational. It is written in a stilted language made up of bolted together phrases, many of which have been handed down, virtually untouched, from the 1950s. The names of TV programmes are abbreviated. It's a compressed and pre-digested discourse. 'Strictly hunk in late-night high-speed mercy dash'… 'Shamed town hall chiefs' … 'Worried Whitehall bosses' … No-one actually speaks like that. Not much thought is required on the part of the reader.

At least half of the pages devoted to Calamity Close consist of pictures. Marcus and Marcella, in their country casuals – denim for her, tweed for him – 'relaxing' at home. They look like waxworks. Their living room has spotless white rugs, antique furniture and well-stuffed bookshelves. Marcus, we learn, is a best-selling author and Marcella is an 'interior designer'. Of course.

The kitchen is a mixture of ultra-modern and faux Cotswolds cottage. Their conservatory, with its wicker chairs, glass-topped coffee table and carefully scattered magazines, is a semi-tropical rainforest of exotic, large-leaved plants.

Marcella is wearing white in nearly all of the pictures. She has clear skin, a cheesy smile and beautifully applied make-up, with heavy use of black eyeliner. I notice something almost at once that catches my breath. In all of the photos, a silver ankh hangs around her neck.

I read on, standing in front of the shop.

The headline says 'How I escaped alive. Tea and cupcakes inside Britain's deadliest address'.

The story continues: Are Marcus and Marcella Gardner the unluckiest couple in Britain? They moved into their brand-new dream home in January. A few weeks later, their neighbours began to die, one by one.

The whole country is speculating how four people in one road could die one by one in unusual circumstances – even Janice Jones' death is now being treated as suspicious.

Mundania Close is intriguing to a nation of amateur detectives. It's a game of Cluedo, an Agatha Christie novel, or an episode of Midsomer Murders.

And now I am sitting in the kitchen of number seven with Marcella Gardner, enjoying a cup of Earl Grey tea, poured from a bone China teapot.

Marcella is pretty and vivacious. Originally from Syria, she grew up in the United Sates, where her businessman father had moved to. She met Marcus while studying in California, where he was lecturing.

Sitting in her luxurious kitchen, with a Persian cat on her lap, she explains that her two-million-pound south London house was a bargain.

'Marcus and I were looking for a doer-upper,' she explains, 'a project. We have always wanted a classic English house. It's what Marcus grew up in in Sussex.'

Their grade-two listed house is in beautiful, quiet little close, with hollyhocks. Marcella explains: 'We both fell in love with it. Of course, it needed a lot of work, both inside and outside. We had to strip virtually everything out and start again.'

Unexplained deaths

Mundania close has become infamous for its unexplained deaths. Did she detect anything strange about her neighbours when they moved in? She replies, sweetly, 'oh no, they were perfectly sweet to us. They all made us very welcome.'

I notice that there is nervous edge to her smile. So, are she and Marcus going to stay in Calamity Close? 'Oh yes,' she says, 'we plan to. The close itself is a community. It's like a village.'

A village in which people are dying in mysterious circumstances. But she insists: 'We have no plans to leave. Marcus and I are sure that the deaths are accidental.

A cat looks up at her, with its hazel green eyes. 'Would you like a cupcake?' she asks. 'I made them myself.'

I stop reading.

The man who sells me the newspaper paper has no idea that he is living virtually on top of Britain's most newsworthy and probably dangerous address, even though a helicopter is buzzing overhead. How dozy is that? There is no point explaining it to him. He simply won't get it.

I look at my watch. It's ten to one. The Nag's Head is a couple of miles away – up one steep hill and down another. My bike, like I said, weighs a ton. It's normal for me to be late and out of breath when I meet people, sweating like Oliver Reed on a late-night chat show. As usual, I tell myself, without actually believing it, that the exercise will 'do me good'. Before I set out, I must make a phone call.

5

Dead Zone

James, my neighbour at number eight, is clearly annoyed that I have phoned him. He doesn't even turn his phone camera on.

'Yes?' he sounds tetchy. He is still in bed.

'Have you seen today's Mail?'

'No should I have? Why?'

'Marcella and Marcus are splashed all over it.'

'I know.' There is a long pause. 'Marcella told me that they were going to run a story, with some nice pictures.'

'She told you?'

'Yeh, she got paid quite a lot, she said.'

I hear a sleepy voice in the background.

'Don't you think that's disgusting, James.'

I hear the voice again. It is Marcella. She giggles the way someone does when they are on coke. Then I hear a male voice that I recognize – Dom, the DJ.

Good grief. Are they in bed together? Something tells me from tones of James's voice that they are.

'Why is it disgusting?' he says, peevishly.

'Because…'

He interrupts me.

'I say good luck to her. They made an offer to me too, but I turned them down. I don't want reporters and photographers traipsing through my house, with their dirty shoes.'

He breathes out through his nose. I can tell that he doesn't want to be on the phone. Yesterday, early in the morning, I saw James and Marcella jogging together. She was wearing figure hugging black leggings, her brown hair was tied in a ponytail. James was wearing a tracksuit and new trainers. They looked like an octopus's tentacles strapped to his feet. The two trotted down the close side by side, like Palomino horses.

'Actually, I'm not phoning you about the Mail, but about another article…'

He does not respond.

'It was in the newsletter of the Honor Oak Society. It says…'

'Christ Daniel!'

He is about to lop me off.

'The thing is…'

'Daniel.' He is speaking while frowning. 'I've been meaning to say this for a while. You need to stop watching people, OK? You're always there at your fucking window, looking out, like a ghost. It's weird. It's creepy. I have to say, it's pissing people off.'

I am shocked.

'Bye.'

He ends the call.

•••

There are times when life slaps you in the face. In these moments, you are granted an insight into yourself from an unexpected quarter – one that causes you to feel uncomfortable or embarrassed. It follows hubris. I have learned, over time, that such moments are extremely valuable. They prompt us to re-evaluate our ourselves.

What am I doing with my life, I reflect, after the phone call? Since the publication of my book on an over-praised pop star, I have, indeed, become a curtain twitcher. I'm the kind of person that I profess to despise – a judgmental suburbanite – a hypocrite, pottering around in the lower reaches of journalism. Yes, I have a lovely house. But I am living there alone. And I'm treading water.

These thoughts flood through my head, as I grab a bag and wheel my bike through the front door, heading for Sydenham. It's five to one, so I am focused on an urgent task – my meeting with Adrian, the chronicler of the weird history of Mundania Close.

•••

The Nag's Head, known as 'the Nags', is what Londoners call a 'proper boozer'. That means that it has carpets, not bare floorboards, that it is patronized by people in the middle and later years of life and that it sells draught beers that were fashionable before the craze for cloudy craft beers and pale ales that are absurdly expensive and all taste faintly of citrus.

Such establishments take pride in their 'traditional' Sunday roasts. Beef, served with roast potatoes, glutinous gravy, Yorkshire pudding and a vegetable is always on the menu.

That is what I am anticipating, as I freewheel down Sydenham High Street, heading for the pub. My stomach juices are gurgling. The Nags is not a microwave place – the food for its Sunday lunches is freshly prepared. They serve a beer that I like, a proper dark brown bitter.

I am about to eat a delicious meal, talking about local history with an expert. And I am to meet Adrian's no doubt charming wife, Charlotte, and take custody of Dixon Granger's intriguing autobiography.

Travelling from Upper to Lower Sydenham means descending the social hierarchy. The poshest houses are those closest to the Victorian railway station at the top of the hill. At the bottom, there used to be a gas works. The site surrounding the former giant gas holder has been replaced by a retail park. But it's still 'lower Sydenham' – a below stairs world in which a faint aroma of town gas lingers.

As you descend the hill, the Nags, well-known for its 'blues nights', is on the right-hand side, next to an Aldi supermarket. It forms a psychological boundary. The top of the hill is 'posh Sydenham', in the middle is genteel, still respectable Sydenham, after the Nags is gangsta Sydenham. You don't want to go there. Especially after dark. OK, I may be exaggerating. A bit.

•••

As I pass the post office, I see that the road has been sealed off. The blue and white plastic tape stretched across the road indicates that a crime has taken place. In London, that usually means a courier knocked off their moped by a car, or a stabbing.

The result is always the same – backed up, irritable car drivers, people on buses jabbing at their phones. But not for the cyclist. The cyclist is invisible – a ghost squeezing between the cracks of the city. As usual, cyclists are not being stopped, because they don't exist. The crime, whatever it was, has taken place in, or in front of, the Nag's Head. The pub is closed.

I see four squad cars. They are slewed diagonally across the road. You can tell from the angle of the cars that something serious has happened.

I like Lower Sydenham. It's one of those second-best or third-best choice suburbs for ambitious incomers which has not yet been fully gentrified. Artists rent empty shops and art school bands play in pubs' function rooms. I've been known to go to gigs there and to frequent the area's second-hand shops, where junk has become re-purposed as bric-a-brac. That Sunday morning, I fall into a normal behavioural pattern. If I am not going to be able to meet Adrian and Charlotte, at least I can have a bit of a wander and pick up some bargains at Aldi, the cut-price supermarket. I park and lock my bike at the rear of the shop.

I phone Adrian while I am waiting at the checkout. The call goes to voicemail. I wonder what has happened. Has he witnessed the crime?

I am about to pay when I overhear a conversation. It's a man who has been in the pub. Yes, he says, it's true. A customer has been murdered, in broad daylight.

The murderer, he says, stabbed his victim with a huge knife and left it protruding from his chest. He calmly exited through the back door. No-one stopped him. The victim's wife screamed hysterically.

I phone Adrian again. Voicemail. Normally, one should dismiss pessimistic and negative thoughts – that's what they told me in my therapy sessions. But this one won't go away.

•••

I linger at the till. There's a strange atmosphere in the shop – a subdued buzz, as the grizzly tale of what happened next door is told and re-told. People are rarely murdered in public places in broad daylight. If the story is true, the event will attach itself to this pub forever – like an invisible plaque attached to the wall.

'It's terrible isn't it,' says someone close to me. I agree that it is.

I drag my feet leaving the supermarket. Lots of people who are vaguely curious or who have been drawn to the grizzly event are milling around.

The Aldi's car park is next to the pub garden at the rear of the Nag's Head. The whole area is sealed off. A forensics tent is in place and a man in white space suit is entering the back door of the pub There is a single ambulance. There is no sense of urgency.

I notice a woman. She is sitting next to a female police officer. There is blanket around her shoulders. It doesn't hide the

59

blood. As well as looking as if she has just finished a shift at an abattoir, she has the whitest face of anyone that I have ever seen and the middle-distance stare of person who has witnessed something terrible.

I am certain that it is Charlotte, Adrian's wife. There's a cotton shopping bag on the table in front of her. I wonder whether Granger's memoir is in it. I observe her for a while. She doesn't see me.

Some thoughts run through my head. Those who get in the way of Marcus and Marcella at Mundania Close tend to perish – mostly horribly. Did getting too close to T.W. Williams cost Adrian his life? This is the kind of brutal, back-off slaying that is the hallmark of the Freemasons, worldwide. A change of tactics is required, if I wish to stay alive. Fuck the memoir. Let the police puzzle over it. It's too dangerous.

I wheel my bike along the side of the Aldi back to the main road. There's a block of weathered stone on the pavement here. Its function was to help people mount horses. The pub is that old.

A television van is squeezing into the car park as I leave, soon to disgorge a reporter of breaking news. A policeman gives me a curious look as I mount my bike. I churn my way slowly, in the lowest available gear, back up the hill.

•••

I arrive back at the close at three o'clock – the dead-zone in the middle of Sunday afternoon, when the search for a purpose to life is most acute. The first thing I see is a police car. At first, I think it's in front of my house – a spasm of panic passes through me. Then I realise that it is visiting next door, the house of Simon the cyclist.

The front door opens A female police officer walks to the car and it drives off, slowly. She barely registers my presence.

The visit could have been about anything – several lines of police inquiry on the traumas of Mundania Close are continuing. The old Daniel would simply have gone back into his house to search for clues on the internet. This isn't the old Daniel – the curtain twitcher. It's the new one – the good neighbour.

I walk down the path and tap on the door of number ten, the house of the holy crotch. I have decided that I won't be nosy. I'll merely ask whether there is anything I can do. Isn't that the sign of a goof neighbour? After all, the remaining residents of this community are suffering from PTSD.

Susan's face is like chalk. Her eyes are red.

'Can I help?'

She doesn't reply. She leads me into the living room. I have never been inside this house. I have barely exchanged more than a few words with Susan in the last ten years. Now I am sitting next to her, on her sofa. She begins to cry. I feel a peculiar urge to touch her. But I don't.

Simon used to ride off on strange missions alone. He would cover unfeasibly long distances on his slim-wheeled titanium machine, like a knight in black Lycra searching for damsels in distress.

Once he told me that he had cycled to Brighton and back – in one day. I was astonished. He was incredibly nonchalant about this journey. Perhaps wearing skin-tight trousers turns ordinary mortals into superheroes.

I know, because he explained it to me, in enormous detail, that he not only measured and logged the miles that he covered on his high-tech bike but his vital signs and the calories he consumed, working out complex coefficients of biology to kinetic efficiency.

•••

The front room is functional. There are no coasters, or mismatched cushions, no family photos or discarded, half-read books. This must be how they live. Susan stops crying. She looks at me, then away, as if she is searching for her husband in the beige room. Then she tells me what happened.

Sometimes, she explains, Simon, in his free time, tested the experimental road schemes and junctions that he had helped to design. Today, he had set out at dawn for Chislehurst, a nearby suburb. He had helped to devise a new road layout there, as part of a 'road calming' scheme – *such an inappropriate term.*

From her fragmentary description, it was a sensor-enabled digitised system, integrating various sets of lights, using an algorithm, so that bicycles and lorries could, in theory, co-exist in the same eco-system – the kind of infuriating traffic intervention that raises the blood pressure of both cyclists and motorists and leads to people writing letters to their local paper.

The police told her that the accident had been an inexplicable event. The section of road that he was on had been closed to traffic at the time of the incident. His body had been found on an empty road – the bicycle's frame was almost folded in two. The police hoped that his helmet camera would solve the mystery.

Normally one would drink tea, or something stronger, on such an occasion. But this is a caffeine and alcohol-free house. I wonder what Susan eats. I bet there isn't much food in her kitchen, apart from rice cakes and energy bars. She tells me that she does not want to stay in the house tonight.

I say that I totally understand. The poor woman is bereft. Her other neighbour, Otto, at number eleven, she tells me, has returned to Germany. He won't be coming back.

She is going to her sister's house in Richmond, on the train. She says that she needs to pack her case. I ask if I can help her. It is a ridiculous suggestion. I feel foolish. She begins to cry again. I want to cradle her, like a baby. But I don't.

•••

Another mystery appears on the national news that day. It is the shocking story of a man who died in a violent incident the Nag's Head public house, in south-east London, while eating a roast lunch with his wife. At first, he is not named. The BBC does not mention the most shocking part of the story – that a zombie knife was sticking out of his heart. By the next day, it's common knowledge in the local area.

It's time for the second phase of my campaign – hold your friends close and your enemies closer. I sit down at home and compose an insincere e-mail, designed to ingratiate myself with Marcella. I push send. With a satisfying swoosh, the message speeds to its recipient. I have written it carefully, affecting a jaunty spontaneity.

Hi Marcella,

I owe you a huge apology ☺. Yes, it's Dan, at number nine. It may appear that I have been spying on you, which would be creepy and weird. Believe me, I haven't. As you know, I am a writer and I work at home. I spend far more time than is healthy looking out of the window – you know, like that character in the Hitchcock film?

Please believe me. I am not spying on you. I'm not a voyeur, or even a particularly nosy neighbour. I'm going to move my desk to face the wall, so you shouldn't see my face staring out again!

I'm so sorry about this. When James picked me up on it, I immediately realized how weird my behaviour must seem. I like you and Marcus. I have since the first day you arrived. I really enjoyed your spring party by the way. Your arrival has been a breath of fresh air, in a dull environment that has not changed for years. English people can be so unfriendly.

I've had some fascinating chats with Marcus. And I hope to have more. We share many common interests. I hope that you can excuse my aberrant behaviour. You won't see my face any more at strange times of day, peering out through the curtains! I promise.

best regards

Daniel

Marcella texts back almost straight away. She must be one of those people, constantly alert to pings and vibrations, who has hyperactive thumbs. She'll be sitting in her beautiful, well-appointed kitchen.

Hi Dan ☺ ☺

Don't be ridiculous. No apology is necessary, my darling. I know that you are not weird!! Marcus and I like you very much you too! He told me that you are most cultured and interesting person that he has met since we have been in London – and that includes people who work for the BBC!

James can be very naughty. He can have a sharp tongue. I don't know what he said to you but, believe me, I have never taken offence at anything you have done. On the contrary. Of course you take a keen interest in the word around you. You're a writer!

Don't worry that you have upset me. You haven't. And please don't move your desk my love. Good news. Marcus and I are planning another party! We have some plans for the close and we've love to share them with you. For example, we think that we should

63

open up the mound, so that residents can party there, and kids play, without having to ask for that stupid gate to be unlocked.

Why don't you pop round tomorrow evening at six? James and I would love you to help us plan the party. Don't give your concerns a second thought. It's good to watch sometimes ☐ 💔 ♥☐! I hope to see you tomorrow.

Sweet dreams my love, Mx 💋 ☐ 🎉 🎈!

It's good to watch. Jesus. Is that swingers' code? Marcella is beautiful and she is as sexy as hell. *I wonder what she, James and Dom get up to, when they… Shut up Daniel!*

Perhaps, one day, people will communicate entirely with emojis, like hieroglyphics.

Should I reply? I wait for ten minutes. *Keep it simple.* Just a thumbs up and a smiley. And a postscript. See you tomorrow. *Oh, Christ what am I getting myself into?*

6

Pink Moon Happening

Monday 29th April, 8.02pm
Daniel, The writer

Marcella's kitchen is warm and welcoming. Her latest painting dominates the white end wall. It could either be interpreted as a juxtaposition of brightly-coloured shapes, or as a sensual dance of bodies writhing in ecstasy on a tropical beach. Which is it?

She spends much of her time here, entertained and assisted by her digital servant, Alexa, close to her sleek Persian cats. Marcella doesn't have a job. I assume that Marcus' private income provides both of them with economic freedom. What is he up to now? Reading up on spells and witchcraft in his study? Who knows? This house, apart from the hallway and kitchen, is a mystery to me.

Marcella's closely-fitting jeans match her contours a little too perfectly. Watching her is tormenting me. She is wearing a faded denim jacket over a white v-necked crop top that makes a feature of her bare midriff and jeweled belly ring. Her amber-skinned face, with its deep brown eyes is always smiling. I have never seen her lips not coated with vermilion lipstick, her hair not shiny and well brushed, her black eyebrows not plucked into perfect crescents.

James and I are sitting on either side of her breakfast bar. I have been trying to read his face, but with little success. James is an inscrutable character, extremely guarded to those who he does not regard as his close friends. That will need to change. If I am to enter the axis of evil and to become one of the 'insiders' of the close.

For the past few minutes, we have been talking about his work, puffing on James' cannabis-loaded vape. He hasn't asked me any questions about mine. I'm old school, I prefer joints to vapes. But, I must admit, the discrete little device creates a nice vibe – the kind that mellows your mood and makes colours a little brighter, without filling your head with clouds. Also, it's more scientific than a hand-rolled joint. You can know, reliably, what you are smoking and how stoned you are going to get – at least in theory.

James explains that he is creating the sets for a forthcoming production of The Marriage of Figaro (yawn) at Royal Opera House.

65

Dom is to design the sound and lighting. It's a step up from DJ-ing and a bit of a gamble. Important matters preoccupy James. Should he and Dom formalise their relationship with a civil partnership, or even marriage? Should they live together? Should they adopt a child? Or more than one? Boys or girls?

Their relationship is fenced in by thickets of unresolved questions. I sense that their answers will be connected to the success of the forthcoming production. Although how can one fail with 'the Fig'? It has everything. Great story. Big tunes. Anxieties have made James' moods brittle and have strained their relationship. The dynamic is obvious. Dom is the easy-going one. James is the worrier.

I make some 'I am-your-friend and I care' type interjections, as James circles his preoccupations. Marcella also comments. I soon notice that he is only listening to and acknowledging her. She is prepping this evening's meal and taking an occasional puff on the vape.

They are comfortable in each other's company. They jog together two or three times a week. Now three of us are sharing James' dilemmas. There are actually, implicitly, four people in the room. I'm pretty sure, from the sounds I overheard on the phone, that James, Marcella and Dom share a bed. Are James and Dom both bisexual, or is it just one of them? What about Marcella?

One of the aromas of the kitchen, is her patchouli oil perfume. Hippy catnip. The aroma reminds me of amorous episodes in damp fields at music festivals, when the fabric of my tent formed a warm orange filter. The other half of me is in the present.

•••

Her manner towards me has always been relaxed but it has changed since the emoji splattered text of Sunday. We seem to have crossed an invisible boundary from friendliness to flirtation. Her white top has a plunging neck. My eyes are drawn like magnets to her exposed, impossibly flat stomach and to the v-shaped-abdominal muscles, that tempt one's eyes ineluctably downwards.

Behind her, as she peels and chops onions on the counter, is the puzzle of her latest painting – one that she has already invited me to admire. To my stoned eyes, the orange shapes are definitely fucking. James is frowning. I understand why. He is jealous. I am intruding into the intimacy that he has created with Marcella, like a stranger at a sleepover. Marcella is pulling me in. James is pushing me out. Dom is somewhere on the periphery. *God, what a soap opera.*

•••

'Is your smoke thing still going, James?' asks Marcella.

He pulls the vape out of his pocket. It never seems to go out. I decline a puff this time. In fact, I ask Marcella for a glass of water.

'So, Dan,' says Marcella, 'James and I were thinking that it would be great to have another party on the close.'

How? Nearly everyone here is dead.

'I think that full moons are always best for parties, don't you, like our last one. And there's a pink moon on the 16th of May.'

'What's a pink moon?'

'it's in April – the full moon of spring. Pink is a great colour theme, don't you think, James, for a party?'

'Er yes.'

He doesn't sound enthusiastic.

'It gives us lots of time to prepare. Oh, Dan, James and I have had some ideas. May we run them by you?'

'Of course,' I say.

'Well, this time, we want to make it a bigger party. We want to have it on the mound.'

'Like you said in your e-mail…'

'That's right.'

She explains the concept. The idea is to remove the spiked iron fence that surrounds the space, now that the orchestra snob at number three is dead and can raise no objections. In future, she proposes, any resident will be able to use it. They will be able to do what they want – barbecues, picnics, parties. It will be great for kids.

'For kids?' I say.

'Like Tallon and Fallon.'

'Who?'

'Don't you know them, Daniel? They are Kaz and Hamish's kids. They also have an adorable baby girl called Fleur.'

'Who are Kaz and Hamish?'

'They live at number one. They are lovely people. Virtually every time their children went outside, that sour old man at number three used to shout at them or phone the police. I've explained to them that Marcus and I are not like that. If their children want to make dens in the bushes or race their bikes round the close, that's fine by us.'

'You've been round to their house?'

'Yes, a few times.'

I'm shocked. The residents of number one are an enigma to me. As far as I can see, she is a faded hippy, dressed from charity shops. He is a grumpy man in a biker jacket, usually holding a can of Special Brew.

Their house is only four from mine, chronologically, but that's a long distance in suburbia. They might as well be living on the other side of the world. Their two semi-wild children, with their sheepdog-like manes are indistinguishable from each other and of indeterminate gender. The whole family has red hair.

Perhaps I have been infected by the hauteur of Egg the clarinettist, the misanthropy of atonal Otto, the end-of-spectrum oddness of Simon Swift, the contempt of Ron 'the bull' Saxby, and the nouveau-riche disdain for the poor of Mandy 'the Mooks'.

I have never wished to connect too closely with the people of Mundania Close – watching them was enough. Is it now changing, under the influence of Marcella and Marcus, into a less uptight, more tolerant community?

'Kaz is a herbalist and a reiki healer. Hamish used to be a guitarist. He was a professional musician before his accident.'

'His accident?'

'He fell off a stage and broke his back.'

'How do you know?' I say.

Marcella smiles.

'Because he told me, darling. You know, I think this party was meant to happen.'

'What do you mean?' James says.

'Well think about it. Marcus and I can invite our Putney and Rye friends. You can design the space, James. Dom can do the lighting. Hamish's band can do the music.'

'Hamish doesn't have a band,' James says.

'Well, he can get one, can't he. By the way, Marcus and I will pay for this. We'll be happy to pay. It's a good idea, don't you think… James?'

She appeals to him with her eyes.

'Yeh, it's a great idea,' he says, like a man facing the prospect of dental surgery.

'We can also open up the chapel.'

'What chapel?' I ask.

'Oh, it's the strangest thing.' Marcella's eyes widen. 'It was built in 1904 when Mundania Close was created, but it's covered by vegetation. It's an actual miniature neo-Gothic church! There are twelve houses in the close. It was supposed to be the thirteenth house.'

'How do you know this?'

'Marcus and I have seen the plans. We got them from the Land Registry.'

'How do you know it's still there?'

'It must be,' she says. 'It will be great to have it revealed in time for the party, won't it. James, you know about landscaping don't you. Can we start the groundwork next week?'

'Sure.' His voice is flat and dead. He is staring into space.

'I'm so excited about this, boys. James is your weed stick still switched on?'

•••

Marcella opens a bottle of red wine. I feel less aroused by her now, even when she is sitting next to me and her knees are brushing against mine. Marcella and I continue to talk through the details of the pink moon party. James makes no contribution to the conversation. I explain that I have dug a few flower beds and mowed some lawns in my time. I assure Marcella that all of my services will be provided free of charge.

I tell her that when I was a kid, in Bromley, there was a large garden at the back of our house and I spent a lot of time in it. I made a treehouse in a crab apple tree, where from the ages of fourteen to sixteen, I read science fiction books.

It's not a surprise when James announces that he has to go home, because he has a headache. In the American vernacular, he is pissed. In the English one, he has the hump. But the 'pink moon happening' has acquired an unstoppable momentum. It will definitely go ahead, with him or without him. That's probably the main reason for his displeasure.

When James has left, I ask Alexa to play the song, Pink Moon, by the melancholy English folk singer, Nick Drake. Marcella has never heard the track. She is enchanted. We move on to something psychedelic and trancy.

She says something that stops me in my tracks.

'Daniel, would you like to go upstairs?'

'I'm sorry?'

'Would you like to go upstairs?' I check her face. Her brown eyes do not avert from mine.

'To see Marcus.'

'Oh.'

'Yeh sure.'

Marcella ushers me out of the kitchen. She precedes me up the stairs. Oh Jesus – her undulating pelvis. I clock the décor of the rest of the house as we walk through it. Part of my mind – one that I rarely turn off – is looking for significant details.

The décor in minimalist. The walls are white, the carpets beige. There are more of Marcella's paintings on the walls, as well as signed lithographs and screen prints.

At the end of the landing, she taps softly with her knuckles on a stripped pine door.

'Yes?' The voice is calm.

Part of me wants to run away. My throat is dry.

'Are you OK James?' Marcella smiles.

'What?'

'Are you OK?'

I nod.

'I'll leave you then.' She walks back to the top of the stairs.

So it's not a threesome.

'Please, come in.'

I push open the door. Marcus swivels his office chair and faces me.

'it's nice to see you again, Daniel.'

He is wearing a maroon corduroy shirt, unbuttoned at the neck, brown leather slippers. His beard is well-trimmed. His eyes are pale blue. He's well preserved for a man of his age. He seems... normal. The room is... normal. It's like the tutorial room of a university lecturer – the friendly type of academic who wishes to get to know his students.

There are lots of books, naturally – paperbacks and hardbacks, nothing antiquarian looking. He invites me to sit down.

He smiles welcomingly.

'I've been thinking about our last conversation. I was really interested in what you had to say about ley lines and how they relate to this part of London. It led me back to Alfred Watkins' book, The Old Straight Track. Have you read it?'

'A long time ago.'

He nods.

'Interesting, isn't it.'

On the wall are framed certificates. They look like qualifications. He observes that I have noticed them.

'In case you wondered, Daniel, I'm an accredited psychotherapist and counsellor. When I was at Berkeley, I became involved in the pastoral care of the students. It's so hard for the Millennials, especially for the women, don't you think? Are they sexual beings or merely sexual objects of the male gaze?'

He studies my reaction.

'What did you teach at Berkeley?'

'Oh?' He seems surprised that I have asked him. 'Well, it began with comparative religions. Believe it or not, I attended a Catholic boarding school. Later, my interests widened. I became absorbed by shamanism and the use of psychoactive substances in religious rituals.'

'It's that kind of place,' I say.

'It certainly is.'

'My doctoral study involved field trips to Brazil, to a region where hallucinogens are used to invoke mystical experiences – ayahuasca. It's the sex vine. Have you tried it, Daniel?'

'No, I haven't.'

'You should.'

I have noticed a particular large format paperback, The Earth Spirit, on a nearby shelf. It's about sacred structures and landscapes. I have it too. His book collection veers from astrology into Nazi mysticism, flying saucers and Freemasonry. Our reading tastes are very similar.

'Marcella, as you'll have observed, is a lot younger than me. She was one of my brighter students. She went to Brazil with me. Did she tell you?'

'No.'

Do you smoke, by the way, Daniel? I mean tobacco.'

'I try not to.'

'Good man.'

Can he see how stoned I am? My pupils must be like tadpoles.

'I used to smoke a pipe, but Marcella insisted that I give up. I was the full English, professorial package when I arrived in Berkely – tweed jacket, beard. I kept the beard.'

He touches it. 'Yanks love that kind of thing. They are extremely predisposed to being led by appearance and taken in by fake gurus and religious charlatans, especially on the west coast – more than the English, I think. We are far too cynical.'

He shifts in his seat.

'I'm telling you my life story aren't I. You are wheedling it out of me. Of course, you're a journalist.'

I've barely spoken since entering the room.

'Anyway, where were we?

'In Brazil.'

'Ah yes. That would have been in 1984 or '85. It was my Timothy Leary moment, Daniel, you know "turn on, tune in, drop out".'

'I've read his book, The Politics of Ecstasy.'

'That's the one. It's the classic story. Tweedy English professor raised by the Jesuits, goes to the jungle and has his brain taken apart and re-assembled. We went back to Berkely but now, instead of teaching people about mystical experiences I was having one.'

'You were still taking ayahuasca?'

'And the rest. The students in the chemistry faculty were extremely inventive. I had changed, Daniel. Some people in my faculty viewed me a drug pusher. An ugly little cabal of them plotted against me. The college authorities said that I had taken advantage of Marcella and that I was screwing students, left and right.'

'Were you?'

He doesn't answer.

'At this point fate intervened. My great aunt died and left me some money. Marcella and I moved back to dear old blighty. We married. We lived in Rye, but it was insufferably narrow-minded, then Putney, but that wasn't right either. Too many prying eyes. Then we found out about Mundania Close. It's perfect for us. This road has an interesting history. Are you aware of it?'

'To some extent, yes.'

'I thought so.'

He studies my face.

72

'Then you'll know – most people don't – that Mundania Close is in a direct lineage of English mysticism – the Golden Dawn, Rosicrucianism, wicca. They all have links to this little road. It's laid out in the shape of an ankh – a symbol of fertility – did you know that?'

'I did, yes.'

'I see that you have done your research.'

I look round again at the surprisingly banal room. He has the usual quota of blue-spined Pelicans, orange and black-spined Penguins. They are cracked and fading. It will be sad when such books crumble.

'Oh, I was going to ask, do you like my wife, Daniel?'

'Pardon.'

'Do you like my wife?'

'Of course.'

'Would you like to make love to her?'

My throat contracts.

'I ...'

7

The Temptation on the Mount

Extract from, Adventures in the Paranormal, Dixon Granger, Honor
Oak Press, 1924

Theophilus William Williams was a rum fellow. Even his name,
derived from an obscure Biblical figure, was odd. The position of
mayor of Lewisham suited him perfectly. He was naturally gregarious
and one sensed that he relished the trappings and modest luxury of
the office – the robes, the gold chain and the gleaming silverware in
the mayor's parlour.

His business ventures, in property and finance, had been
extremely successful. They had paved the way for his rapid ascent in
local government – his appointment to the Metropolitan Board of
Works, his election onto the London County Council and then, in
1901, as Lewisham's mayor.

Men who have attained positions of power and wealth not
through birth but purely by their own efforts are often charismatic.
The people of Lewisham regarded him with affection, especially
those in the poorest districts. In their eyes, a political independent, he
was a champion of facilities for the under-privileged and a prolific
ribbon cutter and speechmaker. The death of his wife, just after he
became mayor, had given a fillip to his career. Some people
whispered that his empire was built on her money.

Williams had been born in a workhouse in the East End of
London. This aspect of his personal history – the sense that he had
overcome adversity and 'made good' – was one of the keys to his
success. To those who knew him well, he did not disguise his
affiliation to Freemasonry. Many people speculated that this had
accelerated his path to riches. I shall say more on this later. Suffice to
say, he once invited me to join 'the craft'. I politely declined.

I was pleased when he offered me a position, just after he had
become mayor, as editor of a weekly newspaper, The Woodsman,
that he had just launched. Its offices were in Forest Hill, only a few
minutes' walk from my house in Sydenham. He had discovered me
because I was putting out a small publication on local history and was
known for giving talks. I said that I knew nothing of newspapers – I

was simply a dabbler in history and natural science, a dilletante, following my interests wherever they took me.

Williams said that my lack of experience did not matter. Many of the staff of The Woodsman, he explained, had worked on Fleet Street. The chief sub-editor, in particular, was an 'old hand' who knew the trade backwards. He would teach me the nuts and bolts of producing a paper. He assured me that, as publisher, he would advise me on the business aspects of the job.

After consulting my wife, I accepted the job.

Seeing one's work in print is powerful drug. From the start of my tenure, I put a great deal of care into my editorials. They ranged over social and artistic issues, folklore and even classicism, as well as topics of local concern. They were well-received. This gave me great a great sense of satisfaction. The paper came out on Fridays. It cost a halfpenny. It did well under my editorship, becoming the heartbeat of the local area.

Williams had travelled in the Middle East and knew a great deal about the Holy Lands and Mesopotamia and their history. He encouraged me to extend The Woodsman's purview from the mundane, everyday world, into spiritual, cultural and philosophical realms. I was more than happy to oblige.

An idea popped into my mind one morning when I was walking to work. It was in the early months of 1903. I was now well established in the job. People from all walks of life would greet me familiarly in the local streets. I had had a telephone installed at home and, to my wife's annoyance, it was constantly ringing. Indulging my creative side, I had recently authored a historical drama set in the first century AD, Elusia the Britain, and had experienced the pleasure of seeing it performed by professional actors. One of my editorials had been mentioned in a Parliamentary debate.

I had regularly asserted my view in The Woodsman, that it is possible to speak to the dead. I held, and still do, that, one day, the practice of spiritualism will be scientifically validated. I am certain, having studied the matter, that conserving with souls who have 'crossed the veil' will become a routine matter, like communicating by telegraphy or radio waves, and that its physics will be understood. My idea, that morning, was to create a society devoted to the field of 'psychic' research. For example, it would conduct seances under strict, scientific conditions.

The society would hold public talks and publish pamphlets. It would be based on the premise that humans have, in some ways, regressed since pre-history. It is my view that we have lost paranormal faculties that we once possessed. In my opinion, our ancestors of the Neanderthal species, with their larger brains, had such powers. Modern humans have become as blind as moles to invisible spectra and wavelengths and scientific progress has caused us to dismiss what we cannot understand.

I was pleased when Williams said that he would like to be involved in The Society of the Ancients and that he would provide financial backing. Its launch in the pages of The Woodsman was widely reported. Several well-known figures expressed an interest in holding *ex officio* positions. They included the Theosophist, Annie Bessant, and the celebrated creator of Sherlock Holmes, Arthur Conan Doyle. He lived nearby and I had recently interviewed him.

One day, I was sitting in the cafe, when the doorbell jangled. I looked up to see a man in a pale grey uniform including a peaked cap. It was Williams' chauffeur. His six horsepower Daimler, an exotic visitation to the streets of south-east London, was idling outside. Williams asked me to go on 'a drive' with him and I was happy to accept.

After ascending the steep hill of London Road, we turned right and progressed along Honor Oak Road – not regally but somewhat in stops and starts. This was where the first Georgian villas that established the suburb that would later be called Forest Hill had been built. At that time, the Surrey hunt sought its prey in the open fields around the new houses.

We stopped at the end of the road, just before the brow of One Tree Hill. It was close to here, I had recently asserted in The Woodsman, that Queen Boadicea had fought her final battle against the Romans in AD 61 or 62, marking the end of her uprising against their occupation of Britain. The information had been vouchsafed to me from the spirit realm, in a seance. I had spoken, at length, to Boadicea herself about what had happened.

'Look around you, Granger,' Williams said.

I did.

'What do you see?'

The area was close to my heart. A square-towered church in grey stone marks the summit of the hill. It stands between trees that have joined remnants of the Great North Wood – the dense forest that formerly cloaked much of south-east England. From the top of hill, a vista stretches for miles in all directions. Close by is the site where Queen Elizabeth I is alleged to have picnicked, beneath the boughs of the original 'honor oak'.

Allotments created on former clay-pits straggle down a hillside to Honor Oak Park railway station. One Tree Hill shows the battle between man and nature. It is the wild wood being turned into a brick and slate dormitory for the people of London. But enough wild wood remains for it to remind one of pre-industrial times and some of their magic.

'I see One Tree Hill,' I said.

'Well I have bought it,' Williams announced.

'You have what?'

'Not all of it, about two and a half acres.'

How this could be, I wondered? Local people had recently concluded a bitter conflict to keep this land accessible, after it had been bought by someone planning to turn it into a golf course.

Williams had deep pockets and good connections. He must have greased several palms. Even so, the coup of buying One Tree Hill attested to his persistence and powers of persuasion.

It was a day to quicken one's pulses, vibrant with the earth spirit that even dulled human senses could detect. Sunlight twinkled from the leaded panes of the church, the green-clad hillside was frothy with May blossom, the sky was a cerulean blue.

'Would you like to see?'

I stepped down to the pavement. Williams indicated that the south-eastern flank of One Tree Hill was now his.

'Please, follow me.'

He used a key to open a padlock in a chain-link fence. We walked down a steep slope carpeted by brambles and ground ivy. I saw the stumps of freshly felled trees.

'Look,' Williams said.

House-sized plots had been marked off with twine. They were arranged in an elongated horseshoe. In one case, footings had already been dug. Next to them were piles of bricks.

'Which one would you like?'

'I'm sorry?'

'There will be twelve houses around the close. One of them could be yours, Granger. Not number six, I've reserved that plot for myself.'

I was dumbfounded.

'They will be beautiful houses in brick and terracotta, built by a local craftsman. He's called Edward Christmas. Do you know him? They will each have a front and rear garden, but the centre of the close will be a communal area.'

He continued. 'I want extraordinary people to live here – people who are open-minded and artistic. I attend to make the houses available to them at favourable rates.'

He explained that the close would offer four-bedroom houses with a servant's room – perfect for an up-and-coming man like me. Mrs Granger would love it, he suggested.

He sensed my main reservation. 'Look, I know that you think that this is where Queen Boadicea fought the Romans – that it's a battle site. That's one reason I bought this land. This way, One Tree Hill, will be protected from any other less sensitive development, in perpetuity.'

He assured me that the builders would retain as many existing trees as possible and, in addition, plant new ones. The houses' foundations, he said, may reveal interesting archaeological finds that would otherwise have remained in the ground.

'These will be modern houses, with electric light and the most up-to-date features,' he said. 'They won't be draughty and uncomfortable, I assure you. Your wife will like that, won't she?'

I nodded. I was speculating how she would react. I knew that she would be excited. Her desire for a house without drafts and a leaking roof would undoubtedly overcome her visceral dislike for Williams. I sniffed the air. The faint scent of woodsmoke that is prevalent in the hop fields of Kent seems to linger in this part of London. We would wake to the cooing of wood pigeons and go to sleep to the hoots of owls.

'So?'

'I'll have to talk to Judith.'

'Of course. Do you think she'll agree.'

'It's possible.'

'Capital. Why not choose your house now?'

We followed the layout of the putative close. I toyed with number seven – a lucky number but it was number nine that caught my eye. Its back garden offered a horizon that extended to the flat green fields of the Weald and it contained a magnificent sessile oak. Williams assured me that the tree would remain.

'Number nine it is. An excellent choice.'

'He smiled. Do talk to your better half. But if she approves, we can settle the details next week.'

The clock in St Augustine's church chimed midday. There are a few moments in one's life when one feels that the stars are aligned. This seemed to be one.

8

The Thirteenth House

Saturday 9th April, 12.02pm
Daniel, The writer

I am not at my best. By nine-thirty in the morning, there is grime on my forehead. My cotton checkered shirt is torn and bloodied. My arms look as if they been attacked by carnivorous insects. I wait at the door for a long time. The nominal front garden in front of number one has received little love for a very long time. Its calf-high grass, beer cans, crisp packets and plastic debris from abandoned children's toys would merit a special category at the Chelsea Flower Show – 'couldn't give a fuck', or 'slacker'.

I'm about to leave. The scuffed door appears to have been attacked with hammers and chisels. It slowly opens. Hamish greets me with no particular warmth. He's a tall man in a black tee-shirt that bears the legend Motörhead, above a fearsome-looking horned skull. Braids are plaited into his unruly beard, which is only a little less fierce in ruddiness than the rest of his hair. He looks me up and down. The air in the hallway is so thick with weed that you could hang your coat on it. I can also smell joss sticks, nappies and unwashed clothes. In a flash of red hair, one of his children – Tallon, or possibly Fallon – rushes past us for the freedom of the open door, like a guinea pig let out of its cage.

'Eh, you wee fucking rascal,' Hamish exclaims. 'Jesus.'

He asks me what I want. I explain that I need help.

'It looks like you need help, pal? What the fuck has happened to you?'

I embark upon a story. He cuts me off.

'For fuck's sake. Come through.'

•••

I don't need to describe the kitchen. You'll be able to imagine the jars of lentils, pulses and rice, the dingy brown light, the cat pee moistened piles of newspaper and the general clutter and disorder. Kaz, Hamish's partner, is holding a baby but she takes an immediate interest in my wounds. She says that aloe vera is the required remedy for my arms. So cactus juice kills bacteria? I'm in no position to argue.

She and Hamish don't seem that curious as to why I am here, but I give them the reason anyway. I explain that Mundania Close's survivors – numbers seven, eight and nine – are organising a party, with live music, the Pink Moon Happening. It's to be held virtually in front of their house, in a week's time. We'll have the services of a sound guy, with stage lighting and mixing gear. We require a band. We'll just need do some jungle bashing on the mound, to prepare the ground for the event. This morning, I have made a start.

Hamish seems interested. He invites me to come through the front room to tell him more. The room smells of damp and skunk. The dingy brown carpet is a black hole of filth. It is so soiled and invaded by particles that even the world's most powerful vacuum cleaner would make little impression on it. The sagging settee, pizza boxes and discarded beer cans attest to the days and nights that Hamish has spent in front of the TV. But hey, what's this? Suspended at eye level on one wall is an Ibanez-style electric guitar – the kind used by shredders – that is, heavy metal players who produce lots of notes, often without knowing what they are. Over the next hour, I receive another life story. Its chapter headings are as follows – Hamish's childhood in the working-class part of Paisley, his art school period, in Glasgow, his first band, Orange Juice meets Alex Harvey, times on the road in a rusty Transit van.

At a gig in a pub in the Old Kent Road, he meets Kaz, a lassie from a well-off family who has inherited a house in south-east London from her grandmother. He moves in with her. It's now that he has his accident. Does Kaz leave him? No. She is a diamond. His long and painful rehabilitation begins at Mundania Close. The twins are born. Then a baby girl arrives.

In a stoned condition, we discuss the recent fatalities in the close. Hamish says that he is freaked out. He has avoided the media circus because of certain matters between himself and the benefits and tax authorities that he would rather remain beneath the radar.

He is enthusiastic about the proposed party. He says that he has lots of musician friends, including a drummer. He has mates who'll be able to help and lend us tools, over the weekend. He adds that he'll come out and help me outside when he has had his breakfast – which, I imagine, will be a joint and a can of Special Brew.

•••

Despite my best intentions, I have achieved little. The mound is at least accessible now. I have removed four railings to create a gap in the fence, but I've cleared, at best, barely ten feet of brambles. It's a far harder job than I had anticipated – one requiring muscles and tools that I don't have.

I am mopping my brow, contemplating miserable failure, when the door of number one opens. Hamish crosses the road with the aid of an aluminium crutch, with a curious swinging motion that makes him look like a pirate. He's dressed in faded jeans and a biker jacket. He's smiling.

'Is that all that you've managed?'

'it's hard work.'

'Aye, I can see that.'

A carrier bag dangles from his walking aid. It contains cans of lager.

'Well, I've come to help pal.'

'Thank you.'

I have brought out two camping chairs from my house. We sit next to each other, like a couple of fishermen. He offers me a can.

'You know we can get money from those railings, don't you.'

'Yeh?'

'Aye. It's ferrous metal, valuable scrap. I have a pal in the trade, Dave.'

He peruses the jungle of the mound.

'We need a rotavator, maybe an excavator,' he says.

'We don't have those.'

'Well, I know someone who does.'

'Dave?'

'Nah, Rob. He's a plumber but he does landscape gardening. He's got a van.'

'Sound like a useful guy to know.'

'Aye, he is.'

He rolls a joint, taking his time, enjoying the sun and fresh air. I am feeling more hopeful now. Hamish's tongue flicks out and expertly moistens the gum strip of his creation.

'Pass us the lighter Danny.'

I reach into the grubby Aldi bag.

'D'you know what?' Hamish says. 'I've had an idea.'
'What is it?'
'You'll see.'

•••

The plan is simple in its conception and execution. Phase one involves elementary house breaking. In Hamish's view, now that Egg, the tyrant at number three, is deceased his worldly goods and chattels are fair game. Egg was the embodiment of what Hamish holds in contempt – a joyless, rule-bound authoritarianism.

The man was a keen gardener. His tools are kept in a brick outhouse in his back garden. It is surprisingly easy to break in. By a man's tools shall ye know him. His implements are arrayed in neat ranks, oiled and ready for use. We see what we need – a jerrycan.

We find a siphon tube. Within 15 minutes we have relieved Egg's Volvo of half a gallon of petrol. We'll be able to requisition other useful items from the shed – saw, secateurs, hedge trimmer, strimmer, spade, axe. All we need is a work party. Hamish tells me that Rob the plumber should be able to help us. So should skanky Dave, the scrap dealer. Clearing the mound is going to be a gargantuan task. Is it achievable? I'm not sure. Hamish is more optimistic.

The close is quiet for a Saturday morning. The grassed areas and flower beds in front of the buff houses made of London brick are already looking unkempt. Only one for sale board has gone up, in front of number five, Ron Saxby's old house.

Mundania Close is still attracting occasional media updates on its 'calamity' status. The property market has yet to pick up to pre-Covid levels. The road, it could be said, has become a symbol for the pandemic – a plague that has thinned out humans, allowing nature to re-assert itself.

'Right.'

Hamish levers himself up, using the flimsy arm of his chair.

'Ready to rumble?'

I nod.

•••

He douses the brambles with fire juice. We return to Egg's Volvo for a second, third and fourth can, to make sure that the tough, thorny vegetation is well-primed. It is Hamish who sets the fire, using a burning rag. With comic rapidity he weaves his way back to his house. As I look back from my front door, a column of flame is rising from the mound, like a Biblical portent.

By agreement, neither of us calls the emergency services. Someone else is bound to. By Hamish's reckoning, the fire will have easily done its work by time that they arrive. The conflagration, he reckons, will be put down to vandals – bloody kids.

I go upstairs to wash and change. The fire is still raging when I look through my front room window. Marcella's front door opens. She stands and gazes at the searing orange flames that are consuming the mound. She sees that I am watching from my window. She smiles.

I decide to text her, professing my surprise at this willful attack. Then I have a better idea. Why not talk to her?

I leave my house.

'Wow Daniel,' she says. 'This is amazing.' She's wearing her crop top and the tight jeans.

Her face shows an innocent pleasure.

'I've phoned 999.'

'Good.'

'I don't think that it's going to spread, do you?'

'No. It can't.'

'How do you think it started?'

'No idea.'

She smiles.

'It's great for our party, isn't it. The fire will clear away all of the bushes.'

'Yeh, I suppose it will.'

The two teenagers from number 12 are standing in front of their house, looking at us and the fire. Both are wearing grey tracksuits and new trainers. They are sharing a joint, making no attempt to hide it. We can clearly smell the kind of fragrant, flowery skunk that can be detected when a hoodie has passed by in Lewisham.

'All right lads,' I lob across to them. They nod. They study Marcella, in her too-young clothes. She says 'hi' to them.

A woman comes out of the house and says something to the boys. She holds back at first. then she acknowledges my greeting and walks to where Marcella and I are standing.

She is Jamaican, in her thirties or forties, friendly, with a nervous smile.

'Your boys certainly like their weed,' Marcellas says. 'It's not a problem,' she adds quickly, to reassure the woman. 'Daniel and I don't' mind in the least. Do we?'

'No, not at all,' I say.

The woman becomes a little more relaxed. Soon, we are neighbours who know each other, chatting familiarly around a bonfire. She says that her name is Carlene. She works for the council, as a housing officer. Her sons are called Tyrone and Marlon. The older one, Marlon, has been excluded from school. He has signed onto a car mechanic's course. Tyrone is in year ten. I get the impression that he is not a frequent school attender.

Carlene greets the news of the party enthusiastically, saying that she'll be happy to come. Her sister is a caterer and can bring some food. Marcella is delighted by the prospect of the pink moon happening having a Caribbean flavour.

Smoke has darkened the afternoon sky like an eclipse. Most of the ash and debris is blowing across to Egg's side of the close, leaving grey smudges on his windows.

By the time we hear the shrill klaxons of the fire service wailing, the fire's initially ferocity has subsided. Two tenders arrive and a single police car. A hose is unreeled. Without urgency, firefighters extinguish the flames. It doesn't take long. Soon, there is a seething hiss as an enormous column of grey smoke rises into the sky.

The mound is now a soggy brown mess, from which half burnt trees protrude. It looks like the aftermath of a World War One battle. There's a sharp, acrid smell in the air. We're questioned by a police officer. He suggests that this is probably the work of juvenile arsonists. Bloody kids. I agree.

Shows over folks. It's time to go inside. Marcella says a warm goodbye to her new friend, Carlene, having exchanged details. Before leaving, she clutches my hand and looks into my eyes.

'Thank you, James,' she says.

I nod.

'That's OK. My pleasure.'

85

Sunday 10th April, 7pm
Daniel, The Writer

We have worked steadily all day. That's Hamish and me, Rob the plumber, who is Scottish, like Hamish, skanky Dave the scrap merchant, who has popped over from Deptford in his flat-bed truck and the two lads from number 12, Marlon and Tyrone – not that they have done much physical work – they are the iPad generation. Marlon, it transpires, knows Hamish already. He is his dealer.

Dave brought an angle grinder with him – the heavy-duty kind that's used to cut up cars. He is making a good impression on the spiked railings that circle the mound. All day, we have heard the whine of the grinder and seen showers of sparks, as it chewed its way through the fence. He has also brought scaffolding poles and planks, to make a stage.

Dom the DJ arrives later, after I phone him. He is dressed for gardening, in a ripped old shirt and a new pair of Timberland boots. Dom surprises me by his cheerful willingness to get stuck in. He and Hamish get on like old mates, discussing the pa and lighting system that they are going to put together for the party.

We have accomplished an amazing amount, considering that this is only the second day. The stage is coming along thanks to bare-chested Dave and his toolbelt, helped by Dom. By midday, they have built a raised rectangular platform with a depth of about ten feet. Soon this structure will be boarded over with scaffolding planks.

We have cut down some sycamores and turned their trunks into benches cradling the stage. We have dug out a fire pit and cleared a flat space for a marquee.

Hamish and I found the chapel this morning. It was in the centre of the mound, freed by fire from its prison of brambles. It's larger than I expected – a brick building with a slate roof. The door and windows are blocked by impenetrable vegetation. We agree to address the problem of how to get in later.

•••

Early evening. The donkey work is done. We're all bushed, sharing beers and a joint by the fire pit. We've just eaten the food that Kaz has brought us – takeaway kebabs and chips.

My body, which is unused to physical labour, is aching all over. My clothes are caked in dirt and blood. I'm feeling a sense of contentment that one does not get from a day chasing letters across a screen.

It feels right – but people aren't supposed to live outside the normal rules and conventions of society. Even fires are discouraged in suburbia. When word gets out that Mundania Close has become an experiment in self-help anarchy, the forces of conformity will move in and shut us down. I hope that won't happen until after our mini festival.

'Should be a good party' I say.

'Aye,' responds Hamish.

We make an inventory of attendees. It includes Hamish's biker and musician contacts, skanky Dave's mates from Deptford, Kaz's friends, DJ Dom's blissed out ravers, Tyrone and Marlon's pals.

'And some swingers,' I suggest.

'What do you mean,' says Hamish.

'Oh, you know, Marcus and Marcella's friends.'

'Marcella. You mean the bird who lives at number seven?'

'Do you know her?'

'Of course. She's been round our house, to see the baby. She's nuts about Fleur. Are you shagging her Danny?'

'Absolutely not.'

'But you'd like to.'

I don't reply.

'I'll take that as a yes. You looked pretty cozy with her yesterday, before the fire engines arrived.'

'You were watching?'

'Aye, through my bedroom window.'

'I'm just pretending to be friendly.'

'By shagging her.'

'No. I'm trying to find out what's going on. Why all of our neighbours have died.'

'Don't you think it was just accidents?'

'Of course it fucking wasn't,' says Dom.

'This road has a very dodgy history,' I say. 'The bloke who built it and who lived at number six was a Devil worshipper. He held orgies and he had a private love chapel. I think that the deaths have something to do with him, but I'm not sure how. I just know that they started when number seven arrived.'

'A Devil worshipper. No way,' says Skanky Dave.

'What private love chapel?' says Hamish.

'That one.' I point to the structure that we have revealed.

'Oh.'

'That's fucking mental,' says Dave.

'Let's go and see, shall we.' It's Dom's suggestion.

'What, now?' I say.

'Yeh, why not?'

Hamish is the most up for it.

I suggest that we'll need a hammer and a saw, to break through the roof, a builder's ladder to climb down into the chapel, and torches.

•••

It's sheer vandalism to a historic monument. There's a gaping hole above us. We are standing inside the chapel. Our torches begin to pick out details of the interior. Our jaws drop.

First surprise. It's all brand new. The small building has recently been renovated. This is, indeed, a chapel. We're standing in the nave. In front of us is a plain stone slab – an altar.

Looking down at us, from recessed plinths, on one each side, are the faces of two pale grey, life-sized statues of women. They are naked. They have voluptuous breasts and thighs. Their arms are raised upwards. They wear crowns. They are smiling.

'Fuck me,' says Hamish. 'They're so fucking real.'

'I bet you'd shag them,' says skanky Dave.

'You'd bruise your dick,' Rob suggests.

Dom steps forward and shines the torch from his phone on the shadowed figures. I see now that they are not exactly the same. The woman on our right has wings. The one on the left does not.

'Fuck. Look at those chicken's feet!' says Hamish. Dom's torch has picked out this peculiar detail on both statues.

'Still fancy a shag, Hamish?'

'Aye… No problem.'

On the back wall, behind the altar, is a tree, in relief. A fat snake curls around its trunk. Above it, looking as if it is about to sweep down on us, is a bird with square-tipped outstretched wings.

Hamish suggests that the frieze depicts the garden of Eden.

'So why are there two Eves, no Adam, and why does one of them have wings?' says Dom.

'Well, there's a tree and a snake,' Hamish notes.

'Yeh, but what the fuck is that?' says Dave, 'that weird eagle. There's no bird in the Garden of Eden, is there?'

'Not that I can remember,' I say, 'but Sunday School was a long time ago.'

'Look at this."

Dom has found something in the apse, the space between the altar and the back wall. He is holding up a trapdoor.

A flight of stone steps descends into darkness. *A secret tunnel. Of course.*

'It's like Jeepers fucking Creepers,' says Hamish.

I love that movie.

What would happen in a horror film? The hapless characters would descend into the unknown, accompanied by ominous music, perhaps a thunderclap – cut to a tree being shaken around in a high wind. Close up of a full moon.

One character would be captured. The others would escape to seek help. There would be no phone network, unfortunately. Cut to a torture chamber, kitted out with pliers, saws and hammers. The captured victim is tied to a chair. His face is filmed with sweat. His wrists and ankles are secured by leather straps.

9

The Theatre of Flesh

Extract from, Adventures in the Paranormal, Dixon Granger, Honor Oak Press, 1924

Rumours persisted that Williams' empire had been built on his wife's money and social connections. Once they were no longer needed, she had conveniently disappeared, following a short illness.

Those of us in his inner circle knew that his amatory proclivities had a darker side. On several occasions, the enraged suitors and husbands of Williams' paramours had appeared at The Woodsman's offices and threatened to blacken his eyes or even to kill him. In one case, the offices were broken into and vandalised. I called the police. They showed no interest in the matter and it went no further.

I was now sure that Williams was using his connections from Freemasonry to sweeten business deals and to silence opposition to his plans. It was said in public houses, late at night, that he had had at least two business rivals beaten, one almost to death.

In August, 1903, Judith and would move into our new house, having secured a loan, on highly favourable terms, arranged by Williams. My sleep had become disturbed. My colleagues sensed that I was battling with my conscience. They were waiting see how I would resolve the conflict.

What to do? The question was not settled when I received an unexpected invitation to visit Mundania Close, just before Judith and I were due to take up occupation of number nine. Williams said that he would love to see me at his house, so that he could show me his billiards room and his theatre. His theatre? I was intrigued by that reference. Perhaps I would be able confide my concerns to him, I told myself.

We agreed that I would present myself at seven o'clock the following evening, which was a Saturday. He asked me to come on my own. There was no need to dress up he said. It was a casual invitation and I was the only guest.

The sight of Mundania Close approaching completion did not excite me. On the contrary. Even on a warm summer evening, the air filled with pollen, it depressed me intensely. I reflected that I may well be living, the following month, next door to a pompous policeman, trapped in a job that filled me with unease.

The raw, new houses rose bleakly from exposed ground. They seemed to me to denote dull suburban respectability rather than art. Number six was more imposing than the other properties. Its principal feature was a corner turret, serving as a viewing room, or belvedere. The house's ground-floor windows were shuttered on the inside. One would have said that no-one was at home.

I tapped on the door knocker and waited. A lump rose in my throat. I was about to turn on my heel and leave, when the door opened. Williams was cheerful. His cheeks were ruddy. To my surprise, he was wearing a white robe, like a monk. I detected incense. He must have registered my shock at what I had encountered. He ushered me inside.

Aside from the incense, there was a musty smell in the hallway. It was lit by dim electric bulbs. A woman came towards us, in a cloud of blue satin. She was coiffed like a fashionable lady in the court of Versailles. Her blonde hair rose to a crescendo of curls. 'Violet,' said, Williams, 'this is Mr Granger.'

The woman had the enthusiasm of a child.

'Oh Dixon!' She clasped my hand tightly. Her eyes burrowed into mine as if she was attempting to extract secrets from my soul.

Williams placed his arm around his consort's waist, 'You will have plenty of time to talk to Granger, my dear. He is my guest this evening. Did we not agree?'

She wilted, her wish slighted.

'It's not fair, Theo. I want to talk to him about his play.'

My play? Only handful of people had seen its only performance, held in a scout hut in some nearby woods, close to a railway cutting. If this child-woman had been there I would certainly have remembered.

'You know about Elusia the Briton?'

'Oh yes. Theo has told me all about it. I do wish that I had seen it.'

'Perhaps you will, my darling.' There was a glint in Williams' eye. 'Why shouldn't it be performed here?'

'Oh yes, oh yes!' She stamped her slipper excitedly. It was blue, matching her dress.

'I should like to be in it, as Elusia!'

'My dear, casting the play is Mr Granger's prerogative as its author, don't you think?

He paused. 'Now, I should like to show him something of the house, if you wouldn't mind.'

She pursed her mouth.

'We'll be back soon, I promise.'

He turned to me.

'What would you like to see first, Granger, the billiards room, or the theatre?'

Williams knew my vanity – that of a hack who wanted his words to be read aloud, in public.

'The theatre?'

I nodded.

At end of the hallway, to our right, was an arched opening.

'Please, Dixon, be my guest.'

He directed me through a bead curtain.

The corridor had been contrived to look medieval. It was faced with pale grey stone and lit by electric filaments that shone from wooden braziers with metal lattices.

The corridor turned back on itself. It led to a further flight of steps and then, through opened doors, to a room of startling size.

•••

The room was so large that one could barely see its sides, as only its middle portion was well illuminated. The sole lighting was provided by candles.

A circle of about nine feet across had been painted in the centre of the floor. It was filled with astrological and runic symbols. The perimeter of the circle was formed by the coils of a snake, edged with yellow. Inside this were four six-sided stars with, yellow points and blue central hexagons. Inside them was a red square, tilted on its side.

On the wall was another, smaller circle. Inside it was the outline of a key, surrounded by further symbols. I recognised the Greek characters eta and theta.

Williams placed his right foot on the red square.

'I see that you are admiring my Circle of Solomon. I must now tell you, Granger, that I have been reborn.' He adopted a loud, solemn voice.

'I am Asmodeus, custodian of Solomon's magic seal.'

'I beg your pardon'

'I am Asmodeus.'

'No, you're not.'

He glared at me.

'How do you think that the Temple of Solomon was built, Granger?'

'I have no idea.'

'It was not made by human hands alone. Now, through my art and craft, the power of the first architect flows though my veins. I am a master of the left-hand path. I have studied the goetic arts for many years. I am well versed in scrying with my black mirror, to unlock the power of sigils. I have succeeded in what only a few men have achieved in the history of our planet. You've heard of John Dee, haven't you Granger? Aren't you impressed? Why don't you step into the circle and join me?'

'This is blasphemy.'

'That is what blind people say. Those who have been intimidated by the pious to be cursed with guilt and to suppress their freedom.'

He smiled.

'The location of my circle was actually inspired by one of your editorials. You see, I do read them. Christian churches are dead places. You only have to hear a hymn to know that. They are sealed off from the odic energy that bubbles through the earth. In most cases, it was never present. But here... you can feel it, can't you. I know that you can. Beneath One Tree Hill is a vent that runs to the earth's core. This is the precise location at which it reaches the surface.'

I was appalled that anything I had written had inspired this sick man.

'My Seal of Solomon gives me powers to call powerful entities into this room. You see that red triangle, Granger? Within its three points, the name of Archangel Michael is inscribed, split into three in order to disempower him. You will be curious about the words written in red. They are Tetragrammaton, Anaphaxeton and

Primeumaton – the three names of god. It is within Solomon's Triangle that blood is offered and that summoned entities appear.'

I clenched my fists.

'Don't Catholics believe in spirits and invest the ordinary with mystical powers, in their sacrament. What's the difference? This is the true religion. The religion of the senses. You have desires, don't you, Granger? Here, you can indulge them to your heart's content. It is a form of theatre – the theatre of flesh. Isn't that what you crave? God gave us our sexual organs. Did he not mean us to enjoy them?'

I pondered this theological question. Williams had simply turned the Christian and Judaic faiths on their head. He had taken their robes, litanies and rituals and re-assigned them to an evil purpose. People like Aleister Crowley, and this preposterous pretender to his dubious notoriety – the man who stood before me – believe that their own will and pleasure are paramount. Their views are not compatible with the norms that bind society. They are dangerous. They must be stopped.

The air rippled and every candle in the basement flickered. Another person had entered the room. It was Violet. She was naked. Her hair flamed into a red corona. Its colour was matched by the vivid triangle at the top of her thighs.

'Why don't you step into the circle and join us? I'm sure that you want to?'

He clasped Violet's fingers and pulled her towards him.

'You disgust me.'

Enough. I strode out of the room. Williams did not follow me. I am sure that by the time I had reached the top of the stairs he was occupied elsewhere.

When fresh air touched my face, I felt an enormous sense of relief. I could sever my ties with Williams now, without any hesitation or looking back

The evening was warm and fragrant and it would be a long time before the sun went down. I took a deep breath. The god in which I believe is manifest in air and sunlight. This god is the force that is found in the wood and the meadow, that sings through our veins.

I had arrived here with a heavy heart but I walked back to Sydenham with a spring in my step. When I got home, I went straight up to my holy of holies, my study.

I sat at my desk, looking out of the window, watching the sun go down.

I heard a tap on the door.

'Dixon, are you alright?'

'Yes, my dear.'

'Would you like some supper?'

'Yes, please.'

It was going to be a difficult meal. I would have to tell Judith that the picture that we had conjured up of living in a beautiful house on a wooded hillside had vanished, and, also, that we had lost our income.

10

Zombie Attack

Sunday 10th April, 2.30pm
The Watcher

Look at them. Look how proud of themselves they are with their hemp cigarettes, their outlandish rags and their profanities. They think they are the first generation to challenge convention and to take drugs. Well, we had Laudanum, cocaine and heroin. We could buy them over the counter.

Over the last two days, I have observed, with interest, this motley crew of casual labourers, hacking back the bushes that cover the mound. At first, it was just two people – the uncouth Scotsman with his ginger hair and the fellow from number nine, Daniel, my rival in watching. I have observed for the past few weeks his attempts to uncover the secrets of Mundania Close – his plotting and conniving.

I have only let him live because of his tenacity and determination. I knew that these characteristics would be useful. I was correct in my assessment. See how he assembled a work party and how they have been doing my bidding – exposing to the light the Chapel of Venus. The young fool has served me admirably. Daniel is malleable. Marcella only has to flaunt her breasts or her crotch at him for his free will do dissolve.

A group of helpers dressed like tramps and gypsies arrived today. They set to work, chopping, sawing and cutting metal. I watched them crawl over the mound like dung beetles. The two youths who live at number twelve, in their shiny grey trousers and jackets and unblemished white shoes, did not break sweat. They are strangers to work. They smoke Indian hemp constantly. It enslaves them as effectively as the shackles that restrained their ancestors.

From high in my tower, looking through its one-way glass, I have watched both of them progress from babyhood. Their lives are dominated by the economy of their mildly euphoric drug. Over the decades, I have observed many forms of rebellion in this little close. Some adherents of new fashions were militaristic. Others adopted the appearance of cavaliers or pre-Raphaelites and took to lotus eating. I am happy to say that the mound facilitated the discovery of tobacco and sexual intercourse for generations of young people, hidden by bushes.

The amplified drumbeats that issued from it became louder and louder, as technology developed. Trouser widths became narrow, then wide, then narrow. Colours turned bright then sombre, then bright again. Beards and hats came in and out of fashion, as I marked off the decades on my wall. People vary their clothes frequently now, like chameleons. Those who cycle or run wear a clinging second skin, that places their genitals on display. Sports clothing, a little less anatomically revealing, is often worn as normal attire. This society of incessant drumbeats has become infantilised. Children do not dress as adults, as they did when I was young. Adults dress like children.

Few people are truly alive. Their senses are dulled, their inner eye closed. How ironic. My fate has been to observe these automata in their witless mechanical repetitions, to watch and not to participate, trapped inside this prison, never to feel the sun on my face.

I know what will happen now that Daniel has found my chapel. He'll come to my basement, with his uncouth companions. They will be like flies blundering into a web. Well, let them come. I'll be ready for them.

Sunday 10th April 8.05pm
Daniel, The writer

A few basic set ups are used in horror movies. There are creepy abandoned hospitals, with their operating wards and surgical instruments inexplicably remaining in situ, and deserted top secret experimental facilities. Other settings are newly-purchased ivy-covered houses out in the sticks, or gothic inner-city tenements, that were suspiciously cheap. Grotty hotels and motels are popular. They nearly always have a creepy desk clerk, who often peers at their hapless guests, using an extensive network of concealed cameras.

This is different. Perhaps it isn't even a horror film. Hamish, Rob the plumber, skanky Dave, Dom and I are walking down a corridor, accessed from the chapel. its walls are faced with the granite surfaces that are used for worktops in expensive kitchens. It is brightly lit.

Hamish, in his biker jacket, and Rob, a grubby yellow tee-shirt straining against his belly, carry improvised weapons that were designed for gardening and DIY. It has been agreed, in an unspoken compact, that they are the muscle on this expedition, should we get into trouble – two fierce Scots who have been in a scrap or two. Dave is a skinny dude. Dom and I are no fighters.

We don't need torches. Discrete concealed lights are activated by conveniently spaced timer switches. This walk-through world doesn't feel spooky or haunted, it's more like a corridor in an oligarch's basement. Forty yards ahead of us, the corridor turns through a right angle. It could easily lead to a games room, a home cinema or a subterranean swimming pool. Perhaps it does.

Marcus and Marcella's money must have paid for the refurbishment of the love tunnel. It must be their intention to use it to access the chapel, from the basement of number six.

Suddenly, the lights go out, thrusting us into darkness. *Uh-oh.* Hamish walks forward to the next time switch and presses it. Nothing happens. *Game on boys.*

Our torches are the powerful LED kind, but their beams are frustratingly narrow. We try the next timer switch. Nothing.

Now, we're in inky darkness, criss-crossed by pencils of light. There is a beat of silence and then… you know that sound that you hear in console games that indicates the approach of zombies – that low, groaning, moaning chorus? That's what we hear – the sound of the undead.

Our torches reveal them.

'Fuck!' says Hamish.

Two zombies are limping and lurching towards us. They are out of the normal playbook – foot-dragging humans, wearing ragged and disintegrating clothes, that are distressed parodies of everyday dress.

The first zombie wears a shredded black blazer, with a jaunty peaked sailing cap. One of his eyes is dangling onto his cheek from its optic nerve. The second is dressed for zombie Zumba. His tracksuit looks as if it has been shredded by giant claws. It is soaked in fresh and congealed blood that follows him in a crimson snail trail.

Scottish Rob has had little experience of video games. Rashly, he dashes forwards. We hear a squelch as the blades of his closed garden shears push into the sailor zombie's belly. The creature looks down, with a hurt expression, at the wooden handles protruding from its abdomen. However, as aficionados know, that's not the way to neutralise a specimen of the undead, *Homo immortui*. It's just going to wind it up.

The zombie's right arm wraps around Rob's shoulders. Its head flicks forward. Decayed, broken teeth economically tear out its victim's throat. Rob drops to the floor like a sack of cement. The zombie brings back it head. It shrieks in triumph, the single eye gleaming, its face a mask of blood.

'He should have gone for the heed, says Hamish. That's how you kill them. You blast the heed off, with a gun.'

'You mean head,' says Dom,

'Yeh, head. Whatever.'

'We don't have a gun,' says Dave.

'Aye. But we have this.' Hamish is gripping a pickaxe handle. He holds the weapon aloft.

What he does is brave – Braveheart brave. He can't easily walk but he stumbles forwards a couple of paces. He waits until the gym zombie is in range.

He lifts his weapon. I think that his plan is to sever the creature's poorly attached head with a sideswipe, like a boxer's haymaker. Hamish howls, as his Highland ancestors must have done, rushing towards King George's redcoats.

The first part of the plan works. The second goes spectacularly wrong. Hamish is not steady on his pins and the floor is slippery. His lead trainer skids like a ski. His body topples back. His head cracks on the floor. He lies still.

'Shit,' says Dave.

The sailor zombie is hungrily feasting on Rob's intestines, which trail from his abdomen like spaghetti. It looks up. The gym zombie glances back. The two creatures are communicating.

What happens now is odd. The sailor zombie suddenly abandons his meal. Dom, Dave and I watch, as the undead drag the two inert bodies back down the corridor. *Zombies two, humans nil.* They disappear round the corner. Perhaps this has merely been a food gathering exercise? Should we follow them into their House of Horror? We conduct a brief debate. Best not, we decide. Discretion is the better part of valour.

We retrace our steps with nervous backward glances. Dave tells me that he has many friends from the biker and festival communities. They will be pretty hacked off, so to speak, when they hear what has happened to Hamish and Rob. We concur that Hamish may not be dead. We agree that, when we come back to rescue him, we'll be armed with some proper weapons.

The smiles of the grey statues in the chapel seem ambiguous. Dave mounts the ladder, followed by Dom and me. We pull it up behind us.

Sunday 10th April 11.04am
Marcus, The Swinger

When Marcella and I moved here, in January, we were not entirely surprised to find that there were people living next door in what was, apparently, an empty house. We had received a message giving us the details of number seven Mundania Close at a séance, which is not exactly normal. We had suspected that something like this might happen.

On the second morning in our new house, I discovered a door in the cellar, connecting it to number six. It wasn't locked.

I was intrigued to see that the floor and walls of next door's basement were painted with circles and symbols. It wasn't the crude graffiti of vagrants or squatters. I recognised both five and six-pointed stars, Greek and Hebrew characters and astrological symbols.

It was like discovering Alistair Crowley's Abbey of Thelema – a 1920s commune in Sicily, in which Crowley conducted ritual magic. This space had clearly not been used for years. It was damp and its walls were swathed in cobwebs.

My heart jumped as my torch touched the shape of a man in the shadows. He stepped forwards.

He was ancient and pallid

I had been half expecting him.

'I have been waiting for you, Mr Gardner,' he said.

•••

Over the next few days, Marcella and I got to know Theophilus Williams and his partner, Violet, as we helped them to clean up their house. First, we renovated the underground ritual room. Marcella used her painting skills to restore the lines and colours of its geometric shapes and glyphs.

Theo was interesting to talk to. The library in his study contained what must be an extremely valuable library of leather-bound books – volumes of magic and commentary on the Bible, its apocrypha and the Talmud, in Latin, English, French and Hebrew. Some of them dated back to the earliest days of printing. Many contained line drawings of figurers who were extremely familiar in medieval times – demons.

His knowledge of these volumes and of deities, demiurges and spirits going back to the dynasty period of Egypt and ancient Mesopotamia, was extensive. He could contextualise Rabbinical debates and quote chapter and verse of multiple esoteric texts, some lost to history. His library contained numerous editions of the Lesser Key of Solomon and its offshoot, the *Ars Goetia* – primers of demonology that have never gone out of print. He would often talk of the Book of Enoch, removed from the Old Testament because of its incendiary content.

Two precursors of his studies, he told me, were the Elizabethan alchemist, poet and spy, John Dee and the nineteenth-century French occultist, Eliphas Levi, author of Transcendental Magic, which was a bridge for many to the grimoires of antiquity.

Williams would often reminisce about the days when he was the mayor of Lewisham – his connections to the rich and famous, the Masonic network that he painstakingly built up, his financial machinations his betrayal, and, finally, the collapse of his empire and his staged suicide.

•••

Once we had finished bringing the ritual room back to life, we swept out and mopped the tunnel that connected it to the chapel. This, too, we restored to a pristine state. Marcella and I were excited. We saw endless possibilities for amatory events – sex parties at the wiccan sabbats, love weekends, hippy handfasting in our Chapel of Love. Blessed with many bedrooms, we would be able to accommodate our guests in comfort. It would be the grooviest and most exclusive shag pad in London. Then an idea was born. Why shouldn't they pay?

From that, came the idea of a company. I have put up the capital. Its four directors are Marcella and me, Theo and Violet. We have a boardroom, on the first floor of number six. We call this room an office, but it is also a space for relaxing. The décor was Marcella's creation. When we first saw the room, it was dingy and neglected. Almost everything was worn out. Marcella replaced the decaying brown wallpaper with modern variants of Victorian patterns, chose comfortable sofas and armchairs in soft brown leather, and subtle lighting.

Non-magical hardbacks take up much of the wall area. The décor of the room is in keeping with the Edwardian heritage of Mundania Close.

•••

Every window in number six, apart from the mirrored glass of the top room of the turret, Theo's belvedere, is boarded up on the inside. The odd thing is, he and Violet have no need of light – artificial or natural. They are quite happy to sit for hours in the dark, and they do so. Also, we have never seen them eat or drink – a topic that we politely avoid. By his own reckoning, Theo is 176 years old. His 177th birthday will be in July. Violet is four years younger.

He says that their bodies were preserved at their then ages in 1904, when he made his pact with the Dark Lord. But time has taken a toll on his face. His pallor is yellowish, his dull eyes have sunk into their sockets. Marcella calls Violet 'the albino'. Her skin is creased like endlessly folded paper. It has become pale beyond mere whiteness, so that her veins and arteries show through, like a roadmap.

Violet's demeanour is eternally saturnine. She is a fizzing firecracker, animated by constant enthusiasms. She is proud of her shapely figure and of her hair, which she often dyes or supplements with wigs. She favours inappropriately sexual clothing – almost transparent dresses and tight miniskirts – and makes no secret of her high sex drive.

Theo and Violet have discovered modern music since we made their acquaintance. Violet loves to dance around the ritual room, in skimpy clothes, or naked, with disco anthems pumping out of the powerful speakers.

•••

Theo requested a meeting in the office early this morning. He was looking pleased with himself. He was wearing a new silk waistcoat.

One of my investments for the close was a high-definition CCTV system. Discreet adjustable cameras now peer into every nook and cranny, 24 hours a day, as Williams used to, from his belvedere.

102

Above the desk in the office is a bank of monitors. I showed Theo how to use the system and introduced him to a modern innovation – the computer. He has a quick mind. He and Violet soon discovered the internet and became patrons of Amazon. They used it to buy new items for their house and their wardrobes, requesting deliveries to our house, number seven, not theirs – its door cannot be opened.

I have never seen Williams look so spruce. It's unnerving. He invites me to share the screen of his MacBook Pro, with its sixteen-inch display.

'Let me show you,' he says, 'I have made a film. I'm sure that you will like it.'

It begins in a low-key fashion. We see a group of casually dressed men in the tunnel connecting the basement of number six to the chapel. One of them is Daniel, the writer who lives at number nine.

'Wait.'

Tentatively, holding gardening implements as weapons, they make their way forwards. Daniel holds back. There are three men in front of him. One is heavily-built, in a stretched tee-shirt, two others wear leather jackets. They have the look of wary explorers.

The light goes off, plunging the corridor into darkness.

'Watch.'

Lit by torches, we see two creatures. They look like freshly dug up corpses.

'Zombies?' I suggest.

'Is that what they are called?'

'Where did you get them from?'

'Just watch.'

The fat man rushes forwards. He spears a zombie with a pair of shears. The creature clamps his mouth onto the man's throat and blood gushes forth in a fountain. Intermittently we see one of the bikers – I think it's the Scotsman from number one – rush the zombies. He falls onto his back and lies still. The segment ends in bathos. The zombies drag two bodies back the way that they have come.

'Why are they doing that?' I say.

'Because I asked them to. I told them to bring back at least one person alive.'

'Why?'

'You'll see.'

He looks pleased with himself.

'Did you like it?'

I don't answer.

'It was Inspired by films that I have seen, on my computer. The human imagination is so rich, isn't it. We made the zombies.'

'You made them?'

'Actually, we adapted them.'

He tells me that he and Violet, through magic in their ritual room, have succeeded in bringing two demons to earth from Hell. They are Shedim, evil entities referred to in the Old Testament, he explains. Neither alive nor dead, Shedim have the wings and feet of roosters and human faces. They fly around in flocks. These horrible creatures like to haunt graveyards, like Goths. They can turn themselves into snakes or lizards, even mammals – generally creatures that live in darkness and corruption.

'Violet made the zombie costumes. We clipped their wings to stop them flying away. That was a messy business.'

'Can they speak?'

'No but they can make sounds.'

I sit back in the comfortable, adjustable chair that my credit card has paid for.

'What if they get loose?'

'They won't get loose. Like I said, we removed their wings.

'See that?'

He pointed to a CCTV monitor.

'That's where I am keeping them.'

'Where are they?'

'They're asleep, in the straw.' He indicates another monitor. A haggard, terrified face looks up. It's one of the bikers.

'This is beautiful Gardner, you'll love this. My Shedim will devour our Scottish friend, while he is still alive – the parts of him that are left after the insects have finished.'

'The insects?'

'They live in the straw. I have purchased some lively creatures from specialist suppliers. I've been feeding them on rotting meat. Now they are in for a treat. We'll be able to watch. And record it. Imagine! We are blessed with technology that has almost infinite possibilities. It's marvellous, isn't it.'

'Look, I think I'll pop home,' I say. 'I've just remembered. We have a delivery coming.'

'But Marcella is there.'

'It's for me.'

'Oh.'

He is clearly disappointed.

'Bet you'd love to see Hamish being eaten wouldn't you.'

Eating the guest. That's not my idea of a dinner party.

'Yes, that would be great…'

Oh shit.

What the hell am I going to say to Marcella?

Monday 10th April 5am

Hamish, The Biker

'Good morning.'

'What the fuck?'

I'm in a small room, sitting on a plank. My wrists and ankles are attached to the wall. It's more like an animal pen than a cell. The wooden door has a gap at the bottom of it. The walls and floor are concrete, painted grey. There's a dim electric light – it never goes off.

It's hot in here, almost sauna hot, and it stinks – God it stinks. It's not the fruity stink of a pig farm. It's worse than that. There's ammonia and a banquet of rotting matter – fish, meat, offal, rotting vegetation. Anything that you can imagine.

The flies are horrible – fat green blowflies. I've spent hours trying to keep them off my head. They can smell the blood. Swarms of them are feasting on the filth outside. The rotting straw that I can see through the bottom of the door is seething with other insects – and rats. I can hear their feet scuttling.

There's a grille in the wall, to my right.

It's talking to me.

'I trust that you slept well.'

Holy Christ.

'I've let you lie in. You've been a busy boy. By the way, on behalf of the close, thank you for all the work that you have done, with your friends, to bring the mound back into use. I want you to know that it is not unappreciated. My name is Theo. I live at number six. That's where you are now. In my sous-sol. You met two of my friends earlier.'

'Fuckin' zombies!'

'That is one word for them. Strictly, a zombie is re-animated corpse. The creatures that you encountered were actually demons.'

'You fucking…'

'Really Hamish. Where is your gratitude? Haven't I kept you alive? Isn't the accommodation to your liking? I imagine that you have spent nights in police and prison cells – a man like you. This is slightly different from those. How? I'll explain.'

'I'm gonna fucking…'

'Listen. I'm going to stop talking in a minute by the way and leave you to your thoughts. You should be aware that the Shedim with whom you are sharing the basement can assume non-human forms – forms that are carnivorous. I can see them now. My beauties. They are not hungry at the moment. They are still digesting the flesh that they have recently consumed. But they will be. Can you see where this going Hamish?'

My ankles. I can't fucking reach them. My head. Fuck…

'The insects will come first, then the Shedim. The insects will devour you, slowly, over several days, beginning with the softest tissue. Eyes are popular, I believe.'

'You fucking sick bastard!'

'I'll be watching… and filming. Perhaps I'll post it on YouTube. Does that appeal to you Hamish? Posthumous stardom? Nothing to say? Yes, rattle your chains why don't you. By the way. It's a sweet baby that you and Karen have brought into the world. Congratulations. I'm sure that fatherhood suits you. Still nothing to say? Very well. I'll bid you farewell then, for now.'

'Jesus!'

11

A Safe Pair of Hands

Extract from, Adventures in the Paranormal, Dixon Granger, Honor Oak Press, 1924

God bless Bill Peevers. Soon after my arrival at The Woodsman, he had been a lodestar guiding me into my new role in life.

Born to a clerk in Deptford, he had worked in the newspaper trade since the age of fourteen, beginning as a messenger on Fleet Street and swiftly progressing into the newsroom. His career matched the rise of the 'penny dreadfuls'. By the end of the century photography, linotype presses, electric telegraphy, typewriters and circulations reaching millions had arrived.

He moved to the Daily Mail in 1901 as a senior reporter – a remarkable achievement for one who had started with so few chances in life. It was a prestigious and well-paid job. He was able to rent a double-fronted house in Norbury with his wife and son, John.

A year later, his life changed dramatically. His wife suffered a nervous illness and was admitted to a lunatic asylum. She died there soon afterwards. He lost his job and house and became estranged from his son. I gathered that his rapid descent may also have had to do with a story that he had written that had angered someone in a position of power.

Forced into rented lodgings in Camberwell, he had, in his own words, 'hit the bottle'.

One would have said that the man I interviewed for a senior reporter's position early in my tenure at The Woodsman was, to some degree, broken down. But Peevers' reporting pedigree was impeccable. It had included chronicling the Jack the Ripper killings, the sorry affair of the Cleveland Street brothel and the Royal baccarat scandal. In his role as a news gatherer, he had been equally familiar with the wealthiest addresses in London and the slums of the East End. Wasn't this job somewhat beneath level of abilities and experience, I enquired? He assured me that it was not. He knew that he would be writing about relatively minor local matters. A local paper, he said, must be a 'journal of record', truthful and reliable, just as much as an exposer of injustice.

I added that the owner of The Woodsman was a rich, vain man who liked to see his name in print but that he rarely interfered in editorial decisions. He smiled wryly. He gave me confidence that he would do a good job. My trust was repaid. He soon recovered his normal equilibrium and fulfilled his role skillfully and diligently. I never regretted my decision.

It was my practice to be at my desk early on Mondays, before the rest of the staff had arrived. This Monday I arrived particularly early. Rather than working, I was staring bleakly through the grimy window. Williams would be sure to dismiss me. Should I leave first? Or should I brazen it out? Should I go to the police? What I had actually seen, while disgusting, was not illegal. It was a quandary. I was relighting my pipe when I heard a familiar tap on the glass panel of my door. It was Bill Peevers.

'Good morning.'

'Good morning, sir. Is there something wrong?'

Where to begin? It was hard for my mind to assimilate what I had seen on Saturday evening, let alone describe it.

Peevers stood by the window.

He was always welcome to come into my office. He was a weathervane of the mood of the rest of the staff. Often, he told me fascinating tales of his time as reporter – for example, how he had pretended to be a tramp to expose corruption in a workhouse in Mile End and bluffed his way into an opium den.

He lit a cigarette. I revived my smouldering pipe.

'You don't need to be concerned about Williams, or your job, you know.'

'Why is that?'

'You needn't worry because Williams' world is about to collapse. I happen to know that he has made an enemy of a senior Freemason in the Metropolitan Police. He has ruffled some important feathers. Consequently, a thorough examination is being made of his business dealings. Criminal proceedings are about to be brought for fraud and improper conduct in public office. By this time next week, he will be ruined.'

I was astonished.

'My guess is that writs will be served by Friday. He will be arrested and taken into police custody.' He paused. 'However, you are still in great danger. I assure you, evil happens in the most ordinary places.'

'Evil?'

'Williams has had three men murdered in the past year. One of them was the man who built Mundania Close, Ted Christmas.'

'Christmas? Don't be ridiculous.'

'He was chasing Williams for money rather too forcefully. He hadn't been paid for months. He was about to apply for a county court judgment. Masons show no mercy to those who cross them. Christmas was strangled with a silk cord. A stake of holly was driven through his heart, while he was still breathing. His flesh and bones were broken up with picks and shovels. What was left of him was buried in the foundations of number nine Mundania Close.'

'Come now. How do you know this?'

'I know the workmen who were on the job. They were secretive, at first, but I am rather partial to Irish stout and I gained their confidence. Don't expect the police to look into it too closely by the way. The service is infested with masons, at all levels. They always protect their own. They are bound, by oath, to loyalty to the Craft and its members, on pain of death. They are as thick as thieves, Mr Granger.'

My mind was beginning to acknowledge patterns in local life that I had previously chosen to ignore.

'You are very likely to be next. For that reason, you and your wife must leave your house, preferably today. Is there anywhere you can go?'

I thought. My wife had the use of a place in Bridport through her family. We used it for holidays.

'I do.'

'Where is it?'

'In Dorset.'

'Perfect. That will give you some grace, until Williams is behind bars.'

I looked at my watch. It was eight-thirty. Carts could be heard on the road on the front of the building. Forest Hill was waking up.

'Will I be able to come back?' I asked.

He lit a fresh cigarette.

'Of course. The Woodsman is a going concern and the liquidators will most likely keep it in business, to pay off Williams' creditors. Its success is because of you, so they will certainly want you to remain.'

'Thank you, Bill. It's because of you too, you know, and young Jack.'

'I'll be happy to mind the shop for you while you are away.'

'Will you be safe?'

He laughed.

'Believe me, I've run up against many men like Williams. I know how to cover my tracks.'

'How long do you think I have,' I said, 'before I join poor Christmas, in the foundations of Mundania Close?'

'Oh, you'll be quite safe today. Williams will have you grabbed when you are least expecting it, in your house, when you are asleep. Just before dawn is the favourite time.'

'That's a relief.'

I had a few hours in which to settle my affairs. I would telephone my wife and ask her to pack for us. There would be an editorial meeting at eleven o'clock. We agreed that, today, Peevers would be in charge. As I sorted out correspondence and items that I would need, Peevers told me something that could have come from a piece of fiction.

'You know the mound that lies in the centre of Mundania Close. Did you notice that there is a small building there?'

'I did. What is it?'

'It's a chapel, Williams calls it his Chapel of Venus. It is designed for depraved rituals. A tunnel has been dug connecting the chapel to the basement of number six. And I believe that Williams has been acquiring the modern equivalent of vestal virgins for the use of his love cult.'

'His love cult?'

I was dumbfounded.

'Are you aware of the Girls' Industrial School, in Dartmouth Road, Daphne House?'

'Yes, I walk past it every day, on my way to work.'

'That is where Williams is procuring his maidens. Do you know who the superintendent of Daphne House is?'

'I don't.'

'Her name is Violet Jones. She was previously the madam of a brothel in West Norwood. Williams met her in her former role. He placed her in charge of Daphne House for his own purpose.'

110

'Which was?'

'Daphne House trains girls from the age of eleven in domestic skills, such as needlework, cleaning and washing, and so forth, to prepare them for domestic service or to work in laundries. They are all orphans who are under the charge of the Lewisham Workhouse Union. They are girls with no parents or guardians to look after their interests. Jones, of all people, has been entrusted with their moral welfare.'

'So, you are saying that innocent young girls will be offered for the depraved pleasure of wealthy men. It's rather far-fetched, isn't it?'

'Mr Granger, I could buy a girl for you tomorrow, for five pounds, or even less. Do you remember W.T. Stead's campaign in the Pall Mall Gazette, on child prostitution in 1885? No-one will miss them and any girls who complain will simply disappear. Williams has devised a perfect way to do evil in plain sight.'

I did not tell him what I had witnessed at number six Mundania Close.

'Should we not expose this?'

'We should, but it will be extremely dangerous.'

For the next hour, we discussed how we would assist in Williams being brought to account for procuring young girls for immoral purposes. There would be much that I could accomplish in Dorset, we agreed. We made a list of individuals to whom I should write. It included the Commissioner of the Metropolitan Police, the Lord Chancellor, the President of the Local Government Board, Lewisham's Town Clerk and local members of Parliament.

I found out train times for the journey to Dorset and telephoned my wife. She was not nearly as surprised as I had anticipated and greeted the news in good heart. I think she was relieved that we would be leaving London.

Peevers said that he would send me a telegram as soon as it was safe to return. He was smiling when I bid him goodbye, just before the delayed editorial meeting was to begin. I slipped out of the building quietly. We did not tell the rest of the staff the true reason for my sudden departure.

On my walk home, I found myself smiling at people who greeted me, rather than looking away. An enormous burden had been lifted from my shoulders and I was confident that I had left the paper in safe hands. Direct trains departed from Waterloo to Bridport every half hour. Judith and I should be comfortably installed in her sister's place by the time it was dark.

12

The Republic of Mundania

Monday 11th April, 3pm
Daniel, The Writer

Now I know how skanky Dave got his name. He's a stick insect of man, with a straggly beard and brown hair that reaches below his shoulders. It's a warm spring morning but he's wearing multiple layers of clothing, in an effort to keep warm. All of the layers are filthy, even his black tee-shirt.

His grime-infested jeans are the shade of coppery mud, even his leather jacket is patched from multiple repairs. It bears the insignia of a motorcycle gang, or could it be a band?

The areas of his rarely washed skin that are visible are heavily tattooed with hearts, daggers and wings. And he's wearing formidable black boots with steel toecaps. It's not really surprising that Dave is dressed like this. He is the owner of a scrapyard. His main interests are motorbikes and heavy metal. His hobbies are also lifestyle choices.

He's the kind of person who starts each day by smoking a large joint, favouring weed that would put most people in a coma. Dave plays in a band. It's more biker than death metal he explains to me. That's how he met Hamish, at a festival. I think it was at the Bulldog Bash.

We are sitting on the mound on camping chairs. We've relived the recent zombie abduction from all sides – what happened, what we could have done, what we need to do now.

'Fucking bastards.' He has used the phrase several times this morning – reflectively, resignedly, aggressively.

'D'you think Hamish is dead?'

'I don't' know'.

'Well, we've got to rescue him.'

'Call the police?'

'Nah, fuck the police.'

Dave stubs out his joint angrily.

'I have a plan.'

'Oh yeh?'

'I know some heavy people and they know Hamish, yeh?'

'Heavy how?'

'They don't fuck around.'

'Meaning?'

He holds up an imaginary gun.

'Blow the fuckers away. No head, no zombie.'

'Right.'

Something tells me that Dave, the general of a putative army of Hells Angels, may be under-estimating his opponent. I choose not to disclose my opinion.

Later that morning, a Portakabin arrives on the back of a trailer. Then a caravan. People turn up on motorbikes and pushbikes, some on foot. Mundania Close is becoming an encampment. It will include music. In Dave's Transit are assorted guitars, a drum kit, amps and a 10,000-watt pa.

•••

There's going to be a hell of a party here on Saturday. Perhaps party isn't the right word. News is spreading far and wide, mainly by word of mouth. This suburban crescent is becoming a festival site – the Republic of Mundania someone called it today.

The police will start sniffing round soon, alerted to this unwelcome and incongruous outbreak of freedom. But serving warrants takes time. The wheels of reaction turn slowly.

I know the drill. I've been to many festivals. By the evening, more tents will have arrived and fires will have been lit. Guitars will come out. My theory is that twinkling lights, woodsmoke and a perimeter of darkness, bring people back to life – they guide us back into the collective unconscious of our ancestors, stored deep in our brains.

Dusk and early morning are the best times at such gatherings. It is a blessing to be freed from the tyranny of clocks and watches – awoken by the sun, propelled to bed by darkness.

I have a tent that I haven't used for years. I'll pitch it tonight amidst the bikers, hipsters, students and anarchists.

The entrance to the close is being guarded on a rota system, organised from skanky Dave's Portakabin. Electricity isn't a problem. Our diesel generator can furnish as much as we will need. Its hum and smell are part of the vibe of the camp. There are sockets for phone charging. Dave, with a walkie-talkie clamped to his ear has become the leader of this ad hoc anarchist collective.

Humans used to be nomads. Life is more fulfilling when the future is uncertain and when one is faced by survival challenges. That's why camping is fun and festivals are great. Put the two together. Magic. It's depressing when you have to drag yourself back into normal, dull, safe reality, after a few days of freedom – like ripping a piece out of your soul.

Egg would have hated what the close has become. So would the Mooks and Ron 'all lives matter' Saxby, Simon Swift and a-tonal Otto. It's hard to remember them now. They seem to belong to a previous era. I wonder what Marcella and Marcus think about what's going on.

Monday 10th April, 4pm
Marcus, The Swinger

Something strange has happened today. I have watched from my study window as a procession of mismatched vehicles and odd-looking people converged on Mundania Close, like Genghis Khan's army. Criminality is clearly involved – at least two houses have been broken into. What's happening here has the hallmarks of a travellers' camp.

At the centre of the mound, a structure has risen, made out of scaffolding poles, like the stockade of an invading army. It grows larger every day. Yes, that's what has appeared outside – an army and its camp followers. Men who look like Hamish predominate. Men wearing leather and denim – the uniform of the disaffected – and women who look like… well I haven't seen too many women.

Some of the bearded throwbacks are musicians. I have glimpsed electric guitars and amplifiers in their vans. They have set up at least one generator. We have heard its low throb all day. This is illegal on so many levels. It's an affront.

It rained last night, adding a new element to this unholy mess – mud. Today has brought dull grey weather, giving the encampment an even more forlorn aspect.

'For fuck's sake, Marcella, have you seen what's going on out there?'

She is sitting on the comfortable chair in my study, her legs curled beneath her.

115

'Woodstock, darling,' she says. 'Or Glastonbury.'

'I think, actually, it's more like Altamont,' I say. 'That was the one where Hells Angels beat someone to death.'

'Oh, Marcus, don't be so negative. Didn't you used to be a hippy?'

'No,' I say, turning into the room. 'I was never a hippy. I like bathing too much.'

'So, what are you going to do? Call the police?'

'You'd like to be out there, wouldn't you.'

'I would, actually. It looks like fun. I'm going to go out later.'

"I'm not going to call the police,' I say, 'we have to deal with the sick psycho next door first. But I think that fate may have delivered a solution.'

'Oh?' her eyes widen.

'This biker invasion is the best thing that could have happened. Theo has one of their own. So what do you think a hairy-arsed biker gang will do? They'll stage an attack and grab him, won't they. Hopefully, they will skewer Theo and his ghastly wife like suckling pigs. The least that Hamish deserves is a bikers' burial. That's what's will happen. Then the police will arrive and clean up this whole sorry mess. I'm going to do something to make life easier for them.'

'What's that?'

'I'm going to disable the electricity supply to next door, by smashing the fuse box. Then I'll barricade the connecting door in the basement.'

'Is that necessary."

Marcella is unaware of the full horror of the freak next door.

She uncurls her legs and stretches. Our eyes connect. God, I feel horny.

Shall we? Why not?

Monday 10th April, 4.30pm
The Watcher

'You fucking prick. I'm going to kill you.'

'Brave words, Hamish. Violet, my love, do come and watch. This is priceless.'

Violet crosses the room from our leather sofa. She stands next to me, looking at the monitor connected to the basement camera. She is wearing a short latex skirt and a clinging unbuttoned blouse.

She is excited by the unfolding spectacle that is being revealed on the screen. Very excited.

Hamish is being eaten alive.

He is now too weak to fend off anything other than rats. His voice is dry and cracked. His head is encased by the shiny wings of flies, like a living wig. Other insects are chewing on his wounds – ants, beetles and the giant centipedes that we bought online, from a specialist dealer. We also purchased parasitic worms that will burrow into his skin and lay their eggs.

Hamish does not just have a wound on his head. The claws of my Shedim slashed his arms and legs to the bone and made oozing ridges across his stomach and chest. Flesh rots quickly in warm, humid environments. These fascinating areas are being thoroughly explored. Columns of creatures are proceeding up his legs. Even slugs will play their part in sucking on his innards. His flesh is a map of torment. The fat tissue that has been burrowed into is livid crimson with streaks of yellow and the gleam of exposed white bone.

'What's your name, you fucking…?'

'Oh, Hamish, I thought better of you,' I tell him, through the speaker which is set into the wall.

It is fantastic that he is still conscious, providing a living record of this event. One that I am recording. He jerks his upper body and tries to wrench his ankles from their chains. Flies lift in a buzzing cloud.

Violet shudders with pleasure.

He wrenches his upper body again. His eyes, encased by swollen lids, are like bruised purple fruits.

The pointed snouts of two animals have appeared in the gap beneath the door of his pen. The creatures leap. Hamish screams. We hear delicious sounds of squelching as their fangs sever ligaments and fracture bone. Soon, the detached head is abandoned. The Shedim tear into the softer parts of the corpse that have been left by the rats and insects.

The lights go out.

•••

117

Gardner has pulled the plug on us. I thought that he would do this. He is a weak man – a sniveling coward. I saw this morning, from his face, that he has no stomach for the Dark Arts. He is merely a curious dabbler.

We have no need for his electricity, I tell Violet. We lived in the dark before he arrived. We can do so again. I had anticipated this. I have laid in a large stock of candles over the past few days, both for lighting and ceremonial purposes.

Not all of Hamish was fully digestible. We have been gifted with something that Demons love – human remains. I have been delving more deeply into The Lesser Key of Solomon. I am now sure, following our successful summoning of the Shedim, that we can invoke one of the Archdukes of Hell into the Triangle of Solomon.

Strenuous sexual magic will be required.

'My dear, we have work to do, downstairs,' I say. 'Are you ready to make demons?'

'Oh yes, yes!' Violet shrieks.

Tuesday 11th April, 10.03am
Daniel, The Writer

I have pretty much everything I need. I popped to the local shop earlier. I have teabags, instant coffee, water and UV milk. I have butter, bacon, eggs, sliced white bread and ketchup. I have a bottle of Merlot for later and sounds and entertainment from my combined cassette player and radio, which is fitted with brand new batteries.

There's a lot going on outside – laughing, music, the occasional crash of what sounds like a pterodactyl colliding with a tree.

My tent has two sections. The front is for hanging out while waiting for the rain to stop. The back is a sleeping compartment. I'm looking forward to my first night under canvas. I love the light that comes through the tent's orange fabric, the sound that raindrops make, the tent's closed-in coziness. I associate it with being a teenager.

It's bound to be noisy until after dawn. That's the only downside. What do bikers say? 'Sleep when you are dead'. I bought some foam earplugs at Boots. They are not particularly effective.

'Daniel …' It's soft, female voice.

'Daniel?' I unzip the door.

It's Marcella.

'How did you know I was here?'

'Dave told me.'

She is wearing jeans, cowboy boots with silver tips, a soft suede jackets with tassels. Beads hang around her neck. Her head lightening perfume contains a subtle variant of patchouli oil.

'May I join you?'

Don't say anything, Daniel.

•••

Thudding bass and raucous laughter have woken us up.

Marcella is lying on top of the sleeping bag, naked.

'Won't Marcus be jealous?' I say.

'Of course.'

'I thought you were swingers.'

She looks at me quizzically.

'We are. But it doesn't mean Marcus doesn't get jealous. He is especially jealous of you.'

'Why?'

'Because you are intelligent. You are a writer. Why are you being so coy, Daniel?'

She guides my hand to the place where all of her angles converge.

•••

Marcella and I are half-awake, half-asleep. Outside, the festival is in day-time mode. Smells of roasting food. Smoke. A band is tuning up.

I hear a voice.

'Good morning.'

It's Dom.

'Can I come in?'

Christ, I should be selling bloody tickets!

'Yeh, why not.'

The door unzips, bringing in light. A head appears, then a body.

'You've got company I see.'

'Hi Dom,' says Marcella.

For a moment, I'm concerned that she will invite Dom to join us.

'Got to go, guys,' she says, glancing at her iPhone, 'Marcus is fretting.'

Thank God.

She quickly dresses, unconcerned about being naked in front of Dom.

She blows a kiss from the tent door.

'Love you both.'

'Christ,' says Dom, when she has gone. Wasn't expecting that. Didn't you tell me that she's a Satanist?'

'I don't think she is now. I think I was wrong.'

'So, who is the grim reaper of Mundania Close?'

'It's Theo, at number six. I also think that he was involved in the killing of my friend Adrian, in Sydenham.'

'How so.'

'Adrian was killed in a brutal, public way. It was a classic Masonic execution. It means, "fuck off, we are untouchable". I know that Theo was a senior Freemason. I think he's communicating with active masons. There's plenty in this part of London, including some extremely nasty gangsters.'

'A man who, you say, died more than a hundred years ago.'

'We've seen his zombies.'

He has no answer for that.

'There's something I should tell you,' Dom says. 'James and I have split up. He was bummed out that I was hanging out with Hamish and the biker guys. I've never seen him so angry. I think he's having a breakdown.'

'Where is he?'

'No-one knows. He's not in his house.'

Oh, Christ, another missing person. Mundania Close has turned into the Bermuda fucking Triangle.

'Shall we get some breakfast?' Dom says.

'Yeh, let's. I'm hungry.'

13

A Coastal Idyll

Adventures in the Paranormal, Dixon Granger, Honor Oak Press, 1924

They say a change is as good as a rest. Our place of retreat was not a stone cottage but a modest house in the middle of a red-brick terrace, with a long garden that swept up the side of a steep hill. Judith and I loved it. We had spent our happiest summers there. At end of our lane was the sea.

Green fields, breathing in fresh air and, at night, being enveloped by an ebony star-clustered sky had their usual effect. After a couple of days, London had worked itself out of my system. My horizons were wider; I felt part of larger universe. It appeared to be a benevolent one.

My working life seemed distant from this elemental world. Fern-covered heaths offered a constantly changing vista and little boats bobbed out to sea from the Bridport's fishing harbour, West Bay. Life had not changed much here for decades, centuries, millennia. To prise a fossil from a cliff that had been a living creature in the Jurassic period is to feel truly insignificant.

Judith has always said that Dorset suits me. Work here was not onerous. I spent each morning writing letters to important people, informing them of the misdemeanours of one T.W. Williams, the former mayor of Lewisham. By midday, there would be clutch of them in manilla envelopes on my desk. A stroll along a delightful lane to the post office followed. The calls of chaffinches and chiff-chaffs serenaded me on my walk.

Each morning, we waited for a telegram boy to cycle down our lane, bearing news from Bill Peevers on what was happening in London. None came. Friday brought a feeling of anxiety. He should surely have contacted us by now. His failure to do so was ominous.

On Monday afternoon, a week after we had left, I took the train from West Bay Station back to Waterloo. My mood was as dark as the sky, as the trained pulled in. I was an ant, joining millions of others engaged in weaving journeys whose apparent randomness was part of a vast pattern.

The tube and a further train journey took me to Forest Hill. I took deep breaths as I walked from the station up the hill. The gas lights were on. I was surprised that the office was locked up, as it was only half past five. The sub-editor and compositor worked until least seven o'clock on Mondays. I decided not to unlock the door. For the moment, the umbilical cord connecting The Woodsman to me had been severed.

There was an obvious place to go. The Pied Horse public house at the bottom of the hill was a supplementary office and a second home to most of the staff, our 'local'. It was where the production team came on press nights to roister, drink beer and play billiards. Sometimes, I joined them.

None of them was in the public bar. They must be in the back room, a space that, unofficially belonged to The Woodsman. Only Jack Kelly, the reporter was here. He was standing at the billiards table. He was collarless and in his shirtsleeves. Three young girls were sitting on a bench at the side of the room. They were wearing white pinafore dresses. They were watching his every move intently.

Jack was a carefree, easy-limbed lad, with a shock of blond hair. His father had abandoned the family and he lived with his mother, as breadwinner. There were traces of Irish in his Cockney accent. He had also learned to speak 'proper English' – as a journalist one must associate with people from all walks of life.

He had taken to his trade like a duck to water. Whether finding a nugget of interest in a dull council meeting, bashing out a story to a tight deadline or steadily drinking pints of beer until closing time and always buying his round, he had never been found wanting. He had painstakingly taught himself shorthand – which was invaluable for capturing the melodramas of the courtroom.

He was surprised to see me.

'Mr Granger!'

'Good evening, Jack. I'm so glad to have found you.'

'We were wondering where you were, sir.'

'I've been in Dorset, with my wife.'

'Dorset? Is it nice there?'

'Very.'

'Well, it's grand that you are back, Mr Granger.'

'Thank you. Do you know where Bill is?'

He didn't answer.

'Is he alright?'

'He um…'

'I think we'd better talk, don't you.'

He placed his cue in the wall rack, glancing at the three girls.

It was a mild evening. We sat outside in the pub garden, which was empty.

'I'm very sorry to say this, Mr Granger, Bill is dead.'

The dingy pub garden with its etiolated weeds and dead geraniums was a miserable place to hear such a devastating piece of information. I had feared receiving such news many times. Never-the-less, it hit me like a hammer blow.

'How did he die?'

'He fell under the wheels a tram, in Peckham. They say that he was almost sliced in two.'

'Oh God, the poor man.'

He sniffed. 'We shut down the paper after that. Nobody much was in last week. We were waiting for you to tell us what to do.'

'What about Williams?'

'He's dead too.'

I felt a mixture of shock and relief.

'How did it happen, Jack?'

He took his own life. They found him in the bath at his home, with his wrists slashed. That was on Monday. The word is, he was about to be arrested for fraud.'

'Have you corroborated that.'

'I have. It's true. Bill had told me about it.'

The world will be better off without him.'

'It will, Mr Granger.'

His blue eyes sparkled.

'So, who are your lady friends?'

'They are called Clara, Beatrice and Lizzie. They are from Daphne House. The place has been shut down, as its superintendent has disappeared.'

'You mean Violet Jones?'

'Yes, that's her. Nobody knows where she's gone. Most of the girls have been transferred to workhouses but these three don't want to go. They ran away. They have been sleeping in an empty shop in Dartmouth Road.'

'And you have been looking after them.'

His smile grew wider.

'You could say.'

'Teaching them billiards?'

'Trying to.'

The girls joined us outside and I purchased lemonades for them and pints of bitter for Jack and me. Clara and Beatrice, who was known as Birdy, had brown hair. They were sisters, aged ten and eleven. Lizzie, who was thirteen, was fair-haired. She had the most to say. She was Irish and had come to London with her mother, who had been killed in a factory accident. Clara and Birdy had been born in the slums of Deptford. Their parents must have died or disowned them.

The dark-haired girls showed extreme deference to me and barely spoke. But Lizzie was soon expatiating upon the capricious cruelties of Violet Jones, at Daphne House. There had been no-one to protect these girls, I saw now. They were wards of the state being equipped for lives as domestic servants or factory hands.

Lizzie explained that Jones bestowed favours upon her 'special girls'. Those who she singled out were provided with nice dresses, curled hair and polished nails. They were being 'prepared', she said. Lizzie was more worldly-wise than the Clara and Birdy. I suspected that she knew the purpose of this treatment.

Jack and the three girls returned to the billiards table, leaving me outside. I could hear them laughing as he demonstrated his dexterity at the game. The four of these delightful young people were living 'in the present', I reflected. Nothing existed for them beyond the confines of the here and now. I envied them.

It was evident that Jack and Lizzie, whose mothers were from both from Dublin, had formed a bond. He confided in me that he and his ma had already agreed to 'put her up' so that she wouldn't be homeless. That left Clara and Birdy. The thought of them spending the night on a hard, cold floor did not sit well with me. I said that they were welcome to come back to my house in Sydenham.

They barely said a word as we walked to my house, even when we passed Daphne House, whose red brick walls were shrouded in darkness. I can understand why. They did not know me. They must have been full of apprehension. My house was cold and there was little food to offer them – only a cake that Judith had made. The bread in the pantry was stale and the milk was sour. I prepared a bed for them in the spare room.

I had seen some letters on doormat the previous night but, exhausted as I was from my journey, I had chosen to ignore them. One of them was neatly addressed in blue ink. I read it the following morning at the kitchen table. The girls were still asleep. The letter was dated from seven days before – the day that Judith and I had left London.

Dear Mr Granger,

First of all, thank you. You picked me up and gave me a fresh start when I was sorely in need of one. You and your wife have been immensely kind to me. I am so grateful for that. The Woodsman reflects great credit on you. Mostly importantly, the staff are contented. You do not rule them by fear, a many editors do, and you have not let your success go to your head. You run a tight little ship.

If you are reading these words, it means that the worst has happened and that I am dead. I asked someone at the office to post it should I succumb to an 'accident'. I have been as discreet as I could, but Williams, like most Freemasons, has friends in every vestry, police station and courthouse in London. His influence, the tentacles of the Craft, extend upwards into the highest institutions of the land – to the palace itself, in fact, and to the Law Courts and both Houses of Parliament.

Do not be fooled if the police break into his house and find him hanging from a strap or with his head in the gas oven! He won't be dead. Why do I suspect this? Let me explain. Williams has complete control over the Rushey Green and Ladywell workhouses. What could be easier for him than to obtain the corpse of an able-bodied pauper of the right age, height and build, to be used as a substitute for himself in a staged suicide! I have heard of Freemasons using this trick before.

It's my guess that he will hole up at number six Mundania Close. The house has been built like a fortress. The police won't go near the place. They have been warned off. Most of Williams' assets, including Mundania Close are owned indirectly through a secret trust. They are held in the name of his wife's family. Her son, who lives in Guernsey, is likely to be named as his executor. This will be conducted through a solicitor who is a big wheel in the Bromley Freemasons and who is as crooked as a shillelagh.

I would not advise you to look into these matters, or to break into number six. God knows what is going on there. There are rumours that Williams has been trying to contact the Mason-in-Chief, the Devil himself, in pursuit of eternal life. I was told, by one of the builders of the close, that he has amassed a library of ancient books full of secret spells and that his Chapel of Venus has a pagan altar.

This is a sad letter to write. in my heart of hearts, I always knew that this story might be my last. I have been sailing close to the wind for a long time now and I have made many enemies. So be it. I have done my bit. You gave me my last opportunity to use my skills to expose skullduggery and I am grateful for that.

Give my best regards to Judith. For God's sake don't let young Jack get wind of any of this. He's a good lad. I don't want him blundering into a situation that is too big for him to handle. If I were you, I would stay well away from London for the foreseeable future. Enjoy the sea air and down a tankard of cider for me!

Your good friend
William Peevers

Light was finding its way into the kitchen through a filigree of ivy leaves. I drank a cup of black tea and pondered my situation. I remembered what Peevers had told me – that early morning was a time when innocent people were often nabbed.

The course of the day was set. I would wake the girls and take them for breakfast in a local cafe. We would then catch a bus or tram to Crystal Palace. From there I would send a telegram to Judith. I would tell here that I was returning to Bridport on the train. The confines of a telegram would not allow me to convey an important piece of information – that I would be bringing two homeless young girls with me.

Clara and Birdy had never been on a train. They had never seen a cow. They stared through the window, greeting the world that was revealed to them in blank amazement. They were still hungry. We ate a generous lunch in the buffet car.

By the time we had reached Salisbury, the external world had become normal to my young charges. They were talking excitedly now, asking me questions. The girls had strong London accents. Sometimes, I could not understand what they were saying. They explained that had not been allowed toys at Daphne houses and that discipline was enforced there with a birch. They were already familiar with grate blacking, laundry blue and scalding water that turned their hands red.

Our arrival at West Bay station offered them a new wonder, the sea. Long before the train had come to a final halt, I had formed an idea that could set them on a new path. My wife and I had not been blessed with a child. How would she greet the idea, I wondered, of welcoming these two waifs from the slums into our lives?

I had told Judith what time the train would arrive. She would be on the platform, waiting. She was in for a surprise.

14

Hells Angels versus Hell's Angel

Tuesday 11th April, 11.15am
Daniel, The Writer

The Republic of Mundania is growing by the hour. New people are arriving all the time. Tents are starting to be pitched. I'm in skanky Dave's Portakabin, transplanted from his scrapyard. It's furnished with battered filing cabinets, office chairs that should be in a skip and a scratched and scorched Formica-covered table. Here Dave, works, eats and rolls joints. His curtained-off sleeping area is at the other end of the cabin.

Kaz has moved in. Since the disappearance of Hamish, she's been too freaked out to stay in her house. Her kids have adopted the Republic of Mundania as their new home. Dom and Kaz, are sitting at the table. Kaz is holding her baby, Fleur.

Dave is frying us up a full English breakfast – sausage, eggs, bacon, baked beans, black pudding, the works. He's wearing a tee-shirt documenting the tour of an obscure (to me) band. His hair is scraped back in greasy strands, tied at the back with a shoelace.

Occasionally, he blows smoke from his joint through the open door, so as not to pollute the air inside. He seems unconcerned by the prospect of ash dropping into the frying pan. Bacon sizzles, intensifying our hunger, even for Kaz – she's a vegan.

She shows no disapproval as Dave prepares his feast. Stress and sleeplessness are marked on her face. Dom and I have reassured her that Hamish is probably still alive. Neither of us believe this.

A sweet smell of sweat comes from my body. I need a shower.

•••

'Marcella!' says Dom. 'Back so soon? Argued with your old man?' Her face has appeared in the doorway.

Her failure to reply means that she has. I guess that the green-eyed god has put in an appearance at number six – jealousy.

The only space at the table is next to me, opposite Kaz. As Marcella sits down our legs touch. She smiles.

'Hi gorgeous girl. How are you today?'

The baby howls.

Kaz looks uncomfortable. She shrinks into her seat, like she doesn't want to be in the same the room as Marcella.

'Christ, I'm hungry,' says Dom.

'Sorry Dave, I have to go home to feed Fleur,' Kaz says.

'You can do it here,' Marcella suggests.

'There's some stuff I need. I really have to go.'

'OK.' Fleur is crying as if her lungs will burst.

Kaz and her baby leave quickly. The good news is that we can now accept Dave's joint and smoke inside. It leaves a toxic coating on my tongue that will soon be joined by acrylamide from the fried food and the tang of stewed builder's tea. Perfect.

Marcella is as crisp and fresh as a walk in the woods. My leg tingles where it touches hers, encased in tight faded denim.

She asks Dave if he has any green or herb tea. To my surprise, he does – the blackberry leaf tea that Kaz has brought from her house – the kind that tastes like infusion of shredded car tyres.

•••

The recue of Hamish has been planned to degree. It has also taken on the momentum of an inevitable escalation – a Hells Angels' arms race.

In the front rank of the raiding party will be Dave, accompanied by his largest and scariest-looking mates. These guys with their insignia covered leather jackets, their arms inked with badges of disaffection, are intimidating. Some of them have tattoos on their faces.

They have arrived on powerful motorbikes, from as far away as the Surrey Hills and North Kent, many meeting up at the Blackheath tea shack. It's close to the spot that was chosen as an assembly point by Wat Tyler for his peasants' revolt, three centuries before.

Some have kept their helmets on. No guns are on view but what they are brandishing is certainly potentially deadly – baseball bats, motorcycle chains, knuckle dusters, knives. Many of them are carrying spears made from the mound's re-purposed spiked railings Some have blackened their cheeks commando style, indicating the seriousness of their mission.

Dave's Portakabin is too cramped for this small army, so they gee themselves up, inside and outside, swigging on bottles and cans, filling the space around them with a fog swirl of dope.

There is no official signal to mobilise them, like a yachting horn, or a whistle. It just happens, through an invisible internal logic. I am watching from the stage, with Dom, as they move in a clanking phalanx towards the centre of the mound. We are not going to be with them. I count them as they climb onto the roof of the chapel, up a ladder. There are fourteen bikers, including their leader, Dave.

As the first disappears through the roof, I consult my watch. It is a little after half-past twelve. At the same moment, we hear, then see, a news helicopter, with Sky markings, hovering above. This prying visitor indicates that Mundania Close has become newsworthy again. Shots of the multi-coloured tents spread over the close, the caravans, bikes and fires must be fantastic.

The helicopter just missed the squad of bikers disappearing through the roof of the chapel. But soon, alerted by TV pictures, the police will be here, in numbers.

Tuesday 11th April, 1.03pm
The Watcher

He is here – Abaddon, the Destroyer, Angel of the Abyss. Violet in her fetching lime green bustier, her hair flaming, has been my able assistant. We consumed the Cake of Light and began our ritual just before midnight.

The air turned to ice and a gust of wind swept through the room, extinguishing every candle. We could hear the buzzing of insects. Abaddon has mastery over locusts and flies. From these signs, we knew that our offering had been successful.

From within the Triangle, his eyes glowed like gemstones. In the near darkness, we could not see his tall, muscular body and his horned head but we could hear his hoarse breath.

Violet quivered. I lit a candle and dared to turn my face to the Archduke of Hell, only one rank lower than Lucifer. With a single thought, he could have cast our bodies into the bottomless pit. By this act I hoped to show him that I was not a mere trifler or dilettante – that I had a purpose in summoning him from the abyss, of far more weight than mere idle curiosity.

Abaddon, the Greeks' Apollo, whose name means 'destruction', stepped from the Triangle. Our eyes met. His power surged through my body. From the expression on his face, I knew that we were safe – for the moment. Violet and I remained within the circle. The Shedim stirred in their pen, sensing the presence of their master.

Yes, I have eternal life, but I am locked in this earthly prison. In return for releasing him from Hell through my Dark Arts, Abaddon will surely grant me a favour. Soon, Volet and I will be the first humans to enjoy true immortality.

His ears twitched, sensing sounds. He pawed at the floor with a cloven hoof, breathing roughly through his broad nostrils.

•••

The attackers have arrived.

Their leader is a puny fellow in a black leather coat, all swagger and braggadocio. He shines a torch into the room, clearly surprised by its size and the curious patterns that are marked on the floor and walls. His clothes are ripped and stained. So are those of the raggle-taggle group of men behind him. Viking raiders must have looked like this.

'What did you do with Hamish?' he says, in a Cockney voice. He is a low, common sort.

'You mean the Scotsman? He has made fine food for my dogs.'

'We're going to fuck you up,' he sneers.

I merely nod.

The fellow is holding a piece of wood, from which nails protrude, like a medieval mace. He walks slowly towards me, glancing down at the Circle of Solomon. I am standing at its centre, my arms folded. His companions fan out to either side.

With a savage whine, locusts stream in from the four quarters of the room – thousands of them. The creatures clamp themselves to the intruders' faces. They begin to bite. I can hear, from the intensity of the screams that fill the room, that this must be agonising. The men claw at their faces.

Abaddon reveals himself from the shadow. He carries a billhook that has been sharpened in the forges of Hell. He moves in a blur. At first, he hacks off heads, snorting hoarsely as they fall to the floor, then hands, then arms, then legs. Some of the intruders have almost expired from the locusts' venom by the time he reaches them. Yellow froth bubbles from their mouths. The smell of death fills the room.

I count the trunks of thirteen men swimming in gore. The gang's leader leans against a wall, his legs extended in front of him. His face is red. A few locusts cling to his swollen cheeks. Life flickers fitfully in his eyes.

Abaddon watches as my Shedim began to devour the corpses. Flies from the filthy straw of their pens are enjoying the feast of their lives from this charnel house. Should the Angel of the Abyss have the pleasure of delivering coup-de-grace to the gang's leader? Or should I?

I am contemplating this question when I become aware that the Dark Lord is standing next to me. My head reaches the height of his chest. He reaches down. His clawed hand is like a knight's armoured gauntlet. His talons pierce the gang leader's eyes. He tears off the man's face, brings the delicacy to his mouth and eats it. The ruffian's body slides to floor.

The attack is over.

I, Asmodeus, Priest of King Solomon and Lord of Hell, have achieved mastery of the earthly sphere. Eternity is now in my grasp. Now I must rid the close of the pestilence of Marcus Gardner, before he can thwart my further progress. I'll use my Shedim for that. I've had an idea.

Marcella is of no concern to me. She is a simpering nobody. And Daniel? He has been a minor irritant for a long time. It has been amusing following his attempts to thwart me – the watcher watching the watcher. I'll enjoy killing him too, in a manner of my choosing.

Tuesday 11th April, 1.04pm
Daniel, The writer

Logistics are essential to the art of war. It takes a while for the men, their weaponry and welding equipment, intended to cut through metal, to descend into the chapel. I glance at my watch. The second hand appears to be stationary. The music has stopped. There is an oppressive silence. We wait. Whatever is happening is too far beneath us for us to hear its sounds. Five minutes pass. Ten minutes.

The sky darkens, as if the sun has been snuffed out by an eclipse. Lightning bolts crash into the horizon. Thunder rolls from swollen black clouds, like surf. From the hole in the chapel roof, a dark column rises up slowly in a twisting corkscrew.

The Sky helicopter is hovering only few hundred feet above us. The column climbs to meet it. Marcella has joined Dom and I. I grip her fingers, sensing what is about to happen. The helicopter lurches like a drunken man, losing altitude. It skims the roof of number seven and flips onto its side, disappearing behind number eight. There's an explosion.

Black smoke rises from James' garden. Petals of ash drift over the close. The air fills with the bitter stench of burning oil.

Tuesday 11th April, 1.03pm
Marcus, The Swinger

I've seen this a thousand times in films. One never expects to do so in real life. It's unnerving when a helicopter crashes. Something that is coherent in its natural element has been metamorphosed. Nothing could be more awkward or graceless. The machine sideslips over a roof. One, two, three – kaboom! Smoke rises from an invisible crash site.

People on the mound point their phones. Many will have captured the spectacle to share on WhatsApp groups. A few of them head for the front door of number six.

The light in the close has been odd today. There has been an apocalyptic, end-of-times vibe out there. Yes, a bunch of Mad Max low-lifes are camped out, with their scrap vehicles and caravans, but it's not just that. One could feel, from an inner sense, that something terrible was going to happen.

Marcella is out there somewhere. She won't answer my calls or text me back. She's probably shagging every tattooed weirdo she can find, as well as Daniel, her new beau, that drug-addled deejay and God knows who else. Look, I don't mind her screwing around, I really don't, but she's rubbing my nose in it.

Sirens. Every light in south London is going to be flashing here soon. There'll be tape and high vis jackets. News crews. There's my doorbell. Maybe it's Marcella, with her tail between her legs. Metaphorically. She doesn't have a tail. Better go down and see.

I open the door. In the background are police cars and ambulances. In the foreground, on my doorstep, is a tall man in a black hoody that hides his face, like a monk's cowl. A plastic satchel dangles from his shoulder. It's a food delivery! *For fuck's sake. Not now.*

I didn't order a pizza. But, actually, I am hungry. Perhaps I should take what's on offer? *Why not?*

I don't' want to be seen. I invite the man into the hallway. He pulls back his hood. *What on earth?* I see a perversion of a human face. Its weird amber eyes have rectangular pupils, like a goat's. They are set too far apart. The head has a pronounced brow ridge. The nose is elongated, the nostrils flared.

The creature brings something from behind its back. It pushes me. I fall back backwards. It stands over me and pins my body with its foot. Its breathing is laboured. The smell of its body is sweet and sharp.

I feel something hard and sharp push against my larynx.

Tuesday 11th April, 11.05pm
Abaddon, The Destroyer, Angel of the Abyss

How easily they perished – the pipsqueaks! How plaintively they pleaded for their pitiful lives. They had festered in their own squalor for more than a century! It was amusing to hear them beg.

The woman offered her disgusting body to me. As if.

The human imagination has been skilled at devising methods of torture. The Inquisition were masters. They used the rack, the thumbscrew, pliers to extract fingernails and teeth, molten lead poured onto skin. A Demon can create such terrors merely through suggestion.

Both of them, screaming in agony, were soon begging for their lives to be ended. I restored their life signs and renewed the torture. The beauty of this torture was that it had no purpose. I knew all of their sins and volitions. They had nothing to confess!

Eventually, I tired of my sport. I explained to them that there would be no death. The pain of being flayed, stretched and burned would last for eternity – the eternity that they had sought. How ironic.

I cast them into the bottomless pit – *nullam requiem malis.*

•••

This house will suit me well. It is a directly linked to the nether world. It will be good to have a base in London from which I can walk amongst humankind, undetected.

15

The Tribulation

Wednesday 13th April
Locusts brings God's wrath to Lewisham
by Sandy Blythe
News Shopper

What the hell is happening at Mundania Close? First, a number of residents at the sought-after address die in suspicious circumstances, in the space of a few days. Then travellers and Hells Angels move in.

Now this. A plague of winged insects makes a Biblical visitation to the disaster-prone address, causing a helicopter to crash, with the loss of three lives. Some people are saying it means that Judgement Day is nigh.

Before the helicopter came, it was reported that the sky turned black. What looked like smoke began to rise from the mound at the centre of the close. But it wasn't smoke.

We have all seen terrible images of stinging insects entering the helicopter's cockpit, the pilot and co-pilot desperately trying to claw them from their faces, as the helicopter span out of control. Images that we will never forget.

On social media the event is being widely interpreted as a fulfilment of the 'great tribulation', described in chapter nine of the Book of Revelation.

A few residents of Mundania Close cling on. Aggressive locusts are the last things they wanted. Is God punishing the world for its sins? Why has Lewisham been chosen? Those are the questions they must be asking? What could possibly happen next?

Wednesday 13th April
End of Times blog. Grayson Tyler.

About me. Son of a preacher man. Trying to save the world from its madness with sweet reason.

Guys, you'll never believe this. More red meat for the nut jobs who see signs of divine intervention in disaster. You've seen the images of the alleged locusts and the crashing helicopter in London – they're everywhere. You've heard and read the endless speculation. A discourse of doom based on the 'fifth trumpet' theory, is spreading around the world like jimson weed.

Many are keen to identify, in these troubled times, signs of the 'end days' that they study endlessly in their Bibles. Like I've said before growing up in North Carolina, in a family of Baptists, this stuff is meat and drink to me and to my blog and you folks seem to like it – the Wrath, the Antichrist, the Mark of the Beast, yada, yada. I grew up with it more directly than most, but it's all around us. Its imagery is infused through our culture. Remember MTV?

This crazy talk is an unedifying spectacle – a bunch of people scrambling to save their asses, while they denounce other churches and sects. They find their 'end days' raw material in some well-thumbed chapters and verses of the Bible – particularly, the so-called Olivet Discourse of Matthew 24-25, Revelation 4-22, Thessalonians 4 (for the 'rapture') and parts of Jeremiah, Ezekiel and Daniel.

Christianity, Judaism and Islam all have versions of the end and the beginning of the world. It's what folks seem to care about most. Their intra-religious bickering has led to mayhem and death for centuries, not least in the Bible Lands. Can't Jews and Christians follow 13:11 and learn the lesson of Lot, who is chastised for selfishly grabbing the fertile land of the Jordan Valley under Abraham's nose. Why not share out the good places? Be nice guys. It's not gonna happen while the cranks with their holy books keep jabbing their fingers.

Banquet of destruction

It's the Book of Revelation that ends the New Testament in a blood curdling finale. This is the part of the Bible that gets the Armageddon obsessives most worked up. We all know the catch-phrases – Fiery Lake, Lamb of God, the Final Judgement etc – the chronology goes as follows. It kicks off in chapter four, with opening of the seven seals (a seal is a scroll). This is the beginning of what religious folks call the Tribulation.

Could be the name of a band! It is the name of a band – they're just called Tribulation. They're from Sweden. Of course. This Hell-inspired musical genre, which sounds, to my ears, like heavy stone crushing machinery, is very northern hemisphere.

The opening of the first 1 (6:1) give us the four horsemen of the apocalypse (white, red, black and pale). The white one is sometimes viewed as the mount of the Antichrist). The sun turns black, the moon turns red, stars fall to earth (6:12). Oh Lord. We already have a bitching CD cover. But this is just an hors d'oeuvre for the banquet of destruction that is about to begin.

When the seventh 1 is opened, seven angels appear, and they blow on seven trumpets. Seeing a pattern here? Seven is God's favourite number. The first blast causes a hail made of fire and blood to burn up a third of the trees on the planet (8:17), the second turns a third of the into blood, killing everything that lives there. Well, it would.

When the fifth trumpet blows (9:1) Satan is given the key to the bottomless pit – an Airbnb for the bad guys. The sky turns black and smoke and locusts issue forth. They are not ordinary locusts. Oh no. With hideous scorpion stings, they torture the unrighteous for five months. Does God, perhaps, have anger issues? Perhaps he is angry with himself?

Wrathful angels

With the sixth trumpet (9:13), God unleashes four very pissed off angels who slaughter a third of the human race – men, women and children. Just like that. Can you believe he's not finished yet? As a final gesture, he tips out seven, yes seven, bowls of wrath, which bring about seven plagues – festering sores, rivers and s turned to blood, a blazing sun that shrivels flesh, and so forth. God blends his favourite ingredients of torment like an inventive chef.

After all of this teasing comes the main event – Armageddon. It's rounded off by the biggest earthquake ever that reduces an entire city to ruins. That city could be Jerusalem, Rome, or Babylon – take your pick and your side folks. God rolls giant, boulder-like hailstones out of heaven, like cluster bombs.

But what's this. A new player appears and ends the Tribulation. Why, it's a rider on a white horse, leading the armies of heaven (19: 11-16). 'He treads the wine press of the fury of God'. Wonderful imagery. The cavalry has arrived. This dude is the King of Kings and this is the Second Coming! The tide is turning. Satan is 'bound', basically grounded, bringing about a thousand years of peace and righteousness begin (20:2). Is it actually a thousand years? Not necessarily folks. Depends on your Biblical interpretation. Righteous people who have died are now resurrected.

You know how it's never safe to relax at the end of a horror movie? You know that there's going to be a jump cut. And there is one. After the 'thousand years' are up. Satan is released from his prison (20:7) He summons a force 'as numberless as grains of sand on the shore'. Nice. There is yet another bust-up. This time. Satan is tossed back into the lake of fire. We're told that he won't be coming out (20:10). Phew! Or will he?

Next, God, sitting on his white throne, opens up the Book of Judgement on the living and the dead (20:11). A second resurrection occurs. Those in Hell are given a chance (13) this time. The Holy City, a New Jerusalem appears (21:1). Here, the righteous will dwell forever. It's the end of the end days.

Past, present and future

So, here's the thing. Have these events – the Tribulation, Armageddon, the Second Coming and the Day of Judgement happened, are happening now or will they happen? It's very important issue, to some people. Oceans of ink have been expended on this subject, wars fought and people put on the rack.

Over the centuries, proponents of different sides have developed their own shorthand. For full 'preterists', all of the events described in Revelation occurred in the past, including the Final Judgement. Far more common for Protestant churches is 'partial preterism'. This is the vanilla option.

According to this school of thought, the nasty stuff has already taken place – the mayhem of Revelation from 4 to 19 and it corresponds to the destruction of the Second Temple of Jerusalem in AD70 – thus, it was all the Jews' fault. The nice stuff – the Second Coming and the Day of Judgement – hasn't happed yet. It's just a matter of waiting. Who knows for how long.

Then we have the 'futurists'. Their creed is modern. It originated in the nineteenth century, took off like wildfire with the advent of radio preaching and came to dominate US Protestantism in the 1970s, in Baptist and Presbyterian Churches whose smart-suited Bible thumping preachers dispensed old-fashioned fire and brimstone, particularly across the Mid-West and the South. A president-friendly, middle-of-the-road version of this discourse was provided by Billy Graham. God wears a tie!

Some futurists maintain that we are still awaiting the Tribulation. Others claim that it has begun, citing the modern 'plagues' of infectious dises, wars and nuclear weapons as signs of God's wrath. This is the socially conservative religion of the Republican states. The scariest most Apocalyptic, adherents are 'dispensationalist'. They believe in the literal truth of the Bible.

They just love the idea of rapture (see Thessalonians 4) in which the resurrected and living faithful will mingle in the clouds in an 'aerial event'. Key to their 'dispensational premillennialism' is a 'pre-Tribulation rapture'. That's important to them.

It means that those who have accepted Jesus into their life – the bar of entry into their churches is very low – will avoid the plagues of boils, the scorpion stings and the angelic slaughter that the rest of us will have to endure.

Most of them believe that the Jews, traditionally hated by Christians, will get to go to heaven, after they have been softened up a bit in the Tribulation. But not Muslims – even though they recognise some of the same prophets, including Moses and Abraham. And not members of unfavoured Christian churches, including the poor old Jehovah's Witnesses, who have been banging on their own cracked drum for more than two hundred years.

The Jehovah's Witness have confidently predicted the return of Christ to earth on at least five occasions. One no show was in 1914. Some of them believe that Satan and his demons were actually cast down to earth in that year, by the big G, hence the First World War and the Spanish flu, and that he rules the current world order. Some of them hate the United Nations, thinking that it's a satanic institution

Blame the Catholics

Never accuse the Catholics of being logical, or consistent. The Church of Rome has promoted both preterist and futurist theology in its long history. It was a defense mechanism. For centuries, Protestants maintained that the Pope was the Antichrist of the Bible. The Catholics had a nifty strategy. If everything bad happened before the Catholic church developed, or is going to happen in the future, the Pope couldn't be the bad guy could he?

So, have humans witnessed the grievous effect of the blowing of the fifth trumpet in London? What do you think?!

Is any of this stuff true? Of course not. It's nonsense. Those who proclaim Armageddon, from the evidence of their interpretation of Biblical texts should show the decency, charity and compassion that is also enjoined by the milder, less hateful adherents of their religions. In my humble opinion, they should shut the fuck up and devote their energies to better things. The hatred that they are stirring up risks helping to bring their end times about – a self-fulfilling prophecy.

Meanwhile, in south-east London... More in my next blog guys. Grayson.

Wednesday 13th April, 6.02am
Daniel, The writer

So, here we go again. I've been watching TV since before dawn. Sky News has one story which it's running virtually continually. It shows one of its helicopters being attacked by killer insects and crashing into a suburban garden – 'warning, the following scenes are of a distressing nature...'

What could these vicious stingers be? An entomologist is interviewed. He talks of global warming bringing unfamiliar species to southern England. The BBC's rolling news has footage of the wreckage. It adds talking heads, saying the same kind of stuff.

The stories refer back to the events of March – the calamitous deaths in Mundania Close. Nearly all of them base their intro on same coy and corny premise. Is the appearance of a plague of locusts in south-east London a signal that the Second Coming is imminent? Blah blah blah.

On later bulletins, evangelists are introduced to the story – oddly earnest people, with staring eyes, representing churches with peculiar names. They speculate, quoting verses from the Bible, about the visitation captured on film of insects smothering a helicopter pilot's face. It makes a nice package – God's wrath or global warming. Maybe global warming *is* God's warning... investigations continue ... etcetera.

Periodically, when it's light, I check my other screen – the window. The police have cordoned off the close. It's no longer a free-for-all outside. The encampment is being removed. Police are interviewing people, taking some of them away. Tow trucks and low-loaders are removing cars and motorbikes. There is an armed response unit on site. A couple of policemen hold submachine guns.

Could the story become any more dramatic? Just after seven o'clock, it does. It's reported that the police have discovered a body of a man in number six, the house in whose garden the helicopter crashed. The details of the death are not given and the man is not named – 'more later on this breaking story later'.

My mobile jumps into life. It's Marcella. She is very upset.

'Oh Daniel, please come.'

'Of course. What's the problem?'

'It's Marcus.'

'What's happened.'

'He's dead.'

●●●

I hope that the police won't stop me going into number seven. All of the focus is on next door, in whose garden the news helicopter has crashed. I'm lucky – no-one seems to notice. Marcella lets me in.

'Fuck.'

At first, I think that the hallway has been redecorated in this son's must have colour – crimson. Blood covers the floor and runs up the walls on both sides. Marcus is lying on his back The leather soles of his brogues point upwards. A metal rod sticks up from his neck. The rod has been pushed into the floor.

There is a blood-covered pizza box next to his body.

'I see you ordered a takeaway.'

'Oh, Daniel. It's horrible.'

'Did you kill him?'

'Of course not!'

'But you didn't call the police.'

'I panicked. I didn't know what to do.'

She begins to cry

'Oh, Daniel.'

I step forwards, failing to find a clear patch of carpet. *Fuck. I'll be leaving crimson footsteps.* Marcus' eyes have rolled back into their sockets – they are blank, opaque. Blood has seeped from the sides of his mouth.

I hold Marcella in my arms and say soothing words. The doorbell rings. It's pushed again after a few seconds. And again. The police.

Wednesday 20th April, 7.35pm
Daniel, The Writer

Mundania Close has changed a lot in the last seven days. The abandoned cars and motorbikes, the scaffolding pole stage and the rubbish caused by the nomadic invasion have been removed. Since no-one is mowing them, grassy areas that have not been flatted have gone wild, lit by the fuse of spring. Sycamore and ash seedlings are popping up everywhere, wildflowers, particularly borage and forget-me-nots, are multiplying.

The close is looking beautiful. It's nice to share it again with jays, lesser spotted woodpeckers and London's noisy invaders, ring necked parakeets – bright green tree strippers that move around in noisy, quarrelsome flocks. There have always been foxes here. They have dens in the mound. People like Egg viewed them as pests and wanted them to be exterminated. Now, they roam around the close unperturbed.

After days of intense, repetitive TV and radio coverage and cut-and-paste stories, the froth of media attention has calmed down. The locusts have not re-appeared, despite intense speculation about a new species of killer bugs that had been brought to London by a warming climate. For a day, a pest control team wearing protective clothing probed and burrowed on the mound. They tried to smoke the locusts out. None were found. There is speculation that they have resettled in the fields of Kent or Sussex, and that the summer will bring killer swarms to the city. The papers love that kind of thing.

As far as I am aware, the police have recovered no bodies from the mound, or from number six. That's odd. I know that at least 14 bikers perished as a result of their ill-fated invasion. I counted them into the tunnel and none came back. Perhaps a conspiracy of silence led to a secret operation with body bags?

The police have conducted a rch of number six. There is a metal door on the property. Kaz and her baby and kids, Carlene, Tyrone and Marlon have left the close. So has James – permanently. His name was made public on Monday. News stories said that he was found hanging in his wardrobe. The death was not being treated as

143

suspicious – code for suicide. A post-mortem examination and an inquest have yet to be carried out.

•••

Most days, at least one film crew shows up. They get shots of boarded up doors and weeds, the half-exposed walls of the chapel. I see people in smart jackets delivering pieces to camera – same words, different languages.

My doorbell is frequently rung by reporters. So is Marcella's. We are the only people left. By mutual agreement, she gives the quotes and interviews, not me. After all, I am writing a history of Mundania Close. I want to keep the best bits for myself.

Estate agent have been sniffing around, showing interest.

Marcella is a widow. She isn't a grief-stricken one, despite having seen Marcus skewered to the floor. I don't think that she loved him. From the coming and goings of expensive cars outside her house, I can see that she already has some new people in her life.

•••

Talking of Marcella, I was surprised, this morning, when she invited me to a dinner party. It's at her house on Friday night.

Friday 15th April, 11pm
Daniel, The Writer

'Daniel. I'd like you to meet my friend, Samuel, Samuel Winter.'

I'm standing in Marcella's hallway. I'm dressed for a relatively informal evening. This guy is togged up for a business meeting.

Marcella is full-on sexy. She's wearing a short little black dress, dramatic eye make-up, lots of perfume.

He's the kind of person that I tend to react negatively to – well-groomed in a dark tailored suit, black shirt, black tie, gold cufflinks, expensive watch, like a successful footballer.

'He's an estate agent,' Marcella says.

Of course he is.

'He works for Croxtons. They are the biggest agents in London.'

144

I know that. Their trick is to make their sales offices look like something from Blade Runner.

'The UK, Marcy,' corrects the man.

His light brown hair has been artfully trimmed with an electric shaver, as if it has been crafted with faint scarifications, in an initiation ritual. His aftershave, or his cologne, treads a balance between his soft feminine side and his desire for rutting. The voice is well-modulated, neither common nor posh, eager to please.

'I've heard so much about you Daniel,' he says, offering his hand and a well-ironed cuff.

'Oh.'

Marcella hovers next to us.

'So, Daniel, before we have dinner, Sam would like to take you downstairs, to show you our plans for the close. I'll wait up here.'

Our plans. What plans?

'Don't worry. Sam's not going to hurt you, are you Sam?'

'I'll try not to.'

It's the first time that I've ventured into the lower parts of this house. They are accessed from the end of the hallway. Soon, I'm in a corridor lined with roughened grey tiles, designed to look like stone. It leads to a further entrance. Sam is carrying a set of keys. He turns back to smile as he opens the door.

He turns the light on. In front of me is a space the size of car showroom. Walls, ceiling and floor are predominantly white with bubble gum colours, assaulting the eyes. It looks like the set of Saturday morning show for sugared up kids. Kids who are into demonology. The floor is dominated by a large painted circle and a lesser-sized triangle. Sections are picked out in vermillion, green and . A yellow snake forms the circle's perimeter. On the wall, a six-pointed star is painted within another circle. Around it are Hebrew characters and astrological symbols.

The room is eye-startlingly bright. The lighting is artfully contrived so that the centre of the room is brightest. The four sides are in shadow.

'This will be the centrepiece of the development,' says Sam proudly. 'It was created for ceremonial magic when the house was built, in 1904. The space is rather bare at the moment. There will be soft furnishings in here, mood lighting – of course.'

'What development?' I ask.

'Didn't Marcella explain? We're calling it Coriander Close. It's going to be a meditation and healing community. We already have a venture capital partner. There'll be facilities for a range of complementary therapies, spaces for ritual and meditation. We're offering a whole new age, mind and body lifestyle package.'

He senses my scepticism.

'You would come here, wouldn't you?'

'Maybe.'

Beer and a game of pool are more my thing.

'What happened to the old couple who lived here?'

'Oh, they've gone. On a world cruise, I think. They were happy to sell up.'

'I see.'

'I know that Marcella wants you to advise us on the re-brand. You're the history man, aren't you? Aren't you writing a book on Mundania Close?'

Am I?

I try to look non-committal.

'That's what Marcella told me. Would you like one of my cards?'

The embossed card tells me that he is Samael Winter 'senior accounts executive'. It comes with a flash of gold watch. The card says Samael, not Samuel. I wonder if it's a typo. Why would such an expensive card have such a basic mistake?

'We'd love you to stay and be part of the journey. Of course, it's totally up to you. You can even get first dibs as an early investor. Marcella thought the idea might appeal to you, Dan. Why don't you discuss it with her?'

There is an implied wink, in his salesman's eye.

I place the card in my wallet.

'Shall we go upstairs?'

'Let's.'

•••

In the kitchen, two women I have never met are seated at the table. Marcella introduces them as Krystelle and Jacinta.

'The same names as your cats.'

'These two came first, Daniel.'

146

It looks as if Marcella has been split into three. They both have dark brown hair, Middle Eastern complexions, red lips, perfect teeth.

She sits me between. Sam is at the end of the table.

Jacinta is the first to speak.

'So, Daniel, I've heard a lot about you.'

'Have you?'

'Marcella tells me that you're an author.'

Christ, not again.

'I wrote a book a long time ago.'

'Darling, you're far too modest,' says Marcella. She positions a serving dish on the table. I can see from her proximity to Sam and the way he is looking at her that they are more than business partners.

'Why are English people so self-deprecating,' Marcella says.

'It's because we're taught not to draw attention to ourselves.'

'Well, that's silly. I've made a chickpea and aubergine casserole. I hope you like it. Daniel, did Sam tell you about our plan, for Coriander Close?'

'He did'

'And?'

Her eyes are fixed on mine.

'I think it's a great idea.'

'That's fantastic. Sam must have done a good job. Did he tell you about the Beltane party? It's going to be next Saturday. It will be the official launch of Coriander Close. Isn't that exciting!'

'My boss is coming, the CEO of Carpe Noctem, the investors,' says Sam.

'I thought you work for Croxton's?'

'I did but he has offered me a job as his sales director. I start on Monday.

There's loyalty.

'It's a wonderful opportunity for Sam,' says Marcella.

'Yeh, we're into lots of projects, all over the world, mainly in the leisure and entertainment space, that's why the company is called Carpe Noctem. It means "seize the night".'

He looks proud and pleased.

'Well, that's worth a toast,' says Marcella, 'Sam, sweetie, get some Champagne would you.'

A thigh touches my leg under the table. I look down and see bare, toned golden flesh. It belongs to Krystelle. Her smile is like Marcella's. Her energy transfers into my body like a line of coke.

16

Adam's first Wife

Sunday 24th April
WORLD EXCLUSIVE
Marcella's moment. Britain's most notorious widow is fighting back
by Lottie Baxter
Mail on Sunday

Marcella Gardner refuses to wear black. 'it's so depressing, so negative,' she tells me, as we drink lapsang souchong tea in her luxurious house, in soon to be re-christened Mundania Close.

Instead, she's chosen a white silk kurta today, gorgeously embroidered with pink, green and patterns. She's sporting her signature bright red lipstick and fingernails. It's not quite the image of the grieving widow, or of a notorious sorceress.

She came into the public eye a month ago, following the tragic deaths of several of her neighbours in what was dubbed 'Calamity Close'. Now three more deaths from the 12-house community have brought further unwelcome attention to what has become a blighted address.

One of those deaths was that of her author husband, Marcus. He was brutally slain in the hallway of their two-million-pound house and left to bleed to death. The police are investigating, but no-one has been arrested for the crime.

She refreshes the tea in my bone china cup. We're sitting in the kitchen in which I interviewed her after just after Mundania Close leapt into the news. It's bright and filled with plants.

Marcella's is an accomplished artist. Her paintings enliven the white walls. Her two sleek Persian cats are never far away.

Peace and quiet

One would not blame Marcella for feeling bitter. After all, many people have said vile things about her on Twitter, in a sustained campaign of hatred, using hashtags like witch, sorceress, hag and far worse.

How does she respond to this relentless vilification? She says: 'It's convenient, isn't it, to blame women when things go wrong. It's part of the patriarchy to associate women with misfortunes, to accuse them of tempting men, with their sexuality and to call them witches. It goes back to the Garden of Eden.'

Her eyes start to mist up. I ask her if it's OK to continue. She takes a breath and offers me a homemade cupcake – the perfect hostess.

Marcus, a respected authority on magic and folklore, was the love of her life. They met when Syrian-born Marcella was studying at Berkeley University, in California. She says: 'He was this dashing English professor, specialising in ceremonial rituals. He was a brilliant lecturer.'

Their relationship and the twenty-year age gap caused controversy within the stuffy academic community. They returned to England to marry, in a country church in Sussex, the county where Marcus' family had lived for centuries.

She says: 'I'm a tremendous Anglophile. When we moved to London, we lived at first in Putney, but we wanted somewhere quieter and with more space so that Marcus could write and I could paint. Honor Oak was perfect for that.'

Vicious campaign

But things started to go wrong soon after they had moved in. The first person to die was Ron Saxby, who lived two doors down. The successful owner of a building firm was run over by his own truck in a tragic accident witnessed by his 13-year-old son.

She says: 'Ron was a sweetie – a Cockney salt of the earth type. He had made Marcus and I extremely welcome. We were devastated when that happened.'

More deaths followed, in quick succession. Victims included a well-known clarinettist, a social media influencer and the much-loved 1970s Jamaican popstar, JJ, who had lived anonymously in the close for decades.

The world's media flocked to Mundania Close. They dubbed it 'cursed'. Following the latest tragedies, the downing of a news helicopter and the apparent suicide of Marcella's neighbour James Barclay, the highly-respected theatre designer, some people are saying that these events fulfil a Biblical prophecy – the end of the world and the Day of Judgement.

Marcella says: 'It's all nonsense. People have taken some unrelated and accidental events and created a pattern that's just not there. As for the religious prophecy thing. I respect those people who are religious, obviously, but this fire and brimstone stuff is a total fantasy.'

Bold new venture

Marcella says that she has news for the haters – she isn't going to be an apologetic grieving widow. What do you do with a road that has been blighted by tragedy that no-one wants to live in? She is helping to launch a bold plan – a multi-million-pound re-development, designed to give the place where she lives a fresh image.

She explains: 'It will be a gated meditation and healing community. I am super excited, not least because I know that this is what Marcus would have wanted. He would have loved the idea of something good coming from the awful things that have happened here.'

The re-born community, Coriander Close, she says, will be devoted to spiritual and physical healing, offering spa facilities and a range of complementary treatments, from reiki to crystals. There will be spaces for meditation and mindfulness, for example yoga and Tai Chi. The development will include short-term accommodation options and houses for sale.

White witch

Marcella says: 'Most of our marketing is aimed at women. We want to release female energy, to "heal" the close. We know that's what is needed. But we are not anti-man. We know that a lot of men will be interested in this, just as much as the ladies, and they are very welcome.'

The first properties, she says, are already on the market. An event to launch the development is coming soon – an open weekend and a party. The date has been carefully chosen – the first of May, known, in the wiccan and Celtic traditions, as Beltane.

Marcella says: 'it's an amazing time, when spring is bursting through. Humans have been celebrating it with fires and other ceremonies for thousands of years. We think that Beltane will be prefect for christening Coriander Close.'

She invites me outside. Her back door leads to an eighty-foot garden, backing onto ancient woodland. Marcella explains that her cultivation of medicinal herbs is based on the astroherbalism. She only plants seeds at the full moon.

She crouches over her beloved plants – every inch the cottage gardener. She turns back and says: 'It was lovely to see you. I do hope that you can come to our party, Lottie. The moon will be waxing. We might do some magic.' She smiles. Perhaps, after all, she is a bit of a witch – a white one, of course.

Sunday 24th April, 11.10pm
Daniel, The Writer

Lottie Baxter has two modes for her newspaper columns – molasses and acid. This one is molasses. It's the kind of gushing prose that the Mail on Sunday pays her handsomely to write. The woman is a mercenary. Her words are available to the highest bidder.

I wonder if Lottie will come to the Beltane party, to dispense her insincere charm. I hope she does. It will be interesting to see her in action.

My eyes linger over photos that accompany the story. The Mail has taken a new set. The main image shows Marcella, looking sad, eyes to camera, holding a framed black and white photo of Marcus. Her filmy dress, opened three buttons, draws one's eyes ineluctably to her breasts, with a silver ankh nestling between them.

From her eyes one divines that she is not just sad. Her expression is more nuanced. It suggests, subtly, that she is coquettish – ready for a bit of fun. *Or is it just me?*

My phone screen lights up with a chirrup. It's Dom.

'Hi.'

'Hi. Are you reading the Mail?'

'I am. I knew they were publishing the story. Marcella told me yesterday.'

'Have you ever read such total crap?'

'It's the Mail on Sunday, Dom. What do you expect?'

'For fuck's sake. You know as well as I do that Marcella is a bitch from hell. She's not Mother fucking Teresa.'

I don't answer.

'Don't you?'

'I don't think she's done anything wrong.'

'She hasn't done anything wrong? Are you serious? Haven't you noticed something? The deaths have stopped, with James. There's no-one left now.'

'I think that T.W. Williams at number six was responsible.'

'But he never left his house.'

'I've been thinking about that. I think that there are a bunch of secret tunnels under the close. We saw one or them.'

'Are you insane? I'm telling you. It's Marcella. It's only because you are shagging her that you can't see it. She's a succubus.'

'A what?'

'A succubus.'

'What the fuck is that?'

He sighs.

'Listen.'

Dom is googling. He reads from his screen: '"a succubus needs semen to survive; repeated sexual activity with a succubus will result in a bond being formed between the succubus and the man. In modern representations, a succubus is often depicted as a beautiful seductress or enchantress, rather than as demonic or frightening." Does that sound familiar?'

'That's disgusting.'

Dom must have spent hours on Wikipedia.

'Listen,' he says, 'you know the love chapel? Well, I took lots of pictures in there, on my phone and I've been studying them. I know what the statues mean. One is Inanna, also known as Ishtar and Venus, the goddess of love. The other is Lilith, Adam's fist wife. She is a demon.'

'Adam's fist wife? He didn't have a first wife.'

'Yes he did. It's in the Book of Genesis, if you read it carefully. Basically, there are two females in Genesis, chapter one, verse 27 and chapter two, verse 21. Adam's first wife was made from clay, like he was, not from one of his ribs. Well, this first lady wanted to be on top of him, not under him, when they had sex. She argued that they were both made from clay, or dust, or whatever, so they were equal. It was demeaning to be underneath. Adam didn't like that. They had a row and she fled from the Garden of Eden. She became a winged demon. She had sex with lots of male demons. God sent three angels after her. They said that God would kill a hundred of her children every day, as a punishment. So, she took her revenge.'

'What are you talking about? That's not in the Bible.'

'More explicitly. it's in a medieval Hebrew text called the Alphabet of Ben Sira. It's also in the Talmud.'

'So, suddenly you're an expert on theology.'

'Of course not. I've just been reading up on this stuff.'

'Well I'd love to spend the whole morning talking to you about the Biblical creation myth.'

'There's more about Lilith in The Epic of Gilgamesh.'

'The what?'

'It's a text from ancient Mesopotamia, from 2,000 BC, a lot older than the Bible. Lilith causes the deaths of babies. She causes wet dreams and she visits men at night to have sex with them. With their seed, she begets more demons.'

'For fuck's sake, Dom, can you hear yourself?'

'I've been studying the photos I took. I can send them to you. The tree we saw in the chapel was not the Tree of Knowledge from the Bible. It was the Huluppu Tree, from Gilgamesh. Lilith is the statue with wings. She lives in the tree. She has bird's feet. The bird in the chapel is Anzu, half eagle and half lion. I've worked it all out, from the photos on my phone.'

'That's mad.'

'You saw the way that Kaz reacted that morning, when Marcella came to have breakfast with us. She couldn't be in the same room. She was freaked out. That's because she sensed, unconsciously, that Marcella is Lilith. She wanted to grab her baby.'

'This is crazy talk.'

'Marcella is evil. You just can't see it.'

'Look, so what if the chapel isn't the Garden of Eden. It just means that T.W. Williams knew about the same books that you've just found out about. I'm not surprised. He was a Middle Eastern scholar. They are just statues.'

'We saw thirteen Hell's Angels disappear into the ground and not come out. That was real. We saw locusts flying out of the chapel roof.'

'Marcella had nothing to do with that.'

He sighs.

'I want you to look at the photos and I want you to read something.

154

'What?'

'The creation story from Gilgamesh.'

'Oh great.'

I say that I will. He WhatsApps me pictures from the chapel and sends me a link. The link directs me to a text called Inanna and the Huluppu Tree. Do I read it? Yes, because it's Sunday and I'm not doing anything else. Sending religious texts is a habit of crazy people – the kind who leave hand-written messages with Biblical citations on bits of cardboard, at bus stops. I hope that Dom doesn't make a habit of it.

In the first days, in the very first days, In the first nights, in the very first nights, In the first years, in the very first years.

In the first days when everything needed was brought into being, in the first days when everything needed was properly nourished, when bread was baked in the shrines of the land, and bread was tasted in the homes of the land, when heaven had moved away from earth, and earth had separated from heaven, and the name of man was fixed; when the Sky God, An, had carried off the heavens, and the Air God, Enlil, had carried off the earth, when the Queen of the Great Below, Ereshkigal, was given the underworld for her domain.

At that time, was planted, a tree, a single tree. By the banks of the Great River, Enki, the Father, the God of Wisdom, did plant the Huluppu-tree. He planted it by the banks of the Euphrates, before he set sail, before the Father departed for the underworld.

The whirling South Wind arose and blew upon the tree, pulling at its roots and ripping at its branches, until the waters of the Euphrates carried it away. A young woman who walked in fear of no man, and would not be owned, Plucked the tree from the river and spoke: 'I shall bring this tree to Uruk. I shall plant this tree in my holy garden.'

Inanna cared for the tree with her hand. She settled the earth around the tree with her foot. She wondered: 'How long will it be until I have a shining throne to sit upon? How long will it be until I have a luscious bed to lie upon?'

The years passed; five years, then ten years. The tree grew thick, but its bark did not split.

Then a serpent who could not be charmed made its nest in the roots of the Huluppu tree. The Anzu-bird set his young in the branches of the tree. And the dark maid Lilith built her home in the trunk.

Monday 25th April, 12.14pm
Daniel, The Writer

It feels really strange to be leaving my house to go to work on a Monday morning. It's the first time I have done so for years. Even more oddly, my new office, at 11 Mundania Close, is only a hundred yards from my front door.

It happened because of a call from Marcella, late on Sunday night. She said that Coriander Close urgently needed a comms adviser, that Sam had been very impressed with me and that he would like me 'on board'. I could work, she said, as a freelance.

When she told me the fee, I almost fell off my chair – a thousand pounds a day.

'A thousand pounds a day?' I responded.

'Daniel,' she spoke sternly. Don't under-sell yourself. Don't ever do that. You are a gifted journalist and author.'

'Am I?'

'Yes, my love.'

'But this is more like being a press officer. I've never done that.'

'Does anyone else know more about this road and its history than you do?'

'No.'

'Well then.'

'Do you have a suit?'

'I have, but I haven't worn it for a long time. The moths have probably been at it.'

'Well, you'll need it for your job. We want you to start next week.'

I tried the suit on. The trousers were tight around the waist and there were some weird stains on the jacket – the result of getting stupidly drunk at a wedding. Can I still wear it?

●●●

So here I am. The centre of operations for today's marketing and sales meeting is Otto's old house. It was chosen because there was virtually nothing in it when he went back to Germany – Otto was a strict minimalist – and because it's located not far from the entrance to the close. It's going to be made into a show home, buffed up, with stylish furniture and a high-spec kitchen.

That's going to mean chaos for the next few days – a constant stream of deliveries.

We're in the front room, sitting on new furniture that's still partially wrapped. Sam leads the proceedings. The other two people are a young woman and a young man – newly recruited Carpe Noctem staff.

Sam is dressed in his expensive suit and black shirt and tie. He is leading the proceedings. He is standing next to a flipchart, equipped with coloured pens.

Parked at the curb outside, is his company car. It's a head turning red Tesla Roadster, with personalised number plates, SAM 616. What does number mean? I wonder how old he is – late twenties? How on earth has he piled up so much wealth?

Sam glances as his over-sized F1 driver's watch. He brings his little team to attention.

'Right guys. First, we have five days to bring this off. That's right. There are five days until the open weekend. It kicks off on Saturday morning and it will conclude with the Beltane party on Sunday night. But our deadline is actually tighter than that, it's 10.45 on Friday. Why? Because that's when the boss arrives.'

There's a gleam in his pale eyes. He is on top of this. 'The boss is Archer Bardon, CEO of Carpe Noctem. He's one of the richest men in Britain. But you've never heard of him. He lives in Bermuda most of the time. He's very off the radar. Who wouldn't be, right?'

I am using paper to make notes, not my phone, and a biro. Sam will have an exquisite fountain pen, designed for high-value contracts, nestling in his suit.

He makes a list on the flipchart – brand values, print, AV, display boards, scripts, guest list, media list, socials…

It's going to be a long day.

Cardboard boxes are stacked along one wall. Some have been opened. They contain polo shirts, fleeces, puffer jackets, baseball caps, tracksuits. They are black and feature the Carpe Noctem logo in gold Gothic script.

Sam is speaking.

'The brand is Carpe Noctem, Coriander Close is the name of the development. I can't stress how important that is. Remember, we're selling the CN brand in everything we do… every phone call, every conversation, got it? And in our clothing.'

He catches that my attention is wandering.

'Daniel, that doesn't' apply to you. You're not on the payroll. You're freelance. You can wear your normal clothes. Nicely turned out, by the way. Like the tie.'

Is he being ironic. It's hideous.

•••

It's eleven o'clock and we're still on brand values. Scribbled white sheets are Blu-Tacked to the wall.

Sam and I are addressing what Coriander Close will be all about. He's holding his hyperactive red marker, which, for the moment, is still. He hasn't loosened his fat black tie one millimeter. Too much strong, acrid coffee is playing havoc with my stomach. But, to my surprise, I am quite enjoying this. He is listening to me.

'So who built the close?'

'His name was Theophilus William Williams. It was in 1904. He was a successful local businessman and the mayor of Lewisham. The close was his concept – the ankh layout, the Arts and Crafts architecture, the quality of materials.'

Sam writes a word – Heritage.

'Great.'

'Number six was his house. It was the centrepiece of the development. We know that he was a Freemason. He probably used the house as a Lodge.'

'What did he get up to there? Do we know?"

'It was a probably pretty standard Freemasons' stuff.'

'What if people say it's Devil worship, Black Magic?'

I know what he wants to hear.

'Freemasonry is incredibly boring. It's greengrocers and bank managers, with their trousers rolled up.'

'Not all boring surely?'

'Well, Williams certainly had an eye for the ladies. And, yes, he built a Chapel of Love in the centre of the close. It's essentially a folly. It's a smaller version of the Watts Chapel, in Surrey.'

'So, he held orgies, right?'

'I would imagine that what went on was a lot more decorous than that. The chapel is devoted to the goddess Venus, also known as Ishtar, with a suitably curvaceous carving. It's pretty standard Victorian stuff, like formal, classical painting – erotic by implication, no more.'

Sam writes 'nice but naughty'.

This proves to be the Eureka moment. The meeting has served its purpose and defined the sub-brand of Coriander Close. It will provide a new age take on health and healing, with a touch of wicca. We'll offer pagan weddings in the chapel. It will be an exclusive environment – target audience, affluent people from their mid-thirties, especially couples It will target a luxurious, high-end market.

Sam attaches loops and arrows to the words he has written down. He asks me to present the results of our brainstorm to the team. I'm happy to do so. It's just before lunch.

I like this. I can do PR. *Who knew?* Even in my below par suit, with its stubborn grease mark, I feel like a thousand pound a day guy!

17

The White Widow

Wednesday 27th April, 5.16pm
Daniel, The Writer

It looks like the weather will be good for the open weekend. With a few blips, preparation for the event has gone fairly smoothly, considering its ridiculously compressed timeline. It was clear, from Monday, that this would be a massive logistical operation, dependent upon a series of events occurring on schedule and in the right order.

Sam is the general of the campaign. He's hands-on, not exactly getting down and dirty in the trenches but geeing on his troops to embrace the barely possible, a calm figure, smiling and well turned out but showing more than a hint of steel. Marcella is the colonel – the senior officer in the field. She's on the phone in her office, Marcus' re-purposed study, from early morning until late at night, wheedling, pleading and threatening by turn, to ensure that the right vans, and people, arrive when they should.

She issues instructions to her front-liners, kitted out in black and gold Carpe Noctem tops and baseball caps and carrying walkie-talkies. A control point with a barrier has been set up at the entrance to the close to allow the check-in of deliveries. Sam's red Tesla has taken up a more or less permanent position in front of number six. He rarely leaves. He's a live-in general, one would guess, and, as evidenced by their body language, sharing Marcella's bed. I try not to think about this.

Because the show house, number eleven, needs a lot of work, we have moved our command and control centre to the first floor of number six. Three other houses, two, three, four and five, have been emptied so that they can be sold. The process was completed by eleven o'clock last night. It involved lorries, so a lot of the grass in front of the houses has been churned up and trampled on.

From early this morning, landscaping began. This is not the amateurish, medieval effort that I was engaged in with Hamish, skanky Dave, Rob and Dom. It involves serious equipment – tabards, plastic helmets, more walkie talkies. Four substantial trees have been cut down and shredded through a chipper. A hydraulic digger is flattening, from what I can see, at least a third of the mound, to turn it into a car park. The front of number eleven has been gravelled, ready for vehicles. Carpe Noctem, for all of its new age credentials, is not very nature friendly.

I realised, yesterday, the importance of the brand. Like a mark made with red hot metal, it's a sign of fealty, not just to an organisation but to a lifestyle – in this case, 'seize the night'. With smiling faces, we are using daylight to build a palace of earthly pleasure to enrich Archer Bardon. Sam has told me that, as well as property in the Bahamas, he owns a casino and leisure complex in the British Virgin Islands. He has a private jet and his own airport.

I also decided yesterday that I want no part of this. It's not just because a great spotted woodpecker that I love has lost its home in a tree that has been cut down. It's because Coriander Close is set to be populated by young professionals who spend a lot of their times in gyms. They are guided by sat-navs, seeking verification and gratification from their phones, pretty much blind to the physical world, including other people and nature. Their new age comes with Astroturf.

The command and control centre is equipped with CCTV screens and squishy settees – ideal for the Carpe Noctem crew to lounge in when they are not rushing around like arsed flies. Marcella has recruited lots of them, some from agencies. Some will staff the gym, spa and leisure facilities, when Coriander Close is up and running. I'm involved in an induction session for new staff tomorrow afternoon. I'll be a veteran by then, four days into the job.

•••

Tomorrow, I'll also supervise the installation of display boards for the show home. I have already proof-read them. They give a potted, censored history of the close – explaining the arts and crafts design and the links to Freemasonry – editing out local businessman T.W. Williams' associations with embezzlement, murder and sexual exploitation, and giving a 'nice but naughty' spin to a beautifully restored Chapel of Love, with its historic statues and friezes and William Morris and Co. stained glass.

I know how these things work from creative projects that I have previously been involved with. Tomorrow, Thursday will be the 'trainwreck' day when delays and mis-timings cause catastrophic collisions. The car parking won't be finished but furnishings for number eleven will still be coming in, plus gym equipment and stock for the bar for number seven. It will be called the Huluppu Bar by the way – my idea. Stressed Carpe Noctem recruits will buzz around in their fly-like black and gold livery.

Tempers will be frayed. Marcella will need to resort to an assertive rather than coercive manner on the phone. I know that's she capable of this – even of being acerbic.

On Friday morning, with any luck, everything will start to come together – damaged verges will be repaired, cushions tittivated, pot plants installed, appliances polished and smiles practiced. There is to be a press conference. I have compiled a contacts list, in double quick time, of print and broadcast media contacts. I have also put together a press pack, including a Q and A. With luck, the press pack will have been signed off, no doubt with annoying amendments made by the snooty West End company that deals with Carpe Noctem's PR.

•••

One flipchart sheet that has not been crossed out dominates the control room. It says Friday 10.45! double underlined. That is when the money man, Archer Bardon, is scheduled to arrive.

As far as anyone can tell, I have become a Carpe Noctem worker through and through. I'm wearing the company hoody and new trainers. This has proved to be easier than making my own clothes conform to brand standards.

So, what's my plan? Quite simply, the money that I am racking up, more than a hundred quid an hour, is amazing – and the more I can earn, the better. It's my nest egg. It will be useful for when I sell up and move. What about Marcella? Yeh, I'll miss her – a lot. But if she wants to throw in her hand with Mr red Tesla and with cocaine-assisted orgies, that's just not me. My heart has been broken before. I'll only miss her for a few years. Pain will nourish my Muse. I'll be another wounded, sensitive artist living in cottage close to a deserted beach, foraging for samphire and picking up interesting pieces of driftwood to bring home. I'll make trips to London to see performances at the Barbican and the Union Chapel and have working lunches with my agent in Soho. Occasionally, I'll swing by Coriander Close to see what's happening with my financial investment. But my main income will come from my books. That's what I hope.

Friday 29th April, 10.31am
Daniel, The Writer

I'm sitting in the empty control room, with its wall of dead screens and stacked carboard boxes, a little nervously, at the invitation of Sam. He texted me earlier. He was supposed to be here at five. He's late. I wonder which buttons I would need to press to access feeds from the CCTV cameras.

'Daniel?'

I swivel my chair to see the general standing in the doorway. I've never been in his company before when he is not dressed for an important meeting. He is jacketless, his tie loosened. I can only assume that has come from number seven, next door, Marcella's place and, from the smile on his face, that they have been having a good time.

'Good time to chat?'

'Yeh, sure.'

He walks across the room and sits beside me. I detect, commingled with the sharp tang of his aftershave, the softer patchouli smell of Marcella.

'Impressive set up isn't it – the cameras,' he says, 'Marcella and Marcus installed them last year. They already had a full business plan for Coriander Close. That's why it was so easy for Carpe Noctem to pick up and run with it so quicky.'

He lifts his voice, to get my attention.

'So, Daniel, how do you think you are doing?'

It's one of those bullshit questions that lays a minefield for the unwary. How do you answer without being too self-deferential or too boastful?

I hesitate.

'Let me tell you. I think that you are doing great. So does Marcella. We've both been very impressed by your performance.

'Oh,' I say.

'I have a proposition for you.'

'Do you?'

'I want to officially make you my head of comms.'

He doesn't wait for me to respond.

163

'One of your first jobs will be to lead the press conference on Friday morning. I'll be there, but just to take the boring financial questions. Marcella will also field questions as ops director. You can do the welcomes, introduce us, then conduct the proceedings, take the lead. I can't think of anyone better, quite honestly.'

'I er…

'I'm not in a position to offer you a full-time job, without running it by my boss, Archer. But what I can do is to double your rather pitiful honorarium, with immediate effect.'

Two thousand pounds a day. Fuck!

'I don't think we would have got where we are without your skills and knowledge Daniel. We are very grateful, believe me.'

'Thank you.'

We shake hands. He's wearing a gold and black Carpet Noctem signet ring on his right hand. It's expensive, custom-made, not like the tacky, made-in-China crap in the cardboard boxes – the mugs, pens, and keyrings.

'So, we're all good, Daniel?'

'We are.'

We shake hands. His grip is bone crushing.

There's something I need to do. I need to explain to him, from practical experience, that it's possible that the press conference will be sparsely attended. We might get some trade press journos, or a under-paid hack from a local paper. The nationals won't send anyone. They never do. And we'll be lucky to get any TV coverage.

'It's OK Daniel,' he says. 'I defer to your knowledge, of course, but you might be surprised. Marcella has what one would call "kerb appeal", doesn't she. Run your media plan by Carpe Noctem's PR director and you can brief Marcella and me, tomorrow evening.'

He departs, leaving me stunned by my windfall, but struck with a sudden, agonising melancholy. I am not thinking about briefing Marcella, but about de-briefing her, something that Sam has clearly been doing.

•••

The press conference is packed. Why didn't I see this coming? The rows of plastic seats in front of me are full. There are cameras. Lots of photographers are standing around the room. Coriander Close ticks several boxes for the media – fitness, leisure, finance, property, lifestyle, health and wellness. These sectors are all covered this morning.

I researched the press list carefully. Yesterday, I gave my new assistant a list of contacts for follow-up e-mails. I phoned people in the afternoon. But that's not why most of them are here, including the press and TV cameras. They are here because Marcella is a hot ticket, at the centre of a sensational unfolding story. She's the white widow. She *is* the press conference.

It's blustery outside and the sky is grey. Carpe Noctem flags are trying to rattle free from their halyards. Landscaping has been suspended. The road has been power-sprayed to remove soil and mud. Most of the journalists here don't care about that. Few have paid any attention to the cleaned-up houses with their open doors.

We're in number eleven, Otto's old pad, the show-home. It's looking great. A wall has been removed, making space for my history panels and AV screens showing the close as it was and as it will be, in saturated colour. No-one seems to be particularly interested. Behind me are Sam, Marcella, a high-up from Croxtons, the estate agents, and the humourless women who is head of media relations at Carpe Noctem. They are seated on comfy chairs arranged against a carefully coloured and lit background, designed to look like a daytime TV set.

They are all dressed to the nines. Marcella is wearing a white dress decorated with strings of red, pink and yellow beads and cowrie shells. It is virtually transparent. Her hair is braided. She's a feast for the senses, even of the most jaded person in the room – a white tablecloth laid out on a meadow, arrayed with fresh bread, cheese, cherries, yellow butter and crisp, chilled Chardonnay.

I'm the roving MC in this gig, not competing with them in status or fashion. On the advice of Marcella, I've selected a black and gold Carpe Noctem fleece and new chinos. This emphasises that I'm one of the work team, front of house, albeit one given extra responsibility – a chief minion.

The event has been timed to the minute, up to the arrival of Archer Bardon, CEO of Carpe Noctem, at 10.45. I catch Sam's eye as he flicks back his cuff to reveal his monstrously expensive watch.

'Thanks for coming everybody.'

My three-minute intro is guided by our newly defined brand values and the sales story. This PR stuff has been surprisingly easy to get my head round, especially on my new rate, £250 an hour.

Coriander Close I explain, briefly, is geared to wellness. Its layout, architecture, natural landscaping and mature trees (the ones that have escaped the Carpe Noctem chainsaw) have time-proven properties to heal mind and body. Add to this, the modern innovations of its pool, hot tubs, complementary therapies, dance, yoga, meditation, 24-hour security and organic food deliveries. It offers a total lifestyle package, for a stressed, over-hurried world. Yada, yada…

A face I know from a blurred by-line photo, Sandy Blythe, from Lewisham's grapevine, the News Shopper, is looking at me. He's eager to ask a question. He's the smallest minnow in this media fish tank. I might as well make his day.

'Didn't the Devil used to be worshipped here?'

Good question.

'I hate to disappoint you, Sandy. Thanks for coming, by the way. I'm honoured that the News Shopper, my favourite newspaper, is covering this event. (There is a ripple of laughter.) To answer your question, maybe you know something I don't? The man who built the close was a Freemason. What he got up to was secretive and ceremonial, but, as far as I am aware, it had nothing to do with anything of that nature. I am pretty sure that it was all rather boring.'

'Isn't there a secret tunnel, connecting his house to his Chapel of Love.'

Don't push it.

'Sadly, Sandy, we haven't found one. The chapel is a historically important architectural folly, from the Edwardian period. I'm happy to say that, with the help of the experts at English Heritage, we have restored it to its full glory, including its amazing interior. We have applied for grade two listing.'

I look behind me. Sam is smiling.

Sandy is anxious to chip in again. *Ignore him. He's had his moment.*

'Yes?'

A woman in the front row is twitching for attention. Her crossed legs are encased in black tights. Her vermillion jacket is the same fierce shade as her lips. Her face is plastered with foundation.

I can see her name badge. Christ, it's Lottie from the Mail on Sunday.

'Charlotte,' I say, brightly. 'It's lovely to see you too. Can I just say, I've been really enjoying your articles.'

'Thank you, Daniel.'

She smiles insincerely.

Here we go.

'A lot of terrible things have happened here. Really terrible things. So much so that people are calling it Calamity Close. Isn't that, inevitably, going to give your development a… negative image?'

'Thanks Lottie. Great question. I actually think that Marcella is the best person to field this one.'

Cameras, pens and tape recorders are poised. I look back.

Marcella centres herself. I know what she will say. She will sigh at the memory of the tragic deaths on the close and say that it has been a terrible strain for her, being the focus of such hostility on social media. But that it is understandable. She'll say that Coriander Close is what Marcus, her former husband, 'would have wanted'.

She explains: 'Marcus was a lifelong student of magic and ritual. But he wasn't just an academic he had many interests – one of them was what he called odic energy, or astral light. He believed that in some places pathways of astral light are very strong. That makes them places of healing and understanding, entry points for new ideas. Marcus said that California, where we lived, was such a place and, remember, that was where Buddhism came to the west. Coriander Close is also one of them – in south-east London.'

She acknowledges a murmur of amusement, before continuing.

'Marcus would have loved Coriander Close. But, I must point out, this could not have happened without the involvement of Croxtons and our financial partner, Carpe Noctem, both of which, I know, share Marcus's vision. I am deeply indebted to them.'

She smiles at the high-ups behind her. There is smattering of applause.

She doesn't wait for it to stop.

'We also need you, guys, to spread the word, if we're going to make this a success. So, truly, thanks for coming.'

Short and sweet. Just right.

Marcella, with her high news value and tragic back story, will appear on TV and newspapers, repeated and responded to on Twitter and Instagram, hashtag white widow. Soon she'll be sofa surfing on morning TV, as an icon of new age feminist empowerment, the new Anita Roddick. This priceless publicity will all be free.

Samael has been applauding himself. I notice how white and perfect his teeth are. His smile could shatter a window.

Friday 29th April, 10.59am
Abaddon, The Destroyer, Angel of the Abyss

How easily people are flattered and deceived. Britain is a country of hat doffers. That's why hats were invented. All it takes is an expensive suit, the right kind of watch and a Bentley Continental GT, in heritage metallic silver. It's the vehicle for an inarticulate man who is highly skilled at kicking around an inflated pig's bladder, a patriotic industrialist whose products are made in sweatshops overseas, a gruff-voiced captain of industry who humiliates sycophants on television, as a form of entertainment. They will be surprised that the great Archer Bardon is driving his own car, not a chauffeur – the common touch. Look at these pitiful brick boxes. Humans are so meagre in their ambitions! To possess a house at all is the highest aspiration for most and to spend a lifetime paying for it. For two-thirds of the year, this dismal road will be wet, cold and miserable, like the rest of this dreary city. The white sand of a palm-fringed beach is more to my taste. Still, needs must. These brick objects of desire are as enticing to humans as expensive cars. They are inexplicably happy to sacrifice their lives for them. They bow and scrape to the rich and compliantly build their own prisons.

It's time to put on my platinum-framed sunglasses. The polarized lenses have 12 layers of proprietary coatings.

Coriander Close is clearly not finished. There are lots of unfinished details, rough edges. Shall I put on a theatrical tantrum and tongue lash my underlings? Yes, but not in public.

Here's number eleven. Flags are flying at the front of the house. How touching. I see that TV crews are here. Lots of mid-range cars made in Japan are parked outside. Journalists. Well done, Samael. I'm ten minutes late – late enough to keep people on their toes but not so tardy as to screw things up. Perfect.

Friday 29th April, 10.48am
Daniel, The Writer

The big cheese has just rocked up in his silver Bentley. I saw him arrive through the window. He has personalised number plates – AB

1. He stands at the entrance to the room, radiating importance. Carpe minions cast frightened glances at him.

AB's lateness has caused heart-stopping anxiety to the PR director, leading to excoriating rudeness to those within reach of her sharp, vulgar tongue. She is a bobbed horror in a pencil skirt, with needle stilettos. Champagne, orange juice and tiny morsels of delicious food on silver trays are waiting to be served. She wobbles over to Archer Bardon and they do a double air kiss. He is wearing sunglasses and has contrived stubble.

The press conference has gone better than I could have expected. Sam is glad-handling reporters skilfully. How suave and charming he is. They are hanging onto his every word, laughing in the right places. Marcella is doing a piece to camera, with one of my display boards in the background. *Great.*

I walk over to AB. I offer him a hand. He shakes but doesn't say anything. From behind his expensive shades he has already assessed me. I realise that I should have put on a suit bought for the occasion. The PR person has clocked his disappointment that I am wearing leisure clothing. I could get a suit made like Sam's with a silk lining. Why not? I can afford it now.

Back to the mic.

'Ladies and gentlemen of the press. I'm delighted to say that Archer Bardon, CEO of Carpe Noctem venture capital, who has made all of this possible, will be more than happy to stay for some photos and to take a few questions before he leaves us. I'm also delighted to say that Champagne and food are about to be served. You've all done well to hang on for so long. Archer has paid for it, so please do tuck in.'

Is that OK? Look back and check. Bardon is smiling. Nice one.

'After that, the Carpe Noctem team will be proud to show you the marvellous facilities that we have created here. Has anyone brought their gym kit? Just me then.'

Laughter. *I've got this.*

His speech is note perfect – modest and self-deprecating, bestowing thanks in the right places, including on the Carpe Noctem team who have 'made the day happen' and Croxtons. Coriander Close, he says, will only be the first of many such developments, worldwide. Someone has written a joke for him. *'I'm known for owning one or two casinos but let me tell you one thing... you can't gamble with your health. Yoga is the new rock and roll. That's what Marcella tells me.'*

Applause. The white widow, basks in Bardon's reflected glory. Lottie grins and claps. No doubt she is speculating on who is screwing who at the top table – not metaphorically, literally.

Arranging the photos is my last official duty before the guided tours. I guide the high-ups as they walk to the chosen spot for the group photo and the 'grin and grabs'. Bardon is drawn to Marcella by the gravitational force of her smile, her scent and her transparent dress. He is devouring her. Samael hangs back in the presence of the alpha silverback.

We are only five minutes over schedule. The press conference has gone like clockwork. *Well done, Dan.*

My phone lights up. It's still in silent mode. Soon I'm pinged with a text message. It's from Dom.

'You are in danger. I strongly urge you to sever your ties with Marcella. I am ...'

Stupid fucker. Not now. At first, I am going to text him back, then I change my mind. Delete. I block him.

18

Business and Pleasure

Friday 29th April, 11.29am
Marcella Gardner, The Bride of Satan

'It's so lovely to meet you again!'

My most enthusiastic publicist is right at the front when it comes to the media scrum, pushing to get a piece of Archer Bardon. Lottie Baxter, Mail on Sunday. Of course! Look at her. There is an English expression 'mutton dressed as lamb'. Poor Charlotte exemplifies this. Her heels are too high. They make her walk like a giraffe. Her skirt is too short and her breasts – well, they require enormous assistance to be thrust up to eye level.

She wants a piece of the CEO, Archer, more than anyone in the room. She fawned to him during the press conference, boasting of her intimate knowledge of Coriander Close. Now, she is actually angling for a free trip to his Caribbean resort for her ghastly newspaper. The brazen hussy.

I can see that Archer is not impressed. He is being non-committal, urging her to direct her request to Carpe Noctem's plank-up-her-ass PR director.

Lottie is carrying her designer overnight luggage. The poor woman has invited herself for the weekend. She's going to write about it, she assures me, in another 'exclusive'. I imagine that it will be something like 'My weekend with the white widow: inside Coriander Close'. I bet she has some suitably clingy, too-small garments in her Gucci gym bag.

Plank-up-her-ass has managed to shake Lottie off. Now she turns her Botoxed cheeks and her pouty red lips to me.

'It's so lovely to see you again, Marcy,' she says. 'By the way, thanks for inviting me to try out your facilities. I'm so excited.'

I bet you are, you bitch.

'Hey, we are honoured to have you.' I reply. 'You'll actually be the first person to use our guest facilities. You'll be getting the whole VIP package. I'll be really interested to see how we do.'

'Does that come with hunky masseuses?' she says, archly.

Unholy fuck. She thinks we're mates.

'I can't guarantee that. But what girl doesn't need a little pampering, Lottie?'

I look round. The room is thinning out. Daniel, bless him, in his ridiculous hoody is plying some hapless news drone with historical facts. I have to admit, he did a good job this morning leading the press conference. The young lamb is smitten with me. I can see by the way that he looks at Sam that he's getting more and more jealous. Oh, Danny boy, you're not going to win in a dick-swinging competition darling.

'Lottie,' I suggest, 'would you like to walk down to number six with Archer, Sam and me? We have to sign some important legal documents.'

Walk? She couldn't get more than a few feet in those shoes.

'Tell you what. Did you drive here? Why don't you move your car. There's parking in front of the house. I can meet you there in five minutes. I think we're about done here. Ok, sweetie?'

She's pathetically grateful. I glance at Sam. He is holding one of those important-looking leather boxes with handles that accountants carry around, like their own mausoleums.

It's supposed to be full of legal documents. It's a prop. Empty. Sam is Archer's shadow today. He's higher in the pecking order than the dreadful PR person, or the grey-haired drone from Croxtons. Fuckwit. I saw him looking through my dress. *Like I would!*

I'll tell Sam to get rid of plank-up-her ass and the Croxtons' perv and we'll walk down to number six with Archer. Daniel is boring the tits of his latest victim. The poor woman is desperate to escape.

I'll instruct Danny boy to take charge of the staff, the Carpe Morons, and lock up. He'll like that. He's such a boy scout.

I catch Sam's eye. He gets it. He'll prise Archer free, so that we can escape.

•••

'So, Lottie,' this is what we call our mind gym. For the body, we're offering a holistic package of chi enhancement, body toning, connective tissue re-alignment. For the mind, we have meditation from both the western and eastern traditions, plus colour. aroma and crystal therapies. We have meditation music from every sacred tradition. Oh, we even have a hot rocks room – that's Mongolian.'

Lottie murmurs her appreciation.

'There is no right route to mind body oneness. It's very much an individual journey. That's why we are offering personalised packages, guided by our enablers – we don't call them trainers, or coaches. You see they are not changing you, they are uncovering something that is already inside you. It's a bit like unpeeling an onion.'

It's scary how easily this new age sales blather slides off Sam's tongue. Lottie is pretending to listen. But she knows that her iPhone is recording it. It's not touching the sides of her brain. Most of what is inside Lottie is in her gut. Donuts.

'I love the colours in here, Sam,' she says.

'Thank you,' he replies, 'they are striking aren't they. We have made them as authentic as we can.'

The fat cow is standing inside the Circle of Solomon, on the yellow serpent that runs around its perimeter, looking around with wide eyes.

'We've added some contemporary looking symbols to the floor and walls.' Sam explains.

For Lottie, it's like dangling mathematical equations in front of a baby. For one who makes a living from writing, she isn't particularly observant.

'I love the Huluppu Bar,' she says.

Of course she does. The planet that dominates Lottie is her stomach.

The bar is recessed discretely into a side of the room – not too obvious but unmissable. It offers our branded, ionically balanced water, health snacks, smoothies, booze tricked out with ginseng and other magic ingredients or, for the straight up desperate, good old-fashioned liquor. In time, most of what we sell in the bar will be branded, like our robes and white towels.

There's also going to be a line of 'Marcella' meditation wear, tight around the erogenous zones but loose around the limbs. It will be a sub-brand licensed to me. My idea. My aim is to be queen of nice but naughty – the Bimbo of Babylon.

Coriander Close will offer tantra weekends for couples who want to add some jiggy jiggy to their spiritual journey. I'll be sure to tell Lottie about that. She'll lap it up for her prurient newspaper. *Memo to self – freebies for new age sex influencers.*

'Would you like to take some refreshment Lottie?'

Sam has her measure. Great euphemism. Like most who follow her occupation, Lottie drinks like a fish. It must be to deaden her mind to the garbage that she writes, the lies she uses to chew people up and spit them out from her fat lips.

Lottie especially enjoys peddling vicious tittle-tattle about other women. It's playground mom gossip on steroids. I know that, without any compunction, she would be happy to sting me with her scorpion's tail. That's why I've got something planned for her. But not until Sunday. I don't want the news to break until after the end of the open weekend.

'Ah here's Archer.'

He walks over to where we are standing. Sam follows him, three obedient paces behind. Archer has decided to be nice to the queen bee. He has flicked a switch to turn on a suave, man-of-the-world charm.

'Lottie,' I say, 'why don't you let Sam take you up to the guest room? He can bring up a drink and anything else you need. We have a lovely Huluppu cocktail which has turmeric and ginseng. Archer and I have some business to finish up here.'

'OK, that's fine,' she burbles.

With a glance back at Archer she waddles away. Sam takes her arm.

•••

I turn to face the CEO.

'What the fuck are you doing here?'

Does he know that the game is up? His face shows no expression.

'You know that I am more powerful than you are, you pitiful wretch.'

In a trice he assumes the form of a Devil. His face is made from putrid flesh. His wings are delipidated, like those of a rotting bird. He has yellow irises, the pupils rectangular,

The pink mouth spits out words.

'Does thou know who I am?'

I shift fractionally, into the centre of Solomon's Circle.

'You are Abaddon, the Destroyer, Ruler of the Abyss. You are one of the Angels fallen from heaven. I believe it was you who

174

planted the Tree of Knowledge in the Garden of Eden, to tempt Eve?'

'That I did.'

He takes a pace on his cloven hooves. His breath carries the stench of sulphur.

'Doest thou know who I am Dark Lord?'

He does not reply.

'I am Lilith, first wife of Adam, Bride of Satan, Queen of Hell, mother of Asmodeus. Samael is my consort for all eternity. I have the power to send you to Hell.'

The advantage is mine.

'My power trumps yours sevenfold and thus I bind you.'

His body is paralysed.

The two Shedim that serve my will enter the room. They are wearing Carpe Noctem tops, the hoods casting their faces into shadow.

'Take him!'

The Shedim drag the frozen Devil into the centre of triangle at the eastern edge of the circle. It is amusing watching his mouth contort as he tries to speak, as if he has been afflicted by a stroke.

I utter a final incantation to banish him.

The Archduke of Hell vanishes – returned to the Fiery Lake.

•••

'Well, that was easy.'

Samael has returned. He too is now in his Devil form. He is winged and cloven-hoofed, like Abaddon. Horns protrude from his fashionably trimmed hair.

'Is Lottie comfortable?'

'She is. Safely tucked up in her bed.'

He twirls from his claws the keys of Archer's Bentley.

Documents have been signed, Carpe Noctem is ours now, the jet, the apartments in London, New York and Paris, the chateau, the private island with its casino and marina, the yacht and now, Coriander Close.

'Early start tomorrow, Sam. If you wouldn't mind?'

'Yes, sorry.'

He flashes back into human form. I don't want those Demon's fingernails scratching my back when we make love.

Saturday 30th April, 9.03pm
Daniel, The Writer

'Well done for yesterday everybody. Great team effort. But, I have to say, today, is equally important. In fact, it's even more important.'

In what has become a daily ritual, Marcella is about to allocate today's tasks and priorities to the Carpe minions. We've arrived early because the show weekend has officially begun. From 8.30 am, Coriander Close has been officially open for viewing and sales. This evening, there will be a reception. After that, the Beltane party will begin. On Sunday, viewings will continue.

The minions in their smart black casuals embellished with the gold company logo, are loading up with caffeine, buzzing with fresh gossip. We're in the carpeted area in front of the now well-stocked Huluppu Bar, whose coffee machine has been gurgling ceaselessly since the lights were turned on.

Most of the minions are female – the kind of fresh-faced students who give out protein bars or health drinks in sales promotions on station concourses, dressed as beverage cans or pieces of fruit. Over the past few days, they've absorbed Coriander Close's corporate identity into their souls. I've taken some of it too. It's an amalgam of ashram, health spa and swingers' night club.

The converted basement of number six is about the size of an average M&S food hall. At its centre is its historically preserved Circle of Solomon, a bold assertion of the power of magic. The northern side bears his magical seal, a key surrounded by mystical glyphs. The room's shadowy recesses hint at hidden transgressions. To the west are changing cubicles, where the Freemasons' robing rooms would have been. The south side has therapy rooms and pool. To the east is the already popular Huluppu bar.

The space is equipped with aroma controls and light and sound can also be subtly adjusted using sliders. Mind and muscles can be flexed to the plangent boom of whales, the twittering of a dawn chorus in Sussex, the strangled gurgling of Tibetan throat singing.

'Daniel.' I hear my name.

'Yes.'

'I want you to take Jacinta and Krystelle under your wing today, since they missed the orientation session on Thursday. I want you to look after them, OK sweetie?'

They are sitting close to me. It is almost impossible to tell them apart. They have adopted their own take on the Carpe Noctem uniform – black crop tops that are little more than bras, exposed golden midriffs, vivid eye shadow, long fake lashes, perfume that would remove barnacles from the hull of a ship.

'They'll be working under you, sweetie. Is that all right?'

Marcella underlines her double entendre, so that nobody misses it, and is rewarded with laughter. It's become part of our company culture that I am always keen to please. She's great at team building, using humour.

•••

Saturday 30th April, 9.03pm
Daniel, The Writer

Same room, twelve hours later. I'm close to the same spot. However, I was seated before, now I'm standing. What a difference. Walls, ceiling and floor pulse with mandalas and sunrays of coruscating light. The light show is co-ordinated with the thud of the bass from the sophisticated 360-degree sound system and shimmering synth patterns of the music. Dots and splashes of pulsed UV dance to the same tune.

In the bar area, Marcella and Sam shine – the brightest stars in the constellation of Carpe Noctem. They are colour co-ordinated, she in a plunging red dress, he in a dinner jacket, whose shiny lapels and breast pocket are picked out with red piping. Marcella's friends, females dressed for a moonlit rave, mingle with invited VIPs – finance and property types, journalists and high value contractors. I can see air kisses, hear greetings, introductions and congratulations.

Lottie Baxter, her lips fiercely vermilion, is in her evening attire – a white dress that clings too tightly and thrusts up her boobs. She's attached to Marcella like a limpet.

Catering staff weave between guests with silver trays. The mainly female minions have been instructed to be in business and pleasure mode. Dressed in their party civvies, they are here to lubricate the guests with chat and drink, emphasising that they would

177

use this place too. I notice that the Circle and Seal of Solomon, normally so prominent in this room, have been masked out. The gold letters of Carpe Noctem, picked out against a violet or black background, flash across floor and wall.

The event is sales-orientated. Purchasers who have put their names down for houses will need to be reassured that they haven't signed up to a 24-hour-a-day rave close to their precious home. But they'll want to have a good time. It's going to be tricky balance to pull off. Later, I can confidently predict, the multi-sensory DJ, hidden in a booth in the darkness, will shift gear to smooch, bump and grind. This will signal the moment when stilettos are cast aside and the lubricated guests engage in a communal affirmation of oneness.

Krystelle and Jacinta have not left me since I arrived. Indistinguishable, they are among the least dressed women in the room. They have started to bump and grind already, pressing against me, one on each side. I don't like Champagne. I associate it with being stuck in uncomfortable gatherings and it gives me an instant hangover. But I have downed four or five glasses of the stuff. At least you feel the effects quickly.

I feel a hand tugging on mine. I look down. Krystelle, or Jacinta, has a twist of paper in her palm. I wash the tiny pill down my gullet with the last of my giggle water.

At every disco, one person, or couple, is always first to unhitch their wagon and head onto the dance floor. Their job is to break the spell of inhibition, so that others will follow.

It looks like it's going to be us. The ladies are propelling me to the centre of the room. Before that happens, something draws my attention – a commotion at the bar. It's Dom.

•••

He catches my eye. I hear his raised voice.

'You know what fucking happened! You know what happened!'

He's standing close to Marcella. His face is sweating.

'You fucking killed James, you bitch.'

'Please Dom…'

'You know it wasn't suicide. Why would he kill himself?'

'Dom, you're being ridiculous, my darling.'

178

'You know what you did and I know what you did – so does Daniel. I've come here to tell everybody in this room, I've already been to the police. You can't fucking stop me.'

Sam is behind Marcella. He steps past her and stands in front of Dom. He doesn't say anything. He simply grabs Dom's wrist and holds his arm down. He places the fingers of his other hand on Dom's neck and applies pressure.

Dom drops to the floor.

The music is still playing. A lot of people in the room won't know what's happened.

Marcella begins to cry.

Sam stands over the body. Two bulky men appear. They are wearing black clothes with no logos. They have dead eyes. They lift Dom by the shoulders and feet and carry him to the door.

Sam consoles Marcella. Lottie Baxter watches, curiously.

The DJ makes the music louder.

Krystelle and Jacinta giggle.

'That was weird,' one of them says. 'Do you know that guy?'

I try to speak but my tongue won't move. I feel light rushing into my brain.

I feel a hot moist, tongue on my check, a hand touching my thigh.

'Come on, Danny.'

We are dancing in stroboscopic light, flashing in frozen flames. My limbs are light. The colours of the music fill me.

19

Bedroom and Boardroom

Sunday 1st May, 07:00am
Daniel, The Writer

'So, how long have you lived here, Daniel.'

I can't believe that Lottie Baxter is interviewing me.

'I moved here in 2012, with my partner.'

'Your partner?'

Lottie has shed her party Spandex. She's changed into a new outfit – a black puffball dress that barely hangs onto to the cliff edge of her bosom. leaving her spray tanned shoulders and arms exposed. We've been told to dress up for a 'special occasion'. I've been forced to pull my suit out of the wardrobe. The trousers are tight around the middle.

'Yeh, Jess.'

'How long were you together for?'

'Oh, about six years.'

'So, you met her before you wrote your book?'

Lottie is doing what I do all the time – conducting a structured interrogation, disguised as chat. I've pulled off the same deception myself, often without consciously meaning to, hundreds of times, working for less exalted publications than the Mammon oven that she is shovelling her calorific prose into.

Are we that different? Not really. I can relate to her earnestness in the relentless pursuit of her story. Look at her body posture. She's sitting on the edge of her seat. Her dark-rimmed eyes are boring into mine like lasers.

Back in the day, when she was a reporter on a local paper, there would have been a shorthand pad in her hand. Now, it's her phone. She's far more successful at this than I have ever been. She's good at it. We both know the score. I'm beginning to see her as a person now, not a monster – a victim of her own falsehoods.

'Do think they have orgies in here, Daniel?' she says suddenly.

I look around. The benches, covered in wipe-down black vinyl, the scattered cushions, funky lighting and softly pulsed mood music would appear to be ideally suited to that purpose. We are in an annexe of the ritual room, accessed through an arched opening. Adjacent to us are a hot tub, showers and the main pool.

'They call it tantric yoga, don't they?' I remark. 'It's not necessarily sexual.'

'Right,' she says, archly, 'like what Sting and Trudie do. So, you moved in with your partner, Jess, and then…'

Marcella enters the room. She too has refreshed her outer garb. She's wearing a dramatically split black dress. Sam's black suit hangs expensively from his broad shoulders. His red shirt and tie match the shade of Marcella's lips.

Kyrstelle and Jacinta follow them. They are identically attired in clinging sapphire jump suits. Their eyelids match the startling shade of their outfits. Their golden cheeks are brushed with glitter. They are both wearing black velvet rhinestone-studded collars. An eye watering attack of olfactory enticement has entered the room. It has been transformed into an upmarket cosmetics counter.

My suit is letting me down. Its lapels have always been too wide. The fabric has a slightly synthetic sheen to it and its shoulders are padded with an unyielding material that feels like a yoke. It's making me sweat. *Nightmare.*

Marcella told me that 'formal wear' would be needed for this part of the evening. Did she pass on the same instruction to Krystelle and Jacinta? Or did they misinterpret it? Perhaps, for them, simply wearing clothes is formal.

•••

The Beltane party ends at 11 pm. It closes, as I had anticipated, with wedding style 'dad dancing' so that that the oldest and least lithe people in the room do not feel left out. Decorum has been observed throughout. The guests depart in an orderly fashion. Marcella says goodbye to each, just as she has greeted them. She is multiply congratulated for putting on a fantastic event. The moment of unpleasantness caused by Dom has already been forgotten.

Now Marcella is focusing her attention on Lottie and me. Sam stands next to her.

'We're so glad that you are here,' she says to Lottie. 'This is the special event that I told you about. It's our first wedding, for Jacinta and Krystelle. Isn't that marvellous.'

181

That's a surprise.

'It will be good "colour" for your story in the Mail on Sunday won't it.'

'Fantastic.'

Marcella attaches pet leads to Krystelle and Jacinta's collars. She hands the end of one lead to Lottie, the other to me.

I see anxiety cross Lottie's face.

Krystelle and Jacinta have been slipping me little white pills all evening. They are not hallucinogenic but they have lifted me onto a cloud of happiness, heightening my senses, as if I am experiencing an aerial rapture.

Both of them have 'snogged' me in isolated parts of the room and allowed my hands to wander. I can't use another analogy – I felt like a fantastically lucky teenager at a disco.

Wet wipes have removed their lipstick from my face but, even after a protracted shower, sweating in my uncomfortable suit, I smell of sex. In my head is a swirling beaker of pleasure chemicals.

'We have a lovely surprise you, don't we Sam,' Marcella says. Sam grins in acknowledgment. 'We're opening the Chapel of Venus specially for the ceremony. By the way Lottie, I have been ordained by the Universal Life Church. I can legally officiate at weddings. Isn't that amazing?'

Lottie smiles uneasily. She starts to say something. It sounds as though a piece of food is stuck in her throat.

•••

We walk into the ritual room – Sam and Marcella are in front, followed by Lottie and me, each of us trailing our slave on a love leash.

The room is fully illuminated now. The Circle and Seal of Solomon are revealed in their full multicolour glory. The harsh light is weirdly chilling.

Lottie attempts to hold back. There is a new expression on her face. Fear. Marcella glances at her.

From behind us comes a noise. Two more figures have joined our procession, the security staff who ejected Dom last night. They are wearing morning jackets with tails, with white carnations in their buttonholes. Their faces are not human. Their features are crude, as if they have been shaped from clay.

182

One of them makes a noise – the low warning growl of a mastiff. The message is clear. Leaving the wedding is not an option.

Lottie begins to cry. The creature growls again. This time we see its canine teeth and red exposed gums.

Lottie is sobbing. Sam turns round. There is enough of the human Sam for us to recognise him, including his faint smile. Horns protrude from his black shining hair.

His eyes, staring from beneath a dense black monobrow, have filled with blood.

'Come now,' he says, 'dry those tears, Charlotte. This is not a time for sadness, but for celebration. Think of the marvellous story that you will be able to write. It's the story that you have always wanted, isn't it? You knew that this day would come, didn't you, my love. Well now it's here.'

Marcella is in the centre of the circle. She intones a phrase, pauses and repeats it twice more. We hear a sound that haunts the human imagination – stone scraping on stone. A hole opens up in front of her.

'Excellent,' says Sam.

Marcella is first to place her foot on the steps. Lottie stumbles. The ushers growl. Sam positions a hand on her shoulder. He smiles like a proud father.

I move off behind Lottie as Marcella disappears into the ground.

The stone steps level into a corridor. Ahead of us a long grey tunnel beckons – the tunnel that is not supposed to exist.

•••

We are in the chapel.

Marcella has a human face. She is positioned between the statues of Lilith and Inanna.

The Red Devil, Sam, stands next to her. A grey owl perches on Lilith's shoulder. It blinks. The coils of the fat snake that is wrapped around the trunk of the Huluppu tree are moving. A long tongue flicks from its mouth.

'Well, isn't this lovely,' says Marcella. 'I guess we should really thank Theophilus. The chapel was his creation. It's a shame that he can't be with us today. Where is he, Sam?'

Sam points down.

'Ah yes. Oh well. Look, why are we being so formal?'

She sits on the stone altar so that her long legs are revealed to their full extent. Sam takes up position next to her. He places a hand at the top of her thigh.

Lottie and I stand in the nave, Jacinta and Krystelle to each side of us. The ushers are guarding the door of the chapel.

Lottie gasps. An usher moves forward.

'My love,' says Marcella, 'there is someone who is dying to eat you. Did I say eat you? Silly me.'

There is a rustling sound as a new entity enters the chapel. It springs onto the altar.

'Ah, here she is.'

An inquisitive triangular head appears between Marcella and Sam. Its bulging eyes extend to each side, each with a small black pupil. I know something of these creatures. The praying mantis, *Mantis religiosa*, is a voracious and fearless carnivore. It is capable of devouring birds, lizards and snakes. This one is the size of a human.

It uses its stereoscopic eyes and its long, flexible antennae to see, smell, feel and hear its prey. The creature's four rear legs are for propulsion. The elongated front legs are lined with sharp spines, superbly adapted to hold their victims.

The female praying mantis is known to deprive the male of its head, by biting through the thorax before mating, thus removing its calculating brain. She impregnates herself from the sexual organs in its still living abdomen. Then she eats her beau.

The insect moves its head from side to side. It is calculating distance. Lottie does not have time to react. Before the movement registers, its front legs flick out to impale her. Immediately, it sets to work, doing what it's good at. The mantis will chew through her face, as she struggles to gain her freedom. Left to its own devices, it will consume all of her soft body parts, until only a skeleton remains.

•••

'Shall we let nature takes its course Sam?' asks Marcella. 'Perhaps we shouldn't. Lotttie's body will be needed for her post-mortem.'

'A body without a head.'

'Whoops. Perhaps a failed beauty treatment? A piece of gym equipment that went tragically wrong? I'm sure we can find a matching body, can't we? All we need is a dark-haired woman.'

Marcella snaps her fingers.

The mantis abandons its grisly task. It looks around the chapel with its alien head and disappears into the darkness.

'Speaking of letting nature take its course,' says Marcella, 'isn't this supposed to be the Chapel of Love?'

•••

The cat brides shed their skins. Marcella slips her skimpy dress over her head. Sam disrobes. The cat bride begin to undress me.

Marcella smiles. But for a fraction of second, I see a sly, corrupted face beneath her beauty.

It is her true face.

A voice inside me is rebelling. Lottie was shallow and misguided but she did not deserve to die in such a hideous way, nor did Hamish, Rob, Dave and Dom, or the brave Hells Angels who were trying to rescue their comrades – or Adrian, the blogger, or any of my neighbours, for that matter, for all of their all human failings.

Not even Marcus had deserved to lose his life – he was an egotistical and lustful man, toying with witchcraft, but he had drawn back from inflicting cruelty.

What is evil? To live for sex, fame and money or sensual gratification, regardless of our moral obligations to other humans.

Choice is what distinguishes us from the other animals.

My hands are clenched in my pockets.

Marcella looks at me, showing contempt that she has always felt. She sends a thought signal.

A green triangle flicks into view above the altar.

One could easily imagine the praying mantis as a pontiff in a ceremonial mitre. It is one of nature's most efficient killing machines. Its spined forelegs grip while its mandibles, like exterior jaws, cut up its prey into digestible pieces, starting from the head.

The insects can jump with extreme precision.

I cross my forearms in front of my body, preparing to defend myself.

•••

185

Wednesday 3rd May, 2023
Success from calamity
by Sandy Blythe
News Shopper

A year ago, I was uncertain that Coriander Close would be a success as a new-age health spa. Under its previous name, the hidden community with twelve houses had gained an infamous reputation.

People talked of a 'curse of Coriander', following the death of a female journalist during the development's open weekend. But an autopsy proved that her death was from natural causes – a congenital heart defect.

The last of the original residents, writer Daniel Robbins has now moved on and Coriander Close has gained an international reputation for it its open-minded approach to mind and body healing.

Marcella Gardner, business co-owner, has become a role model for women. She and her partner, Sam, are a 'power couple', with a seemingly magic touch. They are popular on chat shows and social media for their refreshing take on business and, something that British people are reticent about – sex.

Showing me the Chapel of Love, the close's centrepiece, a popular civil marriage venue, Marcella is quick to quash rumours of sex parties. For historians of the occult, he says, the close's ritual room and its chapel are internationally significant.

Critics, she says, are quick to accuse wiccans and folklorists of immorality. It's an age-old practice, he says. After all, witches were burned in Scotland until the eighteenth century. It's a powerful argument and I have to agree with her. I wish her well.

Hearth and Home

August 17th, 1919, 2.03pm
Dixon Grange, The Paranormal Researcher

We rise early and arrive at West Bay Station before seven o'clock. Judith and Birdy have come to wave me off. There are tears on Judith's cheeks as I lean through the open train window, to reassure her. I tell her not to worry – I'll return, safe and sound, in a week's time.

She is anxious. I am too. I haven't been back to London for more than twenty years. We've been so happy in Bridport. Birdy is a fine young woman now. She comforts her mother and gives me a wave as the train pulls off. It's a glorious day. The sky is cloudless and Bridport Harbour is sparkling. Most of the people travelling on this line will be coming the other way today. The trains will be filled with expectant holiday makers.

•••

First destination in the metropolis – the offices of my publisher at number 15 Waterloo Place, to deliver the manuscript of my book, Adventures in the Paranormal. 'My publisher', 'my book', how pretentious I have become! I carried the MS onto the train like a precious infant, peeping into the bag that held it periodically, to check that it was still there.

Last month, a crowd would have gathered at this grand address – a fine Regency parade dotted with bronze worthies on stone plinths, jostling to see the procession to mark Peace Day pass down the Mall. The crowds would have cheered as columns of soldiers made their way to Whitehall to pass by the new Cenotaph, a memorial for their fallen comrades.

John Murray is based in a porticoed temple of grey stone. There is no one important in situ to acknowledge the delivery of the manuscript that I have brought from Bridport. The company publishes Byron, George Eliot, Thomas Hardy, the Brontë sisters, and, less solemn in tone, the Sherlock Holmes stories of Sir Arthur Conan Doyle. Soon I will join this celebrated pantheon! With a stab of regret, I leave my bundle of type-written papers on a walnut table. I am assured that it will be 'dealt with' in due course.

Murray's acceptance of Adventures in the Paranormal, was made on Conan Doyle's recommendation. I would venture to say that he and I are friends, for we have been corresponding for many years. He is much more of a jingoist than me and he is partial to the abominable practice of shooting birds for sport, but we have much in common. I share with the creator of Holmes a keen interest in matters that defy orthodox understanding. We are both members of the Society for Psychical Research.

I carried his newly-published volume, The Vital Message – an impassioned defence of spiritualism – onto the train in my coat pocket. The book is now embellished with my numerous pencilled underlinings, marginal notes and exclamation marks.

Today's heat, bouncing off the canyons of grey stone, will make London languorous and enervated. Travelling on public transport will be sweaty and uncomfortable. I descend the broad steps that deliver one from Waterloo Place into the Mall. This wide road is to London what the Via Sacra, the Sacred Way, was to Ancient Rome. It is the main artery of the sanguinary campaigns that created the British Empire.

There will be no crowded tube trains for me today. What could be more delightful than the emerald grass of St James's Park and the dappled trunks and feathery canopies of the great London planes that shadow it? I shall stroll down to Trafalgar Square and thence through Covent Garden to Bloomsbury, to re-acquaint myself with the British Museum, before venturing down to Sydenham.

•••

Young Jack – I still call him that – gives me an effusive welcome at the front door. He's delighted when I tell him that I intend to stay for a few days, although my visit will be broken by a visit to Crowborough in Sussex on Sunday to meet the world famous author, Sir Arthur Conan Doyle. He has invited me, I explain to Jack, to stay in his house, Windlesham Manor, in the High Weald. I shall come back on Tuesday or Wednesday.

It's clear from his collarless state that he is at the table with his family, eating supper. He has many questions. Our conversation goes back and forth, as we walk down the hallway to the kitchen.

It is marvellous to see him so happy – the master of his house (my old house) and the head of a growing family. He has recently been appointed as the editor of the South London Press – a well-respected local newspaper – commuting by tram to its offices at Elephant and Castle.

Jack steered The Woodsman on a different course than I had done when he became its editor, in 1908 at the age of 22. Already a seasoned newshound, he was not concerned with the esoteric matters that preoccupied me, but took a practical business-like approach that served the paper and its readers well.

He stuck to the well-travelled beats of the town hall, the local Chambers of Commerce and the courts for his stories. He also made space in the paper for football, rugby and cricket – topics that had been a closed book to me. When our country went to war – I received The Woodsman as its sole Dorset subscriber – he dispensed exactly the practical patriotic spirit that was required.

The house, which I have been happy to rent to Jack and his wife for almost twenty years is filled with the rumbustious energy of their brood. It consists of two teenage boys, Arthur and Eric, their 10-year-old sister, Joy, and a five-year-old boy, Sean. Sean is ruby-cheeked and delightfully mischievous.

The whole family is seated around the kitchen table. They are eating fish and chips. Lizzie beams with delight as I enter the kitchen. She extends her hand. She is wearing an apron. I can see, from her midriff, that she is with child.

It's extraordinary that a pale, thin ward of the Dartmouth Road Industrial School has blossomed into such a fine mother. She notices my downward glance.

'We hope that the new arrival will be girl, Mr Granger, a baby sister for Joy.'

The little girl's interest is piqued at the mention of her name. She turns to look at me, curiously. She has the eyes of her father and the blonde hair of her mother.

'Arthur,' Lizzie says, 'you must go out to buy a fish supper for Mr Granger, so that he can join us.'

I protest that it's not necessary. Lizzie explains that, being Catholic, the Kellys observe the practice of dining on fish on Fridays. Five minutes down the road, she says, is the finest fish and chip shop in south-east London. She hopes that I won't take it amiss to eat a meal from a paper packet. Of course I won't, I assure her.

Jack bids me to sit down at the opposite end of the table to his. Arthur is sent out with thruppence for a battered haddock and chips. I'm extremely hungry. It has been a long, exhausting day and I have barely eaten anything since breakfast. A glass of porter is soon placed in front of me.

Warmth from the range and the sound of children's laughter make this as convivial room as one could possibly imagine. Jack raises a toast. Lizzie joins us. Everyone knows that dark beers are rich in iron and that's good for expectant mothers.

'Thank you, Mr Granger,' she says, 'thank you so much for everything that you have done for us. Jack and I are so grateful. Do you remember the day when you rescued Clara and Birdy and took them to this house?'

'Of course I do,' I said. 'It was the day that Jack taught you how to play billiards, in the Pied Horse.'

'I tried to,' says Jack.

'That is the day that my new life began,' she says. Her face becomes serious. 'And it was because of you. How are your girls, Mr Granger?'

'Clara keeps a public house with her husband,' I reply, 'in Weymouth. 'She married a sailor. He served on HMS Valiant at Jutland. I am happy to say that he returned from the war safely.'

'And Birdy?'

'Ah, Birdy. We are so proud of what she has achieved. She has become an elementary school teacher.'

'What does she teach? Cookery and needlework?'

'No, she teaches English and science. She is very talented at drawing and painting. We thought, at one point, that she was destined to study art. Her sketches of local scenes and fishermen have been greatly admired.'

'I would love to see Clare and Birdy again,' says Lizzie, drying her hands on a towel.

'Well, you shall. You are welcome to visit Judith and me in Bridport at any time.'

'What, all of us?'

'Of course. We have four bedrooms in our new house. We live close to the West Beach. You must come to Dorset for your holiday next summer. There is fine fossil hunting where we live.'

'Fossil hunting, do you hear that, Eric?' Jack says. 'Dinosaur bones.'

The boy is at an age at which enthusiasm in rarely displayed. His father explains that Eric is a keen student of geography. I say that physical geography is of enormous interest on the coast around Bridport. The strata in its rocks are clearly on display. Many of them are teeming with impressions of the plants, shells and marine animals that populated the earth millions of years ago, long before humans appeared.

I can see that Jack is interested. It is agreed that the Kellys will visit the Grangers in a year's time, for their summer holiday, with buckets and spades, jam jars for rock pooling and geologists' hammers. The three waifs, Clara, Birdy and Lizzie, and their progeny, large and small, will be reunited.

It's a fine picture. We have finished eating. Lizzie turns a dissatisfied eye to our plates and cutlery.

'That was a delicious meal,' I say. 'Thank you.'

'That's perfectly... Sean! Stop that!'

Lizzie's commanding voice freezes the five-year-old. The little boy is attempting to insert a chip into each nostril. He has almost succeeded.

'That's disgusting! Joy, tend to your brother.'

The little girl fixes a stern look on the boy. When this fails to quell his mischief, she pinches his arm.

'Joy!' The mother's admonition coincides with a piercing shriek that fills the kitchen.

The dispute is settled with stern admonitions. Joy is sent to her room to reflect on the error of her ways, before she can return. Sean is told that he has disgraced the family and instructed to apologise to me. He does so, although a little reluctantly.

'What on earth must Mr Dixon be thinking of us?' Lizzie inquires. I reply that I am used to such boisterous behaviour, that the children are delightful, adding that I am about to become a grandfather, for the second time.

'A grandfather!' Lizzie exclaims.

'Yes, Clara and her husband have a little, boy, Alfie, and she is expecting another.'

'Clara, who would have thought it...' says Jack.

'Things have turned out well,' I say, 'better than any us could have expected.'

'They have,' says Jack.

'Mummy!' Joy's face is at the door. She has returned already, after a period of silent reflection.

'I'm sorry.'

Lizzie does not say anything. She scoops up the little girl, who is wearing a spotless white pinafore and covers her face with kisses.

•••

My old house – Jack's house – has a long back garden. It begins with a paved area, by the French windows of the dining room and, by way of steps, reaches a strip of grass planted with fruit trees.

The yard is a fine place for growing herbs and for enjoying the contemplative qualities of tobacco. The wrought iron table and chairs that I installed after I moved in, seventeen years ago, are still here.

Lizzie has bid us goodnight, taking the younger children upstairs for their baths and bed.

Jack and I sit outside. The day's fierce heat has subsided but, even so, we are both in our shirtsleeves. One cannot see the stars. They are hidden by the particles of soot that shroud the atmosphere of London, even in summer. How unlike the glorious night-time parade of light that decorates the Jurassic coast, where I live.

I can see, through the kitchen window, a neat row of copper pans hanging over the range – how well Lizzie has conferred order upon this bright space, which is the centre of the house.

'Do you believe in God, Mr Granger?' Jack says.

'Why do you ask?'

'Oh, you know…' He pulls a cigarette from a paper pack. The smoke from his Woodbine twines with that from my pipe, mingling sweetly with the scent of jasmine.

'Did you know that only three men from my squad made it back. We lost almost half of the battalion.'

Jack served in the London Irish Rifles. He joined up in 1915, a year before he was compelled to do so by conscription. He explained to me, in a letter, that he had received white feathers in the post several times – anonymous accusations of cowardice.

I know that he landed at Salonica to fight in the Balkans campaign. It was a bitterly cold winter and the soldiers were poorly equipped. Suffering from severe frostbite, after some fierce fighting, he was evacuated from the front and recuperated in Malta. Fortunately, he never returned to active service. The odds on his survival had not been great. Was it some divine providence that saved young Jack shrapnel or a bullet?

To answer Jack's question, I reflect that there is a need for faith in these times. There has been a prolific harvesting of souls since the end of the previous century. The horrors of Siberia and the pogroms under the tsars, the Russian revolution, the sadistic brutality inflicted by King Leopold in the Belgian Congo, the Armenian massacre, the mechanised slaughter of the trenches – and now, the sleeping sickness that is passing across the world, like a shadow.

'For me a belief in God, or godliness, has nothing to do with religion or churches, one must strip all of that away. It has to do with goodness. I believe that goodness manifests as light and that humanity's hidden purpose, known to some, is to evolve spiritually towards a civilisation of light.'

He stubs out his cigarette and takes out another.

'Do you believe in life after death?'

'Of course,' I say. 'What we call ghosts are souls or spirits that have begun their journey beyond physical life. In some cases, they are tied to a particular place by something that has happened there. I believe that that the experiments of William Crookes have proved this to be the case, incontrovertibly.'

'Who was he?' says Jack.

I explain that he was a distinguished scientist – a pioneer of spectroscopy and that he discovered thallium.

'It is evident to me that, just as there are wavelengths and elements that have not yet been discovered, we will find, in this century, a way to listen to what the dead are saying without the use of mediums or the need for spirit writing.'

Jack is still with me. To some my beliefs elicit no interest.

'Photography has enormous potential. It can show ectoplasm, which is etheric matter that leaves the body at death or during astral projection. Yes, I believe that we will be able to hear those who have passed, just as one can hear a voice down a copper wire, or from a radio signal. We have come a long way since the experiments of Galvani, Faraday and Marconi. Do you think that scientific discovery will stop?'

'Do you believe that we will be able to see the dead?'

'Certainly. The problem with spiritualism is that so many charlatans prey upon the gullible or cloak what is simple in mumbo jumbo, like the false exegetists who sully the the Bible and the Quran. The truth is hidden from us through their obfuscations. The monists and Neo-Platonists understood the nature of godhead. It's all in my book, Adventures in The Paranormal. It is a memoir, but it also delves, in some detail, into Theosophy and psychic science.'

Jack smiles warmly and raises his glass.

'I look forward to reading it.'

'Thank you. I'm glad that John Murray has taken it up. They are a fine publisher.'

'Do you write about your time at The Woodsman?'

'I do, in some detail.'

'And of Theophilus Williams?'

'How could I not?'

'Well, at least he can't sue you. Now that he is dead.'

'That's true.'

I don't share my suspicion with Jack, informed by the letter I received from Bill Peevers, that the rogue may not be dead, that the corpse found at his house was that of a pauper, and that he is hiding, at number six Mundania Close. It would not be fair to implant such a disturbing suspicion in his mind.

'Do you ever go to Mundania Close?' I ask.

His smile is mischievous.

'Why would I, Mr Granger? It is filled with cranks.'

'Is it?'

'It has that reputation.'

'Cranks?'

'People who take their clothes off and worship the sun, who wear sandals in winter, or who only eat vegetables.'

'I see. So, are there such people in Lewisham?'

'Oh yes, they used to write me letters when I was the editor of The Woodsman – usually in green ink.'

'I received my share of those.'

'But you published them, Mr Granger. I refused to. They went straight into the waste paper basket.'

We laugh.

Part of me admires Jack's bluntness and his dismissal of the esoteric, his simple delineation of good and evil. It is typical of most journalists, who have a keen eye for the sham and the specious.

194

I glance at my watch. It is ten past one. My word, how long we have been talking? It is time for bed.

Jack is of the same mind. He stands up.

'I hope that you'll be comfortable, My Granger.

'I'm sure that I shall be. Lizzie has made you a fine wife. You have filled the house with happiness.'

'Thank you.'

We clasp hands. I am aware, suddenly, of his two missing fingers – amputated at a field hospital in Malta. How does he manage to type? Jack is a resourceful and determined character. I am sure that he would have found a way, relatively easily, to overcome his disability.

We bid each other goodnight.

•••

The five bedrooms of this house mean that the Kelly family has room to grow. This one, at the front, overlooking the main road, used to be my study. It's strange to think, as I stare up at the ceiling, how many hours I have spent in this room, with its walls of books, writing at my desk. The books are long gone – many of them are in the study of our house in Bridport.

The room has plain, papered walls and a modest bed that is perfectly comfortable. I read some more of Conan Doyle's Vital Messages, in bed, making annotations that will inform the conversations that I hope to have with him in Crowborough. Then I turn out the light.

I recall Jack's verdict on the residents of Mundania Close – cranks. I assured Judith, last night, that I would stay well clear of the place. But ever since I left Bridport, it has been calling to me, like a flame drawing a moth. I won't be true to my promise.

195

The Summerland

Sunday 17th August, 1919, 7.04pm
Dixon Granger, The Paranormal Researcher

I inform Jack, over breakfast, that I am leaving to see Conan Doyle. It is a small deception. In fact, my plan is to travel to Crowborough in the afternoon from London Bridge. The writer has invited me for supper. I intend to spend the day somewhere else.

He watches as I walk from the house and look back. Does he suspect my true intention? I am making my way to Mundania Close.

Dartmouth Road, on my route, tells the three years of my life when I was editor of The Woodsman. That time was mostly happy. I walked one way in the morning, passing Forest Hill's library, the Industrial School, Daphne House, and a fine public swimming pool. In the evening, I would exactly retrace my steps, nodding and smiling, often at the same people. I was well known by local people. My trade was just as essential to them, I would maintain, as that of the greengrocer or car mechanic.

•••

Time has been kind to Mundania Close. On this perfect August day, with its fleecy clouds and cornflower sky, the road offers a calm, green oasis, a *rus in urbe*. Trees that were here when the houses were built, are of broader girth. They have been joined by new ashes and sycamores.

The brick houses with their subtle, ornate details have weathered in. In form and colour, they complement the woodland green, in a pleasing synthesis or organic and artful, natural and man-made. In the centre of the close on the mound, charmingly shaded, is Williams' Chapel of Venus, formed of the same pale yellow London brick as the houses. The chapel belongs perfectly in its place and time.

Human interventions have further improved the address. Front gardens are bright with hollyhocks, sweet Williams and love-in-a-mist. Cascading fonds of wisteria climb to the eaves of Christmas' fine houses.

That would have been my house, number nine. A black Riley is parked in front of it. How William Morris would have detested the motor car, especially as it gives freedom to members of the lower orders. I glance at the ivy-covered turret of the master house, number six. The windows are boarded up.

I will quicken my place, walk by it and leave. I'll make my way to Honor Oak Park Station and from there to take a train to London Bridge and another to Crowborough.

•••

I hesitate before walking past the house that I almost lived in, my heart beating fast. Perhaps the perfume and colour of the flowers and the drowsy hum of bees have drugged me. I become aware that someone is looking at me. She is in the garden of number seven – a tall woman in an old-fashioned crinolined dress.

Her hair is grey and tied back in her bun. Her eyes are and piercing. Her garden is filled with red Damask roses. Their scent fills this part of the close with an intoxicating sweetness. She is dead heading them with a pair of secateurs. The old lady has been watching me. It would be remiss of me not to acknowledge this.

Soon, we are chatting about her garden. She says that her name is Miss Bird. She invites me in, for tea.

•••

The parlour was a Victorian invention – akin to both dining and sitting room, yet neither. It was, and is, a room devoted to receiving visitors and for special occasions. Even working-class families crammed into small houses keep a parlour, as a sign of their social ambition.

Its furnishing and decoration tend to be formal. The prevalent note is not one of enjoyment but the observance of ritual. If there is a body to be laid out, it will be here. The plant of choice for the parlour is the aspidistra, growing from a ceramic bowl that looks like a chamber pot – a dull plant needing little light that has no purpose other than merely to survive.

197

Miss Bird's parlour, on the ground floor of her large house, is a perfect Victorian interior, frozen in time. Thick partially drawn curtains exclude daylight. There is damp in the air and the melancholy smell of an old church.

The old lady is a meticulous collector, I note, of the spiritualist journals Light, The Truth Seeker and the Two Worlds, some in leather bound sets, going back to the 1870s. That was the decade in which British spiritualism's first formal organisation emerged.

She sips delicately from a china cup. Something unexpected has emerged in the five minutes that I have been here – that we know each other. That is to say, she is aware of my writings, from my time as editor of The Woodsman. We have several acquaintances and points of reference in common.

She explains that she is a member of Lewisham Spiritualist Church which is affiliated to the London Spiritualist Alliance, having severed from the Central Association of Spiritualists. Spiritualist organisations are prone to rupture, like the sects of Christian churches. They normally divide into two factions, denouncing each other as fraudulent.

'Have you visited the library of the alliance at Queensberry Place in South Kensington, Mr Granger?' she asks. 'It was generously paid for by Mr Conan Doyle.'

I say that I have not. Miss Bird contracts her bony brow.

'I must say, I was a keen reader of your editorials. I was fascinated by your account of the Forest Hill soul bird, in 1902.'

'Thank you,' I say. The old lady has an extraordinary memory.

'You have done much for our movement.'

'That is kind of you.'

'May I ask, why you chose to give up such a prominent and influential position as editor of The Woodsman?'

'It was for family reasons,' I say, disingenuously.

'Where do you live now?'

'I live in Bridport, in Dorset, with my wife. We have two adopted children, Clara and Birdy.'

'Oh.'

She elicits no further curiosity in my family life.

A passage of silence is marked by a loud tick of the clock. It chimes a quarter – the hour is a quarter to twelve.

'Would you like to stay for luncheon, Mr Granger?'

It will be a curious concoction, I am sure. The old lady is thin and frail. I could imagine her pecking at a piece of lettuce but not consuming anything more substantial.

'I could not possibly impose on you.'

'Oh.'

This time, the sound denotes relief.

The clock's tick returns.

Her posture is ramrod straight. The chair I am sitting is uncomfortable. Its embroidered surface is scratching me through my trousers.

'Do you pass beyond the veil very often in Bridport?'

I yearn to escape from this oppressive gloomy cave and from this lady, whose manners and vowels are survivors from the era before radio waves and the internal combustion engine. The world of light, with its noble trees, honeysuckle, pansies and sweet Williams is calling me.

'Not often,' I say. 'My interest in the spiritualism is primarily as a researcher. I have been a member of the Society of Psychical Research, since Mr Conan Doyle revived it. I believe that the future lies in spirit photography and other mechanical means of recording that which lies beyond the known wavelengths – and in applying scientific rigour.'

'I see.' The old lady's tone indicates disapproval. She is of the old school.

At last, it's time to escape. I resolve that I shall leave Mundania Close and never return. This evening, I shall enjoy dinner with Conan Doyle, relaxed conversation, excellent claret and Cuban cigars. The old man, I'm sure, will become maudlin. He has never fully recovered since the death of his son, Kingsley, in the war.

'We are holding a séance at my house this evening.'

Her phrase arrests my upward movement.

'It will commence at six o'clock. Would you like to attend?' Her beady eye fixes me.

'I ...'

'We would be honoured by the presence of such an eminent authority.'

'Well perhaps...'

'You are a leading light of the spiritualist movement, Mr Granger. We would highly value your presence.'

How can I refuse such an offer?

I agree that I'll attend, but as an observer, not a participant. Miss Bird is content with this. Her thin lips, fleetingly, make an approximation to a smile. She rises to her feet. She seems to glide towards me on the pedestal of her dress. Her bony hand is as cold as ice.

I can leave now and smoke my pipe. There is a small practical problem. How am I going to occupy myself until this evening?

•••

What a marvellous institution the public house is. I spend the next few hours in the garden of fine example, nearby, the Forest Hill Tavern, reading a newspaper and listening, subliminally, to the hum of conversation and the click of billiard balls.

A pleasant stroll to the brow of One Tree Hill, which offers a panoramic view of London, returns me to the close. Three pints of pale ale have put me in an affable frame of mind.

My intention is to stay at Miss Bird's house for as little time as possible. After that, I shall slip away quietly, whatever extraordinary phenomenon is manifesting in her parlour. This, I calculate, will allow me walk to Honor Oak Park station in time to reach London Bridge for the last train to Crowborough.

•••

As I tap on the door of number seven., I glance at the gloomy exterior of number six, with its boarded up windows, then away.

Thirty minutes, no more.

The old lady is sure to detect beer on my breath.

She is flustered when she opens the door.

'Come, my guests have arrived!'

I follow her. To my surprise, she does not stop at her parlour but continues. A door at the end of the hallway leads to a gloomy passageway.

I pause before following her.

'I thought…'

'The séance is to be held downstairs. Come. We are late.'

We descend a flight of steps into a gloomy region of shadow. She unlocks a second door and motions me through.

200

Through it is a cellar painted with whitewash. I hear the door being locked behind me. *Odd.* I look back. The old lady's expression is blank.

From an adjoining room, come incongruous sounds of laughter and conversation. Jazz is being played on a gramophone. There is a curious sweet smell.

A head pokes through a bead curtain– a cranium of black hair, shiny with Brilliantine, then a body. The man is stockily built. He wears a waistcoat over a striped shirt.

'Mr Granger, you have arrived'

The voice is familiar. My blood freezes. The man I once knew was thin and nervy, with lively grey eyes. This one has a roll of fat around the chin. His face has the waxy pallour of one who lives mainly at night, shielded from daylight.

'I thought you were dead.'

'Oh, I am far from dead, sir.'

He pronounces the last word mockingly.

I begin to speak but words won't come out.

'God, it was hard being sincere, when I was Bill Peevers, the down-on-his-luck hack. You took it all in – my fall from grace, my dead wife, my fictitious son – didn't you. I did work for newspapers. That was true. You are so gullible, Granger. It is a common trait of psychic investigators.'

'Peevers…'

'Theo and I could have killed you at any time after you fled from London. We knew where you were, and exactly what you were doing. You see when you inform one Freemason to another… well, it sets an inevitable sequence of event in action.'

I was so kind to this man.

'Your memoir won't be published by the way. I can assure you of that. It has already been burned to a cinder. You see, the influence of the Craft is limitless. It determines what the public are allowed to read. It was ever thus. How else would senior members of the Royal Family be protected from the consequences of their heinous crimes? We protect our own. Does that shock you, Granger?'

A smile crosses his lips

'How many years is it, since I fell under the wheels of a tram?'

'I…'

'It is fifteen. Those years have been good to me, as you see.'

Time to go. It shouldn't be too difficult to overcome the slight Miss Bird.

Sensing that I am about to move, the man brings his right arm from behind his back.

A revolver points at my chest.

'I wouldn't do that. We knew that you would come. It has taken a long time. Do come and join us, Mr Granger. There is someone who is dying to meet you. Or rather, he is not dying.'

I turn round. Miss Bird's arms are folded. She looks as solemn and stern as a judge.

•••

This room is carpeted. The décor is luxurious, like a luxury hotel furnished for epicurean appetites. Its principal features are embossed wallpaper in maroon and gold, subdued lighting and heavy ostentatious furniture. Velvet-covered ottomans line the walls, spread with black cushions. One wall is dominated by a gilt-framed mirror that reaches almost from floor to ceiling.

The room is as warm as a hothouse. There is a sideboard loaded with bottles and glasses. Four women with bobbed hair and rouged cheeks inspect me. They are dressed in the new style, in straight silk dresses, with no corsets.

Williams' face looks exactly as it did when I last saw him. He is dressed in a black jacket with a velvet collar. Violet wears a plunging purple dress.

'Mr Granger,' says Williams, 'you are here! You are most welcome to join us.'

Violet giggles.

My body tenses.

There is a violent impact on the back of my head.

•••

How long have I been here? I have no idea. I am awake again. My face is aching and swollen and there is a savage pain in my ribs. It jolts through me like a knife being twisted when I strain against the bonds that secure me.

A party is in full swing. The gramophone's volume is unnaturally loud. The opium fumes that fill the room are so thick that my eyes sting. My head pounds as if hammers are beating against it from the inside.

I am aware of white shapes – bodies engaged in a jerking upright dancing, in time to the mechanical syncopations of the music. White changes to pink as the room comes into focus. The women are shedding their flimsy clothes.

Theophilus and Violet are seated on at the side of the room. Violet is naked. Both are sniffing white powder from a hand mirror.

I close my eyes. There is a sharp pressure, as cord cuts into my throat. I am being garroted. I feel warm breath in my ear. It is Peevers'.

'I am not going to kill you. You are here to witness this, Granger. Don't you feel disappointed that you can't join in?'

The women abandon their crazed dancing. They fling themselves to the floor. Williams watches both their bodies and their reflections with a glassy stare as they explore each other with their hands and mouths.

Violet joins the women on the floor.

I close my eyes. The chord cuts into my trachea. I can feel blood trickling down my throat. The gramophone needle meets a scratch. It jumps back. A disembodied fragment of music repeats meaninglessly.

When I open my eyes, I see that Peevers has joined the bodies on the floor. They are merged into a single organism, like an octopus. No one attends to the skipping needle of the gramophone. The limbs of the octopus move in time to its mechanical repetition, as if swayed by ocean currents.

36 Kirkdale
Sydenham
6th October, 1919

Dear Mrs Granger,

I am so sorry that Dixon has not yet been found. I know that the police are conducting inquiries, both in London and Sussex, where he was to meet Mr Conan Doyle. The only thing that is known for certain is that he did not arrive at Conan Doyle's house, as he was supposed to.

My wife and I feel keenly for the anxiety that you must be suffering at that this difficult time. Mr Granger meant a lot to both of us. As you know, he gave me a career and he helped to rescue my wife Lizzie from the difficult circumstances of her childhood.

Our children only met him once, but they are very fond of him and talk of him often. It is almost too much to think that we may have lost him. I can still feel his presence in this house.

I am particularly sorry to write these lines because Dixon had invited us to spend our next summer holiday in Bridport and we had looked forward to meeting you, Clara and Birdy, after all these years.

Let us not be pessimistic. He may still turn up! That would be very like him, wouldn't it Dixon loved a good story and this one would be one of his best!

We hope to see you soon. We'll contact you by telegram should we receive any news.

With best regards
Jack Kelly

Summerland
West Bay Road
Bridport
Dorset

16th October, 1919

Dear Mr Kelly

Thank you for your kind words. They are much appreciated. I know that Dixon was proud of your achievements, not least your brave service for our country, succeeding in your career and raising a fine family and. In many ways, he regarded you as a son.

In my heart of hearts, I don't think that we shall see him again – at least in the form that we know him. The pain that this causes is particularly acute because Dixon's life's work, so nearly achieved, had not been fulfilled.

I have been in correspondence with Mr Conan Doyle to confirm that he did not meet Dixon as had been planned. The manuscript that my husband was carrying was apparently not received by John Murray – they claim to have no knowledge of it being received.

However, there is one small piece of good fortune. Dixon always made carbon copies of his typescripts. I have a full copy of his memoir, although it will need to be proof-read and corrected. I intend to use my full endeavours to see that it is published, as he would have wished. Could you help me, perhaps?

Every day, I wait to hear his key turn in the latch. I long to hear his voice. He was so hopeful and cheerful on the morning when he left Bridport for London, in bright sunshine. That is how I shall remember him.

Please do visit Bridport in the summer. Clara and Birdy will be delighted to see Lizzie the children that you have brought into the world – is it four, or five? We have plenty of room to put you up.

I must break off now to catch the post.

Best wishes
Judith Granger

36 Kirkdale
Sydenham
London

7th November, 1919

Dear Judith

Thank you so much for your kind invitation. I'm afraid that I have come to the sad conclusion that we won't see Dixon again. Police investigations have come to a full stop. It is ironic that he disappeared visiting Britain's most celebrated writer of detective stories. He has left us with a mystery that is worthy of Conan Doyle's pen, hasn't he. But, of course, the pain of his absence is all too real. I can only imagine its intensity for you and your daughters.

Dixon left his reading glasses in his room when he stayed here and a few other personal items. I shall return them to you by post. He was always absent-minded. He was too concerned with his latest enthusiasms to pay much heed to the small matters of everyday life. I can't believe that I am now writing about him in the past tense. I suppose that it is some consolation that he will live on in all of our memories – and in his writings. It is important that his final manuscript is published and brought to the widest audience possible. Yes, I shall be happy to help in this endeavour.

I should like to propose something – that we travel to Bridport at Easter rather than in the summer. The new baby will be old enough to travel then. I can then pick up the manuscript and bring it back to London by hand.

Eric is very keen to hunt for fossils and he has passed on his interest in dinosaurs to young Sean, who is convinced that that they are still commonly seen in Dorset.

Of course, an Easter visitation of Kellys may not be convenient to you, in which case, I shall quite understand. Let me know what you think. In the meantime,

Best regards
Jack Kelly

Summerland
West Bay Road
Bridport
Dorset

12th November, 1919

Dear Jack

Your kind words about Dixon have been an enormous consolation to me. I know that he will be smiling as he looks down on us. He had immense admiration for your skills and perseverance, which I share. As to your suggestion – yes, we should love to see you and your growing family at Easter. Let's hope that the weather will be kind to us! Bring your buckets and spades, just in case.

With regards to the manuscript, it is immensely gratifying to me that it will be in such safe hands. Although Dixon corresponded with John Murray himself about his book, he has failed to reply to any of my letters and cannot be reached on the telephone. It is an enigma.

I hope that you can excuse the brevity of these lines. I am rushing, as usual. Please pass on my best wishes to Lizzie. When is the new baby due? Birdy is very keen to make some clothes for the little boy – or girl! We can't wait to see you.

Fond regards
Judith Granger

Thanks and acknowledgements

I'd like to namecheck Pippa, a continuing source of inspiration, for her no-holds-barred approach to art and life. Jon Heal for his terrific design for the cover, Stu for picking me up when I fall down, Adam for stimulating me with optimism and caffeine, Dylan, my nephew, for his cool music and good vibes, and Paul and Rod at Wild Wolf for making this book happen.

Printed in Great Britain
by Amazon

62182612R00117